TWILIGHT IN A KNOTTED WORLD

TWILIGHT IN A KNOTTED WORLD

Siddhartha Sarma

SIMON & SCHUSTER

London · New York · Sydney · Toronto · New Delhi

First published in India by Simon & Schuster India, 2020
This edition published in 2024

1 3 5 7 9 10 8 6 4 2

Simon & Schuster India
818, Indraprakash Building,
21, Barakhamba Road,
New Delhi 110001

www.simonandschuster.co.in

Paperback ISBN: 978-81-979492-8-9
eBook ISBN: 978-93-86797-93-3

Simon & Schuster: Celebrating 100 Years of Publishing in 2024

Typeset in India by SÜRYA, New Delhi

Printed and bound in India by Replika Press Pvt. Ltd.

'Child Rowland to the dark tower came,
His word was still,—Fie, foh, and fum,
I smell the blood of a British man.'

—Edgar, Act III, Scene IV, *King Lear*

The Marwari's head was magnificent. His ears flared up in two graceful arches, the tips meeting with geometric precision above the forelock. His neck, from the withers to the ears, was straight and noble. His skewbald flanks glistened in the early morning sun, testament to good breeding and a careful diet. As he raised his head from the wooden feeding pail and looked into the distance, poised and perfect, there was a moment when the world was without blemish.

Only Mirza Akhtar saw the horse at that moment, because he had been looking at it for a while. Akhtar was sitting on a charpai in the sarai's backyard after breakfast, while his men were overseeing arrangements before they began the day's journey. It was a brief moment: the horse standing just so in the light, convinced of its nobility and pride, its place in the world and its purpose. Akhtar sought for a moment a kind of kinship with the beast, a shared sense of self-regard, of focus, of privilege and aristocracy, of an ability to wrap their immediate environment around themselves and become the centre of a tableau vivant.

The horse could claim all this. Akhtar knew he could not. But the main reason he had been looking at the horse just then was he had been reminded of its poise in the stance of a man across the yard, on the far corner of the stables.

If Akhtar imagined a shared nobility with the Marwari, the other man would not have had to. He was a thoroughbred, tall and well-proportioned, with handsome, even delicate features. He had long limbs and slender calves of the kind which would, in an earlier age, have fitted well within steel and leather armour. He stood with the grace of a born equestrian. His beard, reddish in the morning light, had been trimmed with care by a barber who valued his craft. Silver threads ran in intricate patterns on his choga. His silk turban was embroidered, as were his shoes. And to wear all that in a village sarai in the middle of nowhere, on what must have been a long journey, meant the man could afford to change his clothes at a halt. Where he stood he became, like the horse, the centre of events.

He appeared to be in some difficulty, however. Akhtar had been watching him speak to a decrepit old peasant for the past few minutes. In his personality the stranger appeared not to be forceful but seemed to be making a request which the younger man had been trying to refuse without success.

Mirza Akhtar looked down at his stubby butcher's hands and the thick muscles of his forearms, and then at his frayed old shoes. He understood duty, and orders, and loyalty to the people who gave those orders. He had few illusions about his place in the world, and no hope of ever equalling the likes of the beautiful young man. He sighed, rose from the charpai and walked across the yard.

'…And I am telling you, abba huzoor, that I wish I could let you travel with us, but I cannot,' the young man was saying. Akhtar wondered when the old fellow had last been addressed as 'abba huzoor' by anyone. He was skin and bone, his face and hands dark and cracked by decades of labour under the sun. His eyes held the accumulated meekness of generations of marginal farmers, an unending line of people who subsisted, and endured, and in whose life there was neither much dignity nor the expectation of it.

'I request you, malik,' said the decrepit one, turning towards Akhtar and speaking in a wheedling tone. 'Please, won't you fine gentlemen allow my troupe and me to journey with you a short way? It is only a few kos, and we shall keep our distance from your magnificent selves.'

Akhtar held up his hands and said he was not with the younger man, but asked what the matter was.

'This gentleman wants me to let his group and he travel with me to a village nearby. I cannot allow people I do not know to journey with me, but he seems to be quite difficult to convince,' said the young man. Even his voice was soft and cultured, as if he just could not give offence.

'Please go away, abba. I do not want to be rude with someone of your age. Please leave the gentleman alone, as he desires,' said Akhtar.

'Huzoor, the two of you have been sent by the Almighty to protect us on this journey. Our blessings shall be with you if you just allow us to follow you to the next village but one from here, to take part in the wedding of the sarpanch's daughter. The roads are dangerous at any time of the day. There are dacoits. They will not spare even us, although we are poor musicians with nothing worth taking.'

Akhtar was about to say that everybody had something worth taking, but felt it would not be appropriate. The young man had turned to him with a helpless expression, as if he was not used to turning down the requests of the meek.

Akhtar gave him a polite salaam with the courtesy that one nobleman expected from another on a country road, even in times such as these.

'I am Syed Ameer Ali of Bhopal,' said the young man, drawing out the words at a gentle cadence. Then he waited.

Akhtar thought he was expected to recognise the name, which he could not. He could see himself through the man's eyes: a low-ranking official, perhaps, of strong physique but not from a family of any great consequence, education or culture. There were many such across the land in those times: people descended from great men if they looked back far enough, but with few prospects, and not much chance of advancement through physical bravery in battle, which had been the making of some of their ancestors.

But Akhtar had to live up to the expectations of his family, and conduct himself with pride. So he said, 'I am honoured to have met you. I am a member of the Maharaja's court in Ujjain.' An exaggeration, it was true, perhaps even a fiction under a certain light. But the nature of reality changed between a great city like Ujjain and a humble sarai such as this one.

Ameer Ali considered Akhtar's clothes, which were a little threadbare and a little loose, as if stitched for somebody else but only borrowed, which was true. Under his gaze, Akhtar felt like a charlatan, a parvenu of modest ambitions, and an ill-prepared one at that. Ameer Ali was polite, but made it clear that he was nobody's courtier. He gave the impression that he held court himself, and had darwaans to deal with peasants.

Mirza Akhtar hoped the man would like the idea he was about to propose.

'Syed Ameer, since we are travelling in the same direction, perhaps I could make a suggestion? There would be no harm in letting this old fellow and his men journey on foot behind us, if we set out together. With our two groups travelling as one, with our matchlocks and swords, we need not fear anyone on the road, and can give protection to these men, which would be a gracious act.'

Ameer Ali was not inclined to agree. He seemed to have the notion that strangers would inveigle themselves with his group and rob him. The old village musician and his troupe of ten men were thin and elderly. If they had ever possessed the capacity to offer violence, or the will, such a time had passed. If this was the mettle of thieves and robbers on the road to Bhopal, thought Mirza Akhtar, sheltered young men like Ameer Ali should have no fears about venturing abroad.

And so Ameer Ali, faced with the wheedling musician and the experienced Mirza Akhtar, gave in and agreed. There were fifteen men with him, but they were lightly armed with spear and sword, on horseback, compared to the twenty with Mirza Akhtar, who in addition to sword and spear also carried matchlocks and had been trained well in their use. Mirza Akhtar himself had two swords, one on each side of his saddle, and could use both quite well on horseback. Not that he was expecting to use them on this journey.

The two noblemen wanted to make the most of an early start and reach the next big town by dusk. About thirty paces behind their retinue and themselves went the old musicians, trying to keep pace with the trotting horses.

It was a beautiful day, one of those just before summer begins in earnest in the foothills of the Satpuras, when the traveller can almost forget that there is such a thing as a scorching midday sun. North and east from the sarai, the group entered a quiet valley and passed through a forest, with the dappled sunlight on its floor. Unknown varieties of birds called in the distance. The horses' legs crunched the leaves and twigs on the path.

'Syed Ameer, where are you coming from?' asked Akhtar.

Ameer Ali thought about this, as if he was not used to people asking him such questions. Akhtar thought perhaps he had been rude. A nobleman was not expected to be rude. He did not want the young man to take offence and part ways so early in the journey.

'We had some work in Akola,' said Ameer Ali, after a while.

Akhtar felt he had to explain where he was coming from. It would not do if Ameer Ali thought he was of little account.

'My men and I have been travelling a long distance. We come from Poona, where we had to perform an important task. And we take a horse as a gift to the young Maharaja,' said Akhtar.

Ameer Ali said, 'It is a fine horse. I was wondering why you would not ride it.' He said this with the air of somebody who had seen many fine horses every day of his life, and did not wish to be impolite towards somebody who had not. Akhtar felt even more of an imposter. His father would have said he was not trying hard enough.

'How is the young Maharaja?' said Ameer Ali.

'He is well, although there have been difficulties with his mother,' said Akhtar. He knew of matters in the higher circles of the court only through indirect means.

'Life in court is full of such incidents. It can be difficult to deal with in the best of times,' said Ameer Ali.

'And how are matters in Bhopal?'

'The Nawab Begum rules with assurance and dignity. The city flourishes, as much as it can in such times. People like us are happier in Bhopal than in Ujjain, Mirza sahib,' said Ameer Ali.

Akhtar was not sure if he meant Muslim noblemen in general or descendants of the Mughal aristocracy.

'It has been a long time since I visited Poona. My father used to go often in his youth, when he was a wrestler. This was before he went to live in the domains of the Nawab of Bhopal. The Peshwa had lauded his skills on the wrestling floor. But in my own sight, the city changed. Once it was the greatest in the land. Now all you will see are fine houses and establishments of British army officers. All you will find a mention of is their name,' said Ameer Ali.

Mirza Akhtar could hear the regret and anger in his voice, almost a lament for a world that had been, and now was not. He did not know enough of that world—he suspected his father's family had been involved in a small way in its demise—but he could not doubt the pain and sorrow that the young man felt. This was a man of honour, a man who saw and understood things in the world far greater than himself. There was little place in Akhtar's world for such men, but he could recognise them when he saw them. They did not last for very long when left to fend for themselves.

Towards the early afternoon the travellers emerged from the valley and passed a small path which appeared to lead to the first village after the sarai. A short distance later, around the shoulder of a rock-strewn hill, they came across a large group of men resting by the side of the road.

Ameer Ali was tense, and remarked on this. Akhtar too saw the men, and knew he need not worry. Around thirty in number, mostly clad in loincloths, they were farmers from someplace nearby and greeted the musicians with cheer. The old musician walked up to the noblemen, accompanied by one of the farmers, and bowed. It was clear that aristocrats seldom passed by this sliver of the countryside, and they were treated like celebrities. Even Mirza Akhtar was touched.

'Huzoor, these men are from our biradari, and are on their way to the wedding. They wish to thank you for letting us travel in your shadow.'

Ameer Ali too was touched, and accepted their thanks.

'We are about to begin our lunch, huzoor. It is nothing, a little gosht and some rice, poor fare for gentlemen like you. But it is part of the wedding feast which we are taking to the village, and it would mean a lot to us if we could share it with you before you continue on your journey,' said the other farmer.

Ameer Ali was in two minds. He was unwilling to eat the food of strangers, even more when they were not of his rank or position. He reined his horse in towards Akhtar and murmured, 'Mirza sahib, I defer to your knowledge of such matters, but we have heard of Dhaturias, who would feed poison to unwary travellers and leave them insensate, robbed of everything. It is vital that we not eat from the hands of strangers, but I do not wish to appear rude in front of these poor people.'

Of such material were high aristocrats made. The Nawab Begum's future was not bright if Ameer Ali was any indication. The man might subscribe to lofty ideals, but could not seem to take a decision in the real world for fear of peril, real or imagined.

Akhtar said, 'Perhaps if only some of us were to eat, while the others stood guard, we could be seen as polite without being vulnerable. Although I do not see any reason to suspect these men, who appear to be just poor farmers.'

Ameer said, 'That is an excellent idea.' He smiled in gratitude. He might have been familiar with kings, but he had much to learn about the road.

The two farmers, who had been standing to attention and ignoring the murmurs of the aristocrats, now came back to life and began shouting instructions to their fellow villagers.

The two noblemen got off their horses and walked beyond the road, through the trees, to a clearing in a grove where the farmers had already begun preparing their food. The armed retinue followed them.

'You do not travel often, I think, Syed Ameer,' said Akhtar.

'It is true,' admitted Ameer Ali. 'Therefore I appear suspicious and perhaps impolite. But one simply does not know who to trust.'

'One should be careful indeed, but if one travels long

enough and often, one knows a thing or two. Just as one nobleman can trust another, we must also be gracious towards poor peasants such as these, even though they have little,' said Akhtar.

Thus they arrived at the clearing, and began their unexpected feast. The food was spicy and flavourful, and if it was hewn too rough for the delicate palates and constitutions of Ameer Ali or even Mirza Akhtar, they gave no sign of it, and neither did some of their soldiers who were allowed to eat in the first sitting. The old musicians now declared they would sing a song in honour of the huzoors. It was loud music, full of drumbeats which echoed in the grove and earthy, peasant words. Akhtar felt Ameer was more comfortable with Urdu poetry in a quiet room, but bore the din with grace.

The day wore on. The two men finished their meal.

'I must say that was unexpected and satisfying, Mirza Akhtar. I am thankful that I met you,' said Ameer Ali, rinsing his fingers with water and running them across his mouth. Akhtar found his gratitude touching.

'In fact, I am feeling a little sleepy,' said Ameer Ali.

Mirza Akhtar smiled. 'You must really travel more often, Syed Ameer. Perhaps you could go on a much longer journey,' he said, and tried to rise. His legs gave out under him and he fell back.

Ameer Ali smiled at Akhtar, and gestured to the farmers. 'Dhar dal,' he said.

Akhtar could not understand what that meant. He wondered what dialect it was. But there were other questions crowding his mind. Strong hands had snaked a piece of cloth around his neck. Other hands now clasped his arms to the ground, and yet others his body and legs. How had they appeared with such speed? He could not tell.

Akhtar was a strong man in his prime. Even when drugged and sitting, he could have been a formidable adversary. But the ruhmal around his neck was held by a man with an iron grip. Akhtar was kept immobile as the scarf tightened. His body began to spasm, but even that was reduced by the grip of the hands on his limbs.

Around the clearing, Akhtar's matchlock men, both sitting and standing, were being strangled at the same time by their hosts and Ameer Ali's men. One after the other, the thrashing victims lay still. Finally, the musicians ended their wails and drumbeats and a silence fell on the grove.

'The chisa was too sure of himself, but his possessions are worth it, huzoor,' said the old musician. His task, and those of the other old men, was now to bury the bodies. One of them carried the sacred pick-axe for this purpose.

'We must be thankful for those who are too sure of themselves and the world,' said the man who called himself Syed Ameer Ali.

'And the Goddess was kind to have given them to us.'

Ameer Ali smiled. 'Yes, one could say that. Please divide the loot as is customary. You will find that the chisa was carrying several valuable items. Dispose of them with care, for some may be easy to identify. And make sure that the sarai owner is rewarded for informing us of the travellers.'

The old musician and the leader of the farmers saluted.

'Huzoor, surely you will take a share of the valuables?' said the farmer.

'I do not seek anything. I will now take your leave and continue,' said Ameer Ali, and turned away, but stopped. They were only poor farmers and did not know much about the world, but they knew of and respected tradition. And without tradition, without myth, what was anyone? He had to accept a morka, and he could choose on his own.

'I think I shall take the horse as my share. It is beautiful.'

So, the man who called himself Syed Ameer Ali of Bhopal placed his own saddle on the skewbald stallion and mounted gracefully. Followed by his men, he turned and trotted away, heading north and east.

The farmers stood by the side of the road watching horse and rider, both erect, proud and certain in their self-regard, about their place in the order of life. And for a moment, for the watchers, the world seemed to be without blemish.

He had brought a shovel, as he always did on these visits, although he had not used it for some time. The layer of rock which he had reached was not suitable for shovels. He had also brought a pick-axe, although it was unkind to his back. The box of much smaller tools, including several types of horse brushes and trowels, would be carried on other days by his wife, who was also the person to wield them. He had never mastered the fine touch and dexterity the smaller tools demanded, or the sculptor's awareness his wife had, the knowledge of what kind and degree of pressure to apply on which kind of stone or soil.

But today the man laboured alone. Neither his wife nor Dr Spilsbury, the other regular visitors to this face of the hill, were present. His wife was at home preparing for the journey to come, and Spilsbury, civil surgeon of the district, had been called away to help a medical officer at a village.

It was evening on a Sunday. The man was on his knees on a broad ledge of the western face of Bada Simla Hill. To his north and west, the ridges of the Satpura range extended beyond the horizon. Behind him the ground fell in undulating, rocky stages to a level meadow, beyond which were the first houses and structures of the Jabalpur Camp. It was a 'camp' for people like him, of a certain time and social class. For others, who viewed the world from the back of a metaphorical horse and whose ancestors had seen the same world from the back of literal ones, it was a 'cantonment'. The man on his knees knew of this distinction, but it had long ago ceased to matter for him.

He was digging in the limestone bed of the ledge with a trowel. Upon a faded cloth on the ground behind him were two irregular pieces of bone, each as wide as his thigh. Neither was complete; only an expert in anatomy would have been able to identify their location on the body. A person unused to cadavers would still not have felt the frisson of revulsion caused by the sight of exhumed remains. Time and untold geological processes had drained the fragments; there was little to distinguish them from the layer of rock in which they had been embedded, and which still covered them in places. They were bone only in shape and structure. They were bone not because they carried on them the sign of once having been the frame of a living creature, but because they could not be rock.

He dug with the trowel along a straight line of thirty feet, marked by thin ropes tied to four sticks at either end, in a rectangle. Other lengths of rope extended from the sticks, creating rectangular grids wherever they intersected. At some spots on the rock bed within these grids were other sticks which marked places.

The grid and the diggings had been the result of two years of patient and slow work by William Henry Sleeman, his wife Amelie Josephine and Spilsbury. But today Sleeman worked alone and was thus slower and more careful than usual. He was in an unfortunate middle ground: he was neither the type who could take a shovel to a rock and terrify it into submission, nor a delicate craftsman who could make the rock reveal its secrets at his pace.

The creature in the hill would have slumbered undisturbed if Brigadier General Joseph O'Halloran, commanding officer of the Sagar division, had not ordered a road to be driven along the western shoulder of Bada Simla, for the passage of gun carriages. On a rather similar early winter afternoon,

Sleeman and Spilsbury were riding past when they found that the work had not been going well. The fickle layers of sandstone and basalt of which Bada Simla was made had slid down the western face after attempts to cut through the shoulder of the hill. Amid the rubble, Sleeman had found the first of the bone fragments, and had started digging on the side of the hill. The gun carriage road was finished to the satisfaction of the general, who had no interest in petrified creatures. The hill became a mild obsession for Sleeman and Spilsbury, more so because it was miserly in giving up its secrets. For each piece of bone they found, for each layer of rock they explored, there were countless geological culs-de-sac.

What the creature was, they did not know. The only safe guess they could hazard was its size, which was gargantuan, and its antiquity. The only point on which Amelie and they agreed was Bada Simla could not be the sole resting place of these giants. Spilsbury said he had found a likely candidate in Narsinghpur, while Sleeman had his eye on another hill spur nearer home.

The afternoon signalled it was about to end with a sudden breeze along the western face. Sleeman, sweaty in his undershirt and long johns, halted his work and put the small tools away, his movements slow. He washed his hands with water from a small goatskin bag, and wrapped the two bone fragments in the cloth. Even a find as paltry as this was rewarding. There had been weeks when they had found nothing at all.

He walked down the hill to where his horse was tethered. His legs were stiff and his hands ached. He was hungry. Lunch had not been satisfying. The days before a long journey always affected him thus. Each monsoon left him weaker, and although still capable of exertions and intense bouts of physical activity, he had become slow and deliberate in his movements. The older he became in his body, and the more frail, the more intensely he wanted to focus on the powers of his mind, as a form of compensation. At least that is what he told Amelie. She was twenty years younger to him, and found such a necessary transaction incredible.

He had never been a natural horseman, but had at least been competent in his youth. Now it was a mode of transport he used with reluctance, for it was not kind on all the joints and limbs which had been worn down the most. He tied the implements and the pouch of bones to the saddle, picked up an old army coat, wore it and climbed on the horse.

The coat's colour had faded from its original bright scarlet to an indifferent red, but Sleeman still found, or thought he did, some kind of meaning in wearing it while riding. He could not quite explain why. Perhaps it was just the residual habit of a former army officer.

He rode down the hill and across the meadow, passing the skeleton of a cannon carriage rusting under the sun, a discarded remnant from one of the Bengal Army's artillery units which practiced on the cantonment range, of which the meadow was a part.

Sleeman's modest house was on the northern edge of the cantonment, between the officers' houses and the civilians', symbolic in the position he occupied: he was the head of the civil administration of Jabalpur district, and assistant to the governor-general's agent who was in charge of the twelve districts which comprised Sagar and Narmada Agency, of which Jabalpur was the capital. Beyond the eastern side of the grounds lay the forest, and spotted deer often grazed near the house.

The first traces of dusk were falling when Sleeman dismounted and entered the house, carrying the tools and the cloth bundle. He stood for a few moments at the entrance to the inner courtyard, listening to Amelie talking to an old woman. Amelie had been visiting the villages near Jabalpur and enquiring about the folk music of these parts. She was compiling an account of the oral musical traditions of the province. The house saw village singers visiting to talk to Amelie, and now that she had finished supervising the household's preparations for the long journey east, she had been revisiting her notes and had more questions for the singers.

It was an animated conversation. Amelie's knowledge of music, or at least the Western classical tradition, was substantial, the result of an education in the Continent in the years of Louis the Desired. She had brought to her studies in Indian folk music the kind of sensibilities that learning classical music required. She still used the same technical terms in her writings, for instance, although she admitted that there were fundamental differences. But she was thorough in her inquiries and her knowledge of Hindi was almost as good as his own, even though he had been in India since before she was even born. Sleeman wished he could understand more of music than he did, but he had long ago come to terms with his limitations. It was enough if he could understand the direction of Amelie's studies.

She looked up when she saw him step into the courtyard, and the old woman stood up. Amelie smiled and pointed to the bundle in Sleeman's hands. He held up two fingers and walked towards her to show the finds.

'They are identical in size. They must be from the lower spine, but the doctor can confirm it,' said Amelie, holding up one of the fragments in the twilight.

'Yes, they must be. I hope your musicians have told you everything you needed to know.'

'Oh, not everything. I should hope not. But the lyrics of some of the songs she remembers from her village and the neighbourhood are similar to what the Bundelas sing in Orchha. Do you recall those songs?'

Sleeman did, or at least the tunes. He had heard them first from some Bundelas in the army: songs about a long-dead prince-saint.

They were to start out early the next morning for Calcutta. It was going to be a long journey, and Sleeman was already exhausted at the thought of it. But he had to go, to present his report to Government House in the absence of the agent, who was unwell. And there had been a letter from the secretary to the governor-general, requesting a meeting in person when he was in Calcutta.

He loved Calcutta as much as he could love any city after all the places he had seen. He would even have agreed with those who considered it the greatest city in the world, a repository of the finest and most murky tendencies of the human species, a great cauldron of activity and purpose. But it wasn't so much the Byzantine corridors of Government House that attracted him as his friends and correspondents in Calcutta. He would go because he had been summoned, but he was pleased with the prospect of the journey only because he would meet people with whom he had been corresponding about the bones for a long time. As far as Government House went, he would have avoided a visit if he could. It was never a good sign when the powerful asked if one would be kind enough to meet them. Great changes were afoot in the establishment at Calcutta, from what he had heard. Such changes often resulted in martyrs, and such martyrs were often drawn from the ranks of the inordinately ambitious, which he was not, or the indifferent, which he was.

The lamps had been lit by the time he had washed the grime off his hands and feet and gone to the study, deposited the bundle on the desk and lit his pipe. He took out one of the bone fragments and turned them around in his hands. The size of the fragments lately had been much smaller than the first few finds. This could be, he had told Amelie, for two reasons. First, because the largest fragments were the easiest to discover. Or second, the bone fragments were part of a whole and tapered in one direction. He knew enough about bones to agree with her that the first finds had resembled a long section of vertebrae not attached to the ribs. Therefore, these were likely to be the bones of a giant animal with a tail, an animal far larger than the largest elephant he had ever seen.

He opened his journal, where he had written about their impressions of the finds and the geological structure of Bada Simla. At a very early point in the excavations he had decided to locate the finds in grids based on letters and numbers. Now, the journal showed the distribution of the bone fragments, the depth at which they had been found and their relative distance from one another. He wished he had studied more geology, if not animal taxonomy. He would have to wait for Amelie to join him. Spilsbury was sure to visit sometime in the evening. He could no more stay away from the creature in the hill than Sleeman or Amelie.

'There is nothing yet,' wrote Sleeman in his careful hand in the journal, 'to indicate the presence of another creature, since all the bone fragments found so far appear to be from the same animal. The sandstone stratum in which the fragments were embedded is of an average uniform depth of…'

He wondered about the age of the creature in the rock, and the age of the rock itself. How much could be known from the bones? When one thought about it, how much could be known from any kind of bone? The ex-soldier in him said: a sword or bullet injury would show in the bones. A cause of death. But what of the detritus of life? If somebody were to study his bones many years after he had been dead and buried, what would they know of him? Not much, beyond his height and gender, and perhaps whether he had been well-fed on an average. What would they know of how he had lived, of his thoughts, or his rise, his fall or how he had striven? Nothing at all. Only the barest signature of his time on earth would remain.

He sat and stared at the bones in the flickering lamplight, waiting for Amelie and the doctor, and for illumination.

It was a place of fictions at once large and small; harmless and profound; meaningless and pregnant with the shapes of futures.

Sleeman climbed down from a creaking carriage at the steps leading up to Government House, the office and residence of the governor-general in Calcutta. Amelie and he, along with their household staff and office assistants, had made a long, wearying and slow overland journey from Jabalpur to Benares, and then by ferry down the Ganga to Calcutta. The great metropolis was almost directly due east from Jabalpur, but there had been no question of travelling through the forbidding forests of Chhotanagpur to Bengal with unarmed civilians.

The small fiction was the governor of Bengal was now the governor-general of India, and therefore primus inter pares among the governors of Bombay and Madras. The large fiction was the reassurance for visiting princes that they were still masters of their dominions. A yet larger fiction was this empire which was still being forged was of the East India Company. Between the courts of the native princes and the directors of the Company, it could not be said who was more wilful in their delusion.

Standing at the bottom of the steps of Government House, the provincial nature of Sleeman's station in life was borne upon him. He was willing to deal only with those changes which affected his district, or the small orbit of his life, but was aware that the great workings of the empire had a way of washing up on a distant shore like Jabalpur as well.

He had been in Calcutta for two days, at the lodgings of the political department at Fort William, before being informed in writing to present himself at the office of the governor-general's secretary. With him were two Indian assistants deputed by the agent, carrying official documents and other effects. The Sagar and Narmada Agency was new, carved out of the debris of Maratha might in central India, but while a portion of the task of restructuring the administration yet remained, it was a tranquil backwater compared to some other places, and the political department had few complaints.

Sleeman walked up the steps, rather stiff in his ceremonial captain's uniform, wearing a girdle to present a trim figure at the waist because Amelie had insisted, although it was unexpected of her. Sleeman never wore a girdle in Jabalpur. It did not seem to matter there in the mofussil. But in the midst of Calcutta's finery, he supposed, he had to make some concessions, even though the girdle made it difficult for him to breathe freely. He wondered how his fellow former officers, now on their way to being fat middle-aged Company men in Calcutta, managed this every day.

Reports had to be presented to nameless clerks and writers in ill-lit rooms at the end of interminable corridors. Assurances had to be made, and messages from the agent conveyed, about the settling of Jabalpur and administration of the province, anomalies with taxation and the functioning of the diwani adalats. The numerous grouses and grievances generated by the process of everyday administration, which sound so much the more alarming when they happen seven hundred miles away.

But at last, all contests were settled, all passion spent, and Sleeman was directed to the office of the secretary, where he was asked to wait on a wooden bench in an ante-room.

Around and beyond was the hum of Government House, the workings of the very insides of the imperial machine. The men who garrisoned this floor were fell creatures with implacable expressions and purpose, headquarters men who would have been at home on the Palatine Hill or Ctesiphon or Qaraqorum. They were either vultures who saw much, missed little and were immune to gore, or homunculi with arcane talents and specialties who laboured in dim burrows and emerged with great reluctance, passing around and beyond Sleeman on mysterious errands.

He waited, knowing that if he waited long enough one of the vultures, if not a homunculus, would remember that they had known Amelie's father in the Continent when they had all been young. He waited, but this did not happen, and he was at last ushered into the secretary's office along with his assistants, who placed their bags on a side table, saluted the figure sitting behind a large desk, and left.

William Hay Macnaghten had aged considerably in the years since Sleeman had seen him last. He smiled, peering over his spectacles, like a keen breed of owl who would have asked an important question if he had not forgotten it just at that moment. Macnaghten was five years younger than Sleeman, but had begun to look a decade older.

Perhaps it was the cares of high office. Perhaps it was the burdens of a difficult decade. An old India hand, born to a judge in Madras, Macnaghten was now the second most powerful man in Calcutta, and therefore the recipient of much of the crown's responsibilities and expectations. From what Sleeman had heard of him, Macnaghten should have been thriving, but perhaps the weight of the crown was beginning to tell.

'Good morning, Captain Sleeman. I believe we last met in Allahabad two years ago,' said Macnaghten.

'We did, Mr Macnaghten. Thank you for remembering.'

'Oh, I would not forget, I would not forget. How is Lady Amelie?'

Of course Macnaghten would remember who Amelie's father was. Noblesse, for the secretary, was eternal. Lady Amelie was well, having prepared a long list of excuses to avoid meeting the luminaries of Government House unless her friends in Calcutta compelled her to. She had inherited a dislike for imperators from her father, who remembered Napoleon. Sleeman assured Macnaghten that she was well, and did not mention the list of excuses.

Macnaghten smiled and gestured at an empty chair across the desk from him. Sleeman sat and waited again while the secretary bent to his work and scribbled on the papers at his desk for a few minutes. Then he pushed them away and looked up. Sleeman was not certain if an assistant was expected to materialise and remove the papers.

'I trust the journey down the river was safe?'

'Safe.' What an odd word to use. Comfortable, perhaps. But 'safe'?

'It was, Mr Macnaghten.'

'Good. That is reassuring. And Jabalpur has been kind to you, after Narsinghpur? I remember being told you had a difficult few years in Narsinghpur.'

Macnaghten had a frightening memory when he chose to have one. Sleeman's two years as magistrate in Narsinghpur had been harrowing, but of no import to anyone except himself, and hardly a matter of interest to Government House.

'One can't, of course, choose one's trials, or know when to expect them,' said Macnaghten and stared at the wall behind Sleeman, who remained silent. Whether it was meant to be in a prophetic vein or a casual remark, he could not tell. The secretary then stared at his desk, as if looking for something he had misplaced.

'So, Jabalpur has been kinder to you. I am glad, I am glad indeed. The mofussils have been administered well, we think. Which is a relief. We have so many concerns on the borders, as it were. We always seem to have unfinished work in Burma, and now we have interests in Afghanistan. It would not do to have restive provinces in the centre, would it?'

Macnaghten peered into the distance again.

'There will be changes, Sleeman. We are working on them, as you must have heard. We have larger responsibilities now. We need to forge a different relationship with the princes, and we need to administer our provinces better. It is not just about the Company any more, you know. The honour of the Crown is at stake. So there will be changes.'

Since Sleeman did not know how to respond to this, he chose to stay silent.

'I do not recall ever visiting the northern coast of Cornwall. You were born there, were you not?' said Macnaghten.

'Yes, at the town of Stratton.' Another odd way to lead up to an innocent question.

'I do hope that part of the coast is doing well.'

'I do not know. I have not visited it since I came to India.'

'Have you not? I see. But you have been to England, at least?'

'No, Mr Macnaghten.'

'Not even once?'

'I do not seem to have managed to leave since.'

'How long ago did you come?'

'I received my commission just after attending college, in 1806. I left England in 1809.'

Macnaghten was silent for a while.

'Your service record is exemplary, captain, as is your record in the political department. We have also been impressed with your surveys and reports on the native society of the

Agency. You have an interesting approach to administration. We need more people like you. Here I have a report from you about the castes and sub-castes of Jabalpur district. It seems you have divided them by population, occupation and income. Am I correct?'

'Only by population and income, although we do not know enough about the income of certain jatis, or how to estimate it. There is no difference between caste and occupation among some, particularly the upper castes. We have also found that caste identities are fluid among some lower castes. In some cases, those who we had been given to consider as Hindu are not thought to be so by the upper castes. It is a complex situation, and I understand only a little of it.'

'Yes, naturally. But you have also, it seems, made extensive studies of the societies in the central provinces, and I am told your knowledge of Hindustani and Persian is encyclopedic. Am I correct in assuming you have the best knowledge of central India among Company officers there?'

'I wish I could say that, Mr Macnaghten. But there are limitations to how much one can know about or study the princely states and the people who live in them.'

'Indeed. And that is another matter that I must discuss with you. The existing arrangement with the princely states, Sleeman, means there have to be strict limits to the inquiries we can make within their territories, unless it affects us in a direct manner. And now, to our regret, we have a matter here which does concern us, namely the Company and the Crown.'

For a moment Sleeman wondered whether Macnaghten was deliberately referring to the Company and Crown together, as a hint that the two were to be seen in the same light, at least in India. Then he remembered that he must not read much into the semantics of Calcutta politicians because their concerns, beyond a point, were not his.

'We have, of course, no complaints about the administration of the Agency, including your own district. Compared to what is happening along the Irawaddy, Sleeman, central India is an oasis of calm. Even Bombay could not claim that.'

Sleeman had heard of rumours that another rebellion had been launched by the Kolis near Dakor, north of the Gaikwad state. He wondered how bad the situation was.

'Therefore, no, we do not have a military problem in your parts, Sleeman, or even a political one, except the fact that when you are in my seat you will find most problems are, in the end, political. No, what we have here is an issue of law and, as it were, order.'

Here Macnaghten held up a finger, stood and walked to a shelf of papers to his left, from where he picked up a sheaf of documents and returned.

'I believe you had written a report about a gang of robbers which were said to strangle people, while you were at Narsinghpur?'

'I did, Mr Macnaghten. There had been some accounts of what the locals call Phansigars, and there had been a reported incident, with an eyewitness.'

'Yes. This is your report. I have read it. This is quite exhaustive, given the paucity of evidence. There were similar reports from other districts over the years, but nothing much seems to have been done about it by anybody. Now it appears that there have been what I can only term as complaints, Sleeman. The princes in your neighbourhood have been writing letters and allegations—and directly to my office, mind you—about each other. Ordinarily this would not be surprising, but they have been, we find, accusing one another of harbouring gangs of robbers, including these Phansigars, who have been preying on travellers in the countryside. Just recently we received a letter from the court of the Scindia himself, in Ujjain. It seems a caravan led by a nobleman, travelling from Poona, disappeared on its way north. Nobody seems to know what happened. The caravan was bringing a very expensive horse to the Scindia's stables, and they are unhappy about it, I am told.'

'A horse, Mr Secretary?'

'That is what the letter mentions. Moreover, the nobleman is from an important Mughal family in Delhi, now fallen on hard times. But the tone of the Scindia's letter suggests the loss of the horse is much worse. And here we have a yaddasht from the Nawab Begum in Bhopal, reminding us of an earlier complaint by her that Phansigars from the state of Gwalior prey on her subjects at will.

'Therefore the governor-general has decided to take some definite steps about it. You will recall reading that it took our armies some time to uproot the Pindaris. I am not saying this problem requires a similar campaign, of course. Far from it. And we cannot have the army chasing every robber and highwayman in the mofussil. But we have, as I am certain you know, an existing Department for the Suppression of Dacoits. We would like you to work for it. This will be in addition to your duties in Jabalpur. You will have certain powers to investigate and suggest courses of action in the princely states. But not extensive powers, you understand. I leave that to your discretion. You can expect all possible assistance from my office. You can choose your men to assist you in this. I believe you have a junior officer from your former regiment also posted at your office, a Lieutenant Reynolds?'

'Yes, Mr Secretary.'

'You can include him in your departmental team for this purpose.'

It was not as if Sleeman had any choice in the matter, since these decisions had been made much before he had arrived in Calcutta. In any case, he would have placed a request to have Reynolds working with him on this.

'Mr Macnaghten, what am I expected to do?'

Macnaghten frowned, as if a difficult problem had been posed to him, or an unexpected reversal had occurred. The frown lasted till he had gathered his thoughts.

'Captain, your province is still being forged out of decades of warfare. There is much we are to learn about it. In this case, the allegations are that the hand of an organised gang of robbers, known for strangling its victims, can be found across the land. These allegations are not new, but we find that nobody has understood the extent of it, or the facts of the matter, or what is to be done about it. The forging of a province cannot happen unless the law, such as it is, can be enforced to the satisfaction of the people. Of interested parties. Therefore, we would like you to understand the problem and explain it to us.'

'Mr Secretary, in the course of my investigations, will I have the power to make arrests and bring the accused to trial?'

'Yes, you will, but only within Sagar and Narmada. For accused persons from other provinces, you will have to involve the respective diwani adalats and magistrates for trial, and assist them regarding the gathering of evidence. Please do not hesitate to ask my office for any assistance you require at any point. I hope that answers your question.'

'It does, Mr Secretary.'

'Very well. We believe you are the right person for this delicate task. One would like to keep the young Maharaja and the Nawab Begum happy, but one would also like to see the task done properly. Please do keep that in mind in the course of your work.'

'I will.'

Macnaghten smiled, clapped his hands and stood up. 'Very well, then. If you would care to accompany me, captain.'

Sleeman was led outside and down the corridor to doors guarded by two sepoys and a dwarf palm of uncertain provenance, which opened onto a broad staircase. The doors shut behind them and they walked upstairs to another set of guarded doors and entered a large, sunlit room with open windows. A man stood with his back towards them, staring out at the gardens. He turned around when he heard them enter and walked towards them.

'Captain Sleeman. I am delighted to meet you once more,' said Lord William Henry Cavendish-Bentinck, the former governor of Bengal province and, for the past year-and-a-half, the first governor-general of India.

In Sleeman's experience, difficult though it was to believe, extreme privilege could, on occasion, give rise to people of exceptional drive. Bentinck was such a person. However, exceptional privilege also meant people like Bentinck were fated to be surprised that the world was not always prepared to understand their vision. Disappointment, or even failure, did not sit easily with them. Sleeman had found that the world only made sense when it was compelled to do so. The Bentincks he had known often did not understand this.

Sleeman had last met Bentinck during the same Allahabad visit where Macnaghten had been present. Over the years, Sleeman had met Bentinck a few times, with greater frequency when the former had been posted in Calcutta while in the 12th Regiment of the Bengal Army. As Sleeman drifted into civilian posts around the country, he had followed accounts of Bentinck in Italy and other distant parts of the world.

Power sat with ease on the governor-general, and he had a certain kind of charisma, Sleeman was aware. But it was not the mere fact that the son of a former prime minister had now found himself in the possession of power more concentrated than what any other man in India had wielded since the Great Mughals.

It had always been clear to those familiar with him that Bentinck had vision. He had ideas about what he wanted to do in India. It was true that not everything he did had the expected results, such as at Vellore in 1806, when he had been the governor of Madras. Hindu and Muslim soldiers, angry at not being allowed to wear caste marks or forced to shave their beards, and made to wear hats which looked like those worn by Christian converts, had mutinied, and although it had been put down, Bentinck had to be relieved of his post.

That had been then. It was not that India had rejected Bentinck. Rather, Bentinck had made a tactical retreat. The India of his imagination could still be forged, some said. Old Calcutta hands were known to add that he had been chafing to shake things up, and now he had been given the opportunity. Vellore had been an unfortunate anomaly. The sons of the Enlightenment were going to light the lamp in India the way they wanted to.

'Please have tea with me, captain,' said the governor-general, gesturing to a table.

Sleeman had not quite expected to have such an informal meeting. They sipped tea in silence, till Bentinck cleared his throat.

'I trust Mr Macnaghten has explained matters to you. I hope you have agreed to take up the additional work for the

Dacoits Department. It should not be a hindrance to your normal administrative duties.'

Sleeman assured him that it would not be.

'Have you ever wondered why we are here, captain?'

'In what way, my lord?'

'I mean, why we—that is, our generation of the British—are in India? Have you given some thought to it? I see from your reports that you are a thoughtful man. I am certain that you, whilst in Jabalpur, have had occasion to reflect on what is called the larger scheme of things. Have you wondered why we are here?'

'You mean, my lord, what our purpose is here?'

'Not if by purpose you mean a form of destiny. That is a type of speculation I shall leave to the indefatigable soldiers of the Church of England. I mean, why we came to be in this situation. We are ruling over this land now. One might say, by accident. Wouldn't you agree?'

'I would not say quite by accident, my lord.'

'I am certain it was not by design, captain. I doubt the Honourable Company, when it first arrived here, ever dreamt of ruling the land. And yet here we are. But what I am saying is, we are here, and we need to understand the difference between ruling and administering. It is not enough to let matters continue the way they have been. Consider the tea that you drink. Do you like it?'

'I like the taste, my lord.'

'It makes a fine cup, even for someone like me who might not be considered a connoisseur. Where would you say it comes from, if you were to hazard a guess?'

'It must have been harvested somewhere in China, my lord. I regret that I do not know enough to be more specific.'

'It is indeed tea originally from China, but not harvested there, captain. This is a small batch from a harvest at the

Botanical Garden in Kandy. We have for some time been trying to grow tea plants on the island, and I am happy to say that efforts are beginning to produce results, although it would be premature to disclose this to a wider audience. You must have heard the expression, "You cannot take tea to China". As you can see, we might no longer need to bring tea from them either. And thus the world changes, but we have to give direction to such a change.'

The governor-general, having made this statement, sipped his tea in silence and contemplated his idea of change for a few moments before continuing.

'As Mr Macnaghten must have told you, we are in the midst of great change here, captain. These changes will of necessity begin from Calcutta, but very soon they will reach your province and the others. There will have to be extensive reforms. Administrative, political. The state of education at colleges here is intolerable, I have always held. The way we have permitted some…gross inequities to persist among the people is intolerable. The condition of women is deplorable. They are still being pushed into funeral pyres. We can't begin to educate them unless we can save them from such horrible deaths. There have to be reforms.'

Sleeman understood that Bentinck believed the most difficult part of social reform was legislative, followed by the administrative and the logistical. It was not such a simple matter, particularly in the provinces.

'Since you will hear of this shortly, I feel I can tell you about it in confidence. We will introduce a regulation prohibiting the practice of sati, and making it a criminal offence, very soon. Perhaps you will need to enforce it in your district, although I hope you will not have to take punitive action for this.'

Sleeman nodded. The decision had been expected for

some time, and was certain to have consequences in Hindu society. He would have to wait and see how the civilians in his district reacted to it.

'Captain Sleeman, we need a better class of administrators. In fact, we need a better kind of administration. And we will need to reconsider how we are treating with the princes. We must intervene wherever relations among them are affected because of a failure in law and order, or other causes.'

'Yes, my lord.'

'But we must also change the way we approach the law here in India. It will not be enough to remove a few judges and expect everything else to fall into place. We need better enforcement of the law as well, and how officers of the law connect with the people. I am certain you understand what I mean.'

Sleeman was not sure if he did, and said so.

Bentinck picked up a bound volume lying next to him on the cane settee and passed it over to Sleeman. The cover said: *The Metropolitan Police Act, 1829*.

'I am not certain in what detail you have been following recent news from England, captain, but I recommend you take a look at this. It is a copy of an Act of Parliament setting up the Metropolitan Police in London. I find the spirit of this Act, and the idea at the base of this police apparatus, to be quite inspirational. There is no reason why we can't have something similar here. Our police departments in the provinces are rude, rudimentary and haphazard. This situation has to be remedied.'

Sleeman said he would read the document with care.

'Your responsibilities with regard to the Department for Suppression of Dacoits, Captain, require the application of a different kind of mind. Army officers tend to think in terms of campaigns, as you know. Law enforcement of the kind needed here is different. One will need to understand the people as much as crimes and criminal groups. The surgeon's scalpel, if I may, and not always the cavalryman's sabre. I am convinced that you are a thorough man. But for a task of this nature, we need a wise man in addition to a thorough one. There will be many pitfalls. Mr Macnaghten must have told you about the complaint we have received from the young Maharaja. He appears to be having some problems with his mother. She blames us for interfering beyond necessity. His court believes we do not intervene as much as we should. Now there is the possibility that the court will use this incident as an excuse against the Nawab Begum of Bhopal. We cannot have, as the princes allege, stranglers ranging the countryside and attacking the innocent. But we also cannot have princes harbouring resentments against one another, and ultimately against us. I am, I fear, passing on a political Gordian knot to you, and unlike in the myth it is not always advisable to slice through such a knot and move on. Sometimes knots need to be unravelled. We would like you to examine this problem of the stranglers, tell us the extent of it and what needs to be done.'

Sleeman, when he rose and said his goodbyes, assured the governor-general that he would give his best efforts.

From one governor-general to another took the better part of half an hour. Sleeman let his assistants return to their quarters and took the carriage north up Chitpore Road, beyond the crowds on Mughal Bazaar, and then east to Cornwallis Street. The carriage stopped at the gate of a small compound a short distance from Christ Church. It was late afternoon and the street was quiet.

Cornwallis Street occupied a kind of middle ground in Calcutta's geographical hierarchy. Its larger houses were owned not by the powerful among the Company's or British officers, who clustered around Government House, farther south in Alipore, or in rambling estates outside the city. The houses from here to Upper Circular Road belonged to merchants who had achieved modest success, senior professionals or retired army men whose careers, despite their best efforts, had been mired in the plains of colonelcy.

A gatekeeper opened the portals for Sleeman's carriage and he was deposited at a trim brown door. It was opened in turn by a manservant, who led him through the house to the rear garden.

They said there was a woman, now. They did not know much about her, beyond idle speculation, for the owner of the house would not volunteer news or satisfy their curiosity. A pahadi woman of considerable beauty, said some. A Kumaoni, perhaps, or from Kinnaur. Not so, said others, but a Muslim from Kashmir, without much in the way of evidence beyond second or third-hand witness testimonies.

Amelie's friends made wagers on her identity. Amelie had wanted to visit with Sleeman, but not to settle the wager.

'I do not see how her identity should make any difference. It would not matter to me,' he had said.

'You say that because you have been taught not to notice women,' she had said. Amelie had such a curious way of stating opinions sometimes.

It was a house and at once an archive for a man whose heart lay somewhere else; for a reluctant visitor to the great metropolis. The sitting room through which Sleeman was ushered had walls lined with sketches of landscapes, beasts and birds. The landscapes were of mountains, as if signifying a constant longing. The beasts and birds were a mix of the familiar and the unknown for Sleeman, who was neither hunter nor naturalist. A passage was filled with shelves of dried leaves and boards with pinned butterflies. Occasional small mammals preserved in animated poses by taxidermal cunning crowded around Buddhist icons in bronze and wood. If there was a woman present in the house, he did not come across her. Did he anticipate meeting her? Did that make him just as distasteful as Amelie's friends? He was not certain. If there was such a thing as a woman's touch, it was absent from the rooms through which he passed. The only presence was that of a supreme intellect at the height of its engagement with the natural world.

The host sat at a cane table in the sun at the far corner of a wide backyard and smiled on seeing Sleeman.

'Welcome to Calcutta, captain. It is a pleasure to see you here, and a greater pleasure to see you in the winter. It was such a pleasant day that I decided to stay here. I hope it is all right,' said Brian Houghton Hodgson.

He was a decade younger to Sleeman, but had an old man's stoop, caused by poor health. He had kind and thoughtful, if tired eyes, and had grown a beard which was now in the process of becoming unkempt. There were smudges of ink on his fingers and shirt because he had been writing since the morning and had forgotten about them.

'It is a pleasure, Mr Hodgson,' said Sleeman, joining him at the table. He enquired after the scholar's health.

'I am not as well as I would have liked, I am afraid. The plains no longer agree with me, and I shall have to return to the mountains soon, this time for an extended duration. I was hoping to meet Amelie before you returned to the province. I have read her study of folk music with considerable interest. Do visit once before you leave.'

Amelie's friends had waylaid her for the day. Some of them were daughters of the kind of men who were certain to have known her father in the Continent.

'Certainly, Mr Hodgson. She was disconsolate for not being able to accept your invitation. Meanwhile, I thought you would like to see the results of our excavations over this year.'

It was a small table, so from his bag Sleeman laid out the two largest bone fragments that had been found on Bada Simla since the last time he had visited Calcutta.

'How delightful! The rocks continue to reveal their secrets. The good news, as I mentioned in my last letter, is we have so many bone fragments by now. The scientists I am corresponding with in England and France have been most forthcoming in their views. The bad news, if I may call it that, is the fragments are all from the spine of a single creature. Nevertheless, this is worthy of further study, captain. I am sure to visit you in Jabalpur soon, and will take a look at the hill,' said Hodgson.

'We have identified another spot nearby which has a similar geological structure, at a place called Lameta Ghat. I have brought some survey maps with me, if you would look at them and guide us about other likely places.'

'I will go over the maps. My advice is to keep searching near the approximate area where you found these bones. At almost every place in England and Europe where such remains have been found, people have identified several different creatures. Sometimes, one just needs to know what to look for. That reminds me: please excuse me for a minute.'

Hodgson returned in a few minutes, carrying a thin document which turned out to be an academic journal.

'President Buckland of the Geological Society of London had written this last year. I had not received it in time for your visit then. You will remember that I have been corresponding with the woman, Anning, who has made several discoveries at Lyme Regis, near Exeter. She had mentioned a peculiar kind of bezoar stones which have been found to contain fish bones and other objects. Now Professor Buckland has written that these stones are petrified faeces in the stomachs of these ancient creatures. He has called them "coprolites". Here are some drawings of them.'

Sleeman took a look at the proffered page.

'Therefore, do not lose hope. I am certain you will find these coprolites, and possibly more bones, somewhere on that sandstone layer.'

'Can we tell how old the creature is, Mr Hodgson?'

'I cannot, but I have invited two gentlemen who have taken an interest in it, and could help us ask the right scholars in Europe. I still think the spine is not mammalian, and is very likely from some kind of large reptile of great antiquity, similar to the recent finds in Europe. I am still awaiting Buckland's reply to my last letter. It might take a long time, for he is a busy man.'

'Buckland, you had said, believes the antiquity of these creatures indicates the age of the earth is far greater than had been thought. He has written that the story of Genesis must be considered metaphorically, and not literally,' said Sleeman.

Hodgson chuckled. 'Yes he has, hasn't he? I should say...'

The conversation was interrupted by a maid announcing the two guests who were expected. The older of them was of Sleeman's vintage, but thin, with the sallow complexion of somebody who spent almost all his time indoors as far as could be helped. The younger man was tall but just as thin, with an open, friendly face and a hoarse voice, as if he had a permanent cold.

'Captain Sleeman, may I introduce you to Dr Horace Wilson and Mr James Prinsep. Dr Wilson, who I believe you have met earlier, needs no introduction. Neither does Mr Prinsep, who has recently returned to Calcutta from Benares. I believe you will be the deputy assay master at the Mint here now, James? Shall we consider it a certainty, then?' asked Hodgson.

Prinsep smiled and took his seat. 'I think we may, Brian. I shall be assisting Dr Wilson in his duties at the Mint from now on. I will be periodically visiting Benares, but only for my studies, and if time permits.'

Hodgson had once described Prinsep as the most formidable intellect of their time in Calcutta. This was ironic, for Horace Wilson had once described Hodgson in a similar manner. Prinsep's achievements had begun to acquire the status of legend, even among the small circle of interested persons in a place like Jabalpur. From studies about ancient Indian coins to arcane metallurgical experiments, from paintings to architectural history, it appeared to Sleeman that there was no year when he had not heard of some significant scholarly breakthrough by the young man, who had now turned his attention to revitalising the activities of the Asiatic Society.

Dr Wilson, his mentor, was no less formidable: at that point, he was the foremost scholar of Sanskrit literature in Calcutta, in addition to being a historian, linguist and metallurgist.

Prinsep shook Sleeman's hand and apologised for interrupting the conversation.

'Oh, you must not apologise. We were just discussing the writings of the geologist Buckland, who says, what with all these ancient creatures we are digging out of rock everywhere, the age of the earth might be longer than six thousand years.'

'It does appear to be so,' said Prinsep, smiling.

'Buckland, of course, thinks Genesis refers to two eras of land formation separated by thousands of years,' added Hodgson.

'And you do not agree with that, Brian?' said Prinsep.

'Buckland wants to arrive at some kind of balance between Scripture and empirical evidence. I can assure you that if I were to speculate on the antiquity of the earth, I would not use Scripture to aid me in such a speculation,' said Hodgson.

'The Hindus in their Puranas say the age of the earth is vast, several hundreds of thousands of years. The story of Genesis is not the only creation myth to be considered, I suppose. But I must defer to Brian, who alone among us knows of the Puranas as much as he knows of natural history,' said Wilson.

'Now you are being modest, Dr Wilson. But I find it helpful to conduct my studies of the natural world and mythology in isolation. The understanding of myth requires a certain amount of whimsy which does not help in the study of natural phenomena. Consider Lamarck, about who at least the three of us do not differ. I cannot speak for you, captain. Lamarck says certain acquired attributes can be inherited by succeeding generations, leading to changes in the physiology of species. A perfectly reasonable argument, I should think, even if Scripture does not agree. But returning to Buckland, what do you think, James?'

'About the age of the earth? I would not know at all. I prefer not to speculate. But I do know people like Buckland would like to reconcile their empirical findings with Scripture, or their long-held beliefs, even if this requires considerable acrobatics.'

'Do you have any long-held beliefs at all?'

'Just that empirical evidence is the only reliable truth.'

Three men laughed. Prinsep smiled. Sleeman contemplated the idea of reliability of the truth, and realised these conversations were what he had missed most about life in Calcutta.

'But in any case, Captain Sleeman, I am delighted to meet with you. I have heard so much about your excavations and findings. These must be some of the bone fragments which Brian had told me to expect to see. And I have read your wife's studies on the folk music of the central provinces with considerable interest,' said Prinsep.

'James, is there any possibility at all of publishing them in your journal?' said Hodgson.

Prinsep was a regular contributor to a small journal called *Gleanings in Science*, edited and published from Calcutta by an energetic army captain. They said it would not be published at all if Prinsep did not write for it.

'It does not carry studies on folk culture, Brian. The Society would be interested in accepting her writings. But, Captain Sleeman, the Society needs to bring out a journal of its own, where such writings and findings like your own can be accommodated. That is one of the matters I hope to discuss with Brian today,' said Prinsep.

'Captain, as you must have heard, our progress has been glacial. We have only recently admitted native scholars into the Society's ranks, with no excuse for the delay of several decades. We have acquired an enormous number of artefacts and manuscripts, and contributions from diverse correspondents, but have as yet no means of publishing studies on them,' said Wilson.

'I wish the Society could be persuaded to have a reading from Amelie's studies, or perhaps a discussion by those interested in folk culture. But it is a difficult task. First, because she is a woman, and it is almost impossible for the Society to conduct a discussion on a paper written by a woman. In that respect, at least, there is no difference between Calcutta and London,' said Hodgson. There were unsaid bitter notes in his voice.

'That may be remedied sometime in the future,' said Wilson. 'The second problem, however, will take a much longer time to be resolved. Captain, you must understand that there is, shall we say, a varna system in the workings of the Society. If you were to publish a study on the Vedas, there would be considerable interest among the learned of Calcutta and London. But a study of the songs of some farmers from central India might not spark much interest among them even if we begin publication of our journal shortly. This is a state of affairs that cannot be remedied even by James. I have not been able to change it in the eighteen years that I have been the Society's secretary. As with the matter of inducting native scholars, to bring reform among the members is a daunting task, and perhaps I have not been equal to it.'

The answer had been expected, but disappointing nonetheless. It was testament to the limits of Wilson's influence among the powerful who composed the core of the Society. And perhaps, Wilson was one of those well-meaning scholars who were better suited to academic pursuits than to administration. Sleeman would have to explain it to Amelie, although he suspected she would take the news better than he had. Amelie did not care much about the opinions of some of Calcutta's intelligentsia, curmudgeons retired from the bench or mercantile humanists, and their hidebound manner of functioning. This had driven her from Calcutta to central India in the first place.

'What about you, Dr Wilson? What occupies your attention at present?' said Sleeman.

'Economics, I should say. I am compiling a study of the external trade of Bengal over the past decade and half, from 1813. I believe the current set of gentlemen at Government House might find it of interest if they can stir themselves to read it. They seem to not have learnt any lessons in avoiding fiscal misadventures after the recent campaigns in Burma. Speaking of them, I hear that you shall be meeting with the governor-general.'

Sleeman said that he had just come from Government House after meeting Bentinck and his secretary.

'What do you think of Macnaghten?' asked Wilson.

Sleeman hesitated. Trading confidences on such matters with a man he had only briefly met in the past, even if the man was the assay master of the Mint, was a little difficult.

'I will have to report to him, so I hope he is a fair taskmaster, as I have heard,' he said.

'He might be fair, but he has always struck me as being more impatient than is safe for any man. He appears to think that the only two choices for dealing with a native prince is a show of strength, or a lot of gold in the right pockets. The real world is a little more complex than that, and human motivation is boundless in its variety. That man will either scale great heights or come to a bitter end. And what of the governor-general? Did he give his "rule as opposed to administer" speech?' said Wilson.

'He did, in fact. He also gave me a copy of the Metropolitan Police Act for reference about my new duties.'

'Did he also offer you tea from Kandy, and say how change needed to be given a direction?'

'Yes, he did.'

'Perhaps he did not mention how it was grown from plants stolen from China. Or how the people of Kandy are in the process of having their land stolen from them by his friends who are plantation owners.'

'No, he did not, Dr Wilson.'

'As you can see, the nature of change is different depending on your point of observation. You may want to read the wording of the Police Act, but I do not know how much it would help. Keeping the peace in Britain is different from here. You know it far better than the three of us. In Britain it is understood that it is the King's peace. Now this new law makes it the responsibility of all citizens to ensure the King's peace is kept. In other words, an officer of the law has to keep the people's interests in mind. Whereas in India, you will first need to know whose peace you are keeping: the Crown's, the Company's, or the princes'. Not to mention the people. What works on the streets of London will not work in Benares...or Jabalpur. You can walk around London and believe you are working for the community. In Benares, as James here will tell you, you will first need to know which community you are thinking about, or are permitted to think of. The truth has many sides, but its worst enemy is always he who knows, but is not concerned.'

'I will keep that in mind, Dr Wilson,' said Sleeman.

'Regarding the governor-general, I fear his zeal for reform will have unfortunate consequences. The day is not far when those who have his ear, and of Whitehall and Parliament, will introduce English as the medium of instruction in India,' said Wilson.

'I wonder if that would be such a bad decision, Dr Wilson,' said Sleeman.

'It would be a catastrophe, captain. It would create unfathomable tensions within the communities of the Hindu castes and Muslims, not to mention those outside the varna fold. Already there are murmurs among the sanyasis and the ulema about Lord Bentinck's reforms, real and imagined. Persian and Sanskrit scholars have always held English in contempt, partly for fear that its wider use would erode their power, and such a move will convince them that they were right. Any attempt to force them into what they think is cultural subservience to the West would be most unfortunate. Moreover, English as a medium of instruction would create a class that would, in time, be deracinated, as uncomfortable among the people as the Englishman born in Calcutta, who has lived here all his life, but wishes for a home in the hills in summer.'

'At the very least, English as a medium of instruction could help Indians study science and modern thought. But I understand what you mean by Englishmen who wish to escape India's summers,' said Sleeman, who knew of at least one such Englishman and often wondered about this phenomenon.

'I trust you are not among those who believe that Persian and Sanskrit literature cannot compare with the works of European scholarship, captain, or are not worthy of study,' said Wilson, with a smile.

'I do not know enough to venture an opinion, Dr Wilson. I have heard similar views from some people at Government House in the past. I only wonder if it would be easy to study modern subjects or thought in any language other than English. And whether the higher judiciary or administration can be run in any other language.'

'Yes, that is a legitimate concern. But what if there are

reforms at the lower judicial levels? Would you have diwani adalats conduct their affairs in English? I cannot imagine how you will be able to explain that to a local qazi or pundit. But for education, we already have functioning institutions where subjects are taught in Sanskrit and Persian, to the benefit of students. But there is also the matter of texts in these languages. There has always been a faction at Government House and in Leadenhall Street which has believed that Sanskrit and Persian texts are not worthy of study. I do not begrudge them anymore, nor do I have the will or strength to contest their policies. Among the Brahmins of Benares are many dear friends who believe—with evidence, they say—that a single shelf of parchment in any tol or math has more knowledge than in an entire wing of any large library in London, Paris or Berlin. It is human nature to believe in the superiority of one's own culture, of what one is familiar with or to which one is emotionally bound. I cannot be expected to feel for Latin classics what I experience when I read Sanskrit texts. But I have contended for far too long with those who would like to do away with Persian and Sanskrit studies, and I am afraid we have lost. Government House no longer listens to our views, even if Lord Bentinck is not unreasonable when he chooses to be. Whenever London approves of the new education policy, it will be English as medium of instruction in our universities, and not Persian or Sanskrit.'

'And I believe neither the Anglophiles nor Dr Wilson are correct, at least on this matter,' said Hodgson. His tone was still gentle and wry, as if he had had this argument countless times with Wilson, which must have been the case.

'If one were to seek a just education policy for India, the language of instruction has to be the native tongue of the student. Imposing Sanskrit or Persian would be as unfair as imposing English. It would be similar to forcing English schoolchildren to have their lessons in Old English, or perhaps a Frisian dialect, or compelling a Highlander to learn the King's English, a crime which has been committed already. You may ask the captain here whether he learnt Cornish at school, or anywhere else except from his mother,' said Hodgson.

'Your solution would be difficult to implement, Brian. You must have considered the variety in the languages of India. Even if one were to introduce the language spoken by the majority in a province, the sentiments of linguistic minorities will need to be considered, not to mention determining what the standard forms of these languages of instruction are to be. In the captain's own province, would it be fair to impose Hindustani as spoken in Awadh hundreds of miles away, or Bundeli or even Bagheli? And, to refer to Captain Sleeman's original problem, texts in English will need to be made available and comprehensible to students,' said Wilson.

'That is the task of translators like you and I, Dr Wilson. But I cannot support the imposition of any language, modern or ancient, eastern or western, over the native language of a student. Of all the impositions on a people, an alien language must be among the most cruel. Almost as cruel as permitting the acolytes of Charles Grant to proselytise in the countryside, and thus foment unrest among the sadhus and fakirs. I should like to know who will accept the blame when all these resentments fester, as they will, and erupt, as they are likely to,' said Hodgson.

Sleeman wondered how much of this was the wide-eyed alarm of people who understood ancient texts and inscriptions better than the workings of their contemporary humans, and how much was based on actual information from people on the ground. He knew that Hodgson, Wilson and Prinsep corresponded with a vast array of well-informed, perceptive and well-travelled individuals across the subcontinent. Therefore, he could not dismiss their fears. It was just that, sitting there in a Calcutta winter, after reading about the end of yet another grinding campaign in an inhospitable land, it was difficult for him to believe that Government House was blind to the possibility of native resentment festering to such an extent. He tried to imagine the sadhus of Malwa and Baghelkhand leading a rebellion over real and imagined grouses. Of qazis in Bhopal preaching jihad. It seemed fanciful just then.

'Gentlemen,' said Prinsep, his hands raised. 'I do not believe Captain Sleeman finds our debate entertaining at present. We can continue this vexed discussion afterwards, as I am sure we will, although we can agree that it will make no difference to the makers of policy at Government House. Captain, you mentioned that secretary Macnaghten would supervise your new responsibilities. I gather these concern the enforcement of the law?'

Sleeman did not think such distinguished scholars would be interested in the minutae of administration in Jabalpur, but Wilson would receive the news anyway, it being pertinent to the work of the Mint.

'I have been asked to assist the Department for the Suppression of Dacoits, and inquire into the activities of a class of criminals in the Agency, known as Phansigars, who are said to waylay and strangle people. There have been a few cases, but there were jurisdictional issues, and the crimes were never solved in a satisfactory manner, in my view. I will be able to take a fresh look at them and, because of the department, be able to work around the problem of jurisdiction.'

'So, we should not expect the gallant captain to dash

off on horseback on a campaign against some murderous dacoits in the forests, like the Pindaris?' said Wilson.

'Indeed not, Dr Wilson. There will be no such armed campaign. This is just a matter of enforcing the law and communicating better with the princes.'

'Did you say these gangs waylay and strangle people?' asked Prinsep.

'That is what they are said to do. They have acquired considerable notoriety in the past,' said Sleeman.

'This reminds me of a report I had read in the Society's office some weeks ago. In an old journal, from Madras I think. If I recall correctly, there is some mention of the character and activities of stranglers in that region. I will try to locate and send it to your lodgings.'

Sleeman thanked him.

'And now, gentlemen, the light is failing, so let us re-enter the house and continue the conversation before dinner,' said Hodgson. 'We have a lot to discuss about these petrified bones that are being discovered by everyone. I find them a far more pleasant topic of conversation than the missteps and hubris of Government House. Captain Sleeman, I must visit your province as soon as I can, and I shall be delighted if I can convince both Dr Wilson and James to accompany me.'

Calcutta's most formidable intellect took two days to find what he had mentioned to Sleeman. The delay was not the result of a lapse in Prinsep's powers, but a testament to the huge number of unarchived and uncatalogued documents and objects which had been accepted and stored by the members of the Asiatic Society at its sprawling house at the corner of Chowringhee Road and Park Street. Accepted with an indiscrimination which matched the enthusiasm of the Society's members, and stored on the assumption that someone, at some point, would clear the Augean stables without the necessity of diverting a river through them.

Prinsep was not up to this task just yet, being preoccupied with analysing the iconography and text of his own collection of antique coins, but he took it upon himself to wade through the rooms of documents and unearth a thirteen-year-old copy of *The Madras Literary Gazette*, which he then sent to Sleeman's quarters. The publication contained a report compiled by a doctor named Robert Sherwood, titled 'Of the Murderers Called Phansigars'. It was the most exhaustive study of stranglers that Sleeman had ever come across.

In his decades in India, and particularly his time in the central districts, Sleeman had been acquainted with the numerous classes and categories of criminals which beset travellers in the countryside, or in the crowded roads and alleys of the cities. From confidence tricksters, burglars and poisoners to highwaymen and dacoits, the types of organised and professional criminals ranged from the merely clever to the disturbingly violent. Sleeman himself, in his ordered, methodical manner seemed to recall concluding to himself that there were eight or nine such categories of criminals. Phansigars, he had supposed, were one of them, distinguished only by the means by which they murdered their victims. Sherwood's report made him begin to realise there was much more.

At around the time when Sleeman had received his commission in the Bengal Army, Government House had begun to receive reports of the disappearances of sepoys on leave, while they were travelling to their homes in the villages, or were on their way back to the barracks. Some were said to have been waylaid and murdered by stranglers for their pay. The number of disappearances had risen so much that sepoys had been told to travel in large groups and not carry much cash, neither of which was always possible.

Over the years, these cases had been noticed by administrators in provinces from north to south, but little had been done, and not much was understood.

Sherwood was a surgeon from Madras who had travelled everywhere in Tamil lands and a bit of a naturalist and antiquarian, but his main interest was in the social structures of those parts.

'The Phansigars or stranglers are thus designated from the Hindustani word "phansi", meaning a noose. In the more northern parts of India these murderers are called Thugs signifying deceivers; in the Tamil language they are called Ari Tulucar or Muslim stranglers,' the old doctor had written.

In Kannada, they were called Tanti Calleru. Sherwood had explained that this meant 'thieves who used a noose or a wire'. Meanwhile, in Telugu they were called Warlu Wahndlu, or 'those who used the noose'. They were believed to be votaries of various forms of the Mother Goddess, even, noted Sherwood, the Muslims.

What had attracted the doctor's attention as far as Sleeman could gather was: first, the extensive geography across which these stranglers could be found; second, that there was a similarity in their methods, beliefs and weapons and third, that they straddled a very specific divide in the Stygian world of criminals. That they were murderers and well-organised was obvious. But unlike the more common murderous dacoits and highwaymen to be found in every human society around the world, the Phansigars were also reliant on deceit and elaborate cunning to entrap their victims. This made them an aberration. For the violent professional criminal did not depend on the fine scalpel of deceit to ply his trade, relying instead on the blunt instrument of violence, or its promise. And the trickster did not kill.

The Phansigars did both as a matter of principle, said Sherwood, who had studied in detail four cases which had achieved considerable notoriety in Madras, because of the circumstances surrounding the crime and the particulars of the victims. In 1805, five men travelling from a village to Coimbatore, a distance of not more than two dozen kos, had been befriended by a group of harmless traders proceeding in the same direction. They had then been strangled by the traders and robbed of 2,500 pagoda coins which they had been transporting.

Sleeman did a quick calculation: the coins were worth eight thousand seven hundred and fifty rupees. An amount so substantial that its loss was bound to be noticed by somebody, even if the disappearance of the five men was not. And the somebody who did notice was the collector of Coimbatore, principally because it had been his money, and the victims had been clerks in his office.

Later the same year, two well-regarded and wealthy merchants of Kannur, travelling on horseback from Madras with five armed attendants, had been killed and robbed. In 1807, five persons transporting some valuable property owned by a senior British army officer were killed on their way to Bangalore Cantonment, along with two other men who they had met some hours previously. And in 1815, three government employees carrying two thousand and five hundred rupees had been killed in the district of Masulipatnam. Sherwood had happened to be on hand when the bodies had been discovered. All three had been expertly strangled. None of them appeared to have put up a fight.

All the murders had been committed in isolated places, with no sign of the furtiveness and haste with which an urban criminal ventures out if he has to in the daytime. There was, the old doctor felt, an element of ritual in the crimes, like the performance of a macabre ballet. The culprits had never been seen or identified, leave alone caught. There had only been the faintest of whispers about groups following the victims, or being seen in their company, or emerging elsewhere much later. If it had not been for extraordinary circumstances—the army officer had convinced his regiment to deploy an entire battalion to scour the area, and had obtained the services of the best hunting dogs from among Bangalore's British residents—some of the bodies might never have been found.

Sleeman imagined the doctor methodically going over the evidence to compile the report in 1816. He would have liked Sherwood, who reminded the captain of Spilsbury.

Sleeman thought about where he had been when the report was published. It did not require effort. After the end of the Anglo-Nepal War, during which he had seen action with his regiment in the terai, he was recovering from a second, severe bout of malaria, and had been invalided to Calcutta, where he had spent several days in delirium, hallucinating, wondering if he had died and had been placed in limbo. He did not care to recall that year.

Sleeman imagined the locations of these crimes, spread in a wide arc from Madras through Coimbatore and Bangalore to Masulipatnam. And if such well-protected, influential persons could be murdered with impunity, he could imagine the number of poorer travellers, carrying less valuable cargo or property, who had been similarly waylaid and never heard from again.

In all this, Sherwood had noted, the Ari Tulucar had not shown excessive violence, if such a phrase could be used for murder. There was no indication that the victims had been attacked by dacoits, with swords or sticks. There were no signs of blunt force inflicted on the bodies, of broken bones or sword strikes, of torture. In fact, the old doctor had noted from his own observations and from conversations with those who had seen the bodies of the other victims, it had appeared that the victims had been unaware of their fate up till the moment they had been strangled. Somewhere on a routine journey, on a familiar road, these seasoned and worldly-wise travellers had fallen among people cleverer and more cunning than themselves, who had convinced them to let their guard down, and who had killed them without giving them the time to mount a resistance.

If Sleeman was to enforce the law across the districts neighbouring Jabalpur, and inquire into the allegations of Phansigars in these areas, he would have to understand what was going on in these parts, and how extensive the problem was. Nothing much seemed to have happened after Sherwood's report, and it was doubtful that many people had even paid attention to it.

The return upriver to Benares and then upcountry to Jabalpur found Sleeman reflecting on the vast geography he had been asked to contend with; on the complex nature of politics there; on the diverse royal egos and political fictions which fed this complexity; and on the difficulties of enforcing what passed for law in what passed for Company-administered territories. He reflected on what he knew of the people and societies across the vast hinterland. But Sleeman also thought of an old man he had met once, long ago, and of a story that straddled the meandering line between the macabre and the tragic. The longer he thought of the old man, the more morose he became, until even Amelie grew worried and asked if he was feeling poorly.

On the morning after his return to Jabalpur, he arrived at his office so early that his chief munshi had to run from his house nearby on hearing that Sleeman was on the way. The munshi found Sleeman in the armoury behind the adalat, searching among the old records. It was an armoury only in name. Since his office and the court were just a few dozen feet from Jabalpur Camp, the muskets and matchlocks which were the poor weapons of the district constabulary had been stored in the Camp's magazine. The armoury, with thick brick walls and a sturdy roof, had been given over to the storage of official papers and records. People had forgotten whether it had been Sleeman's idea or the agent's, but the papers stayed safe in the monsoon.

Sleeman emerged from the armoury with an old sheaf of documents, told the munshi that he would see visitors later in the day and shut himself in the office.

In 1823, at the beginning of his second year as magistrate at Narsinghpur, and suffering from recurring bouts of poor health, Sleeman had been sitting in his office on a day of comparative quiet when an army officer acquaintance had dropped by and requested his time. Accompanying the officer had been an old Indian man, and the officer had requested

Sleeman to give him a hearing. With many profuse thanks, the old man had started his story.

After years of service in the officer's regiment in the Bengal Army, the man had returned to his desh, not twenty miles north of Chhindwara. Here he had resolved to spend the remaining years of his life with his son and his family, his wife having died many years earlier. Shortly thereafter, however, tragedy had struck the family, and the son and daughter-in-law had both died of cholera in one of the waves of the epidemic Sleeman remembered well, leaving a teenaged grandson as the only remaining family for the man. The old soldier had been supplementing his income from the small family plot through his ancestral occupation as a garpagri, employed by the village to perform the appropriate rituals to keep hailstorms away.

'My grandson, sahib, was impatient as young men are, and wanted to make his way in the world. I told him to join the army in that case, but he refused. He wanted to travel to Bhopal and start a trade suitable for a Brahmin. I do not know where he got the idea from. Perhaps someone in the village put it in his ears. Perhaps an evil spirit spoke to him in the night. And I could not convince him otherwise,' said the old man, his rheumy eyes squinting in the afternoon sun as he sat at Sleeman's feet under a tree outside the magistrate's court.

'But sometimes a young man can see sense after some time, and my grandson might have not left if it had not been for the cursed Sukh Ram. This man would frequent the village, and was said to have helped many young men from other villages travel to big cities elsewhere. He was said to be a musician in a nautch court in Bhopal, and would travel often. Finally, after months and months, and a difficult dry season, my grandson convinced me to let him go, so I gave my blessings, and he travelled with Sukh Ram for Bhopal. On the way, he was to stay at my brother's house in Pipariya, and was to return in a year. A little more than a fortnight later, my brother and his wife visited me to enquire after us, and I was told my grandson had never arrived.'

Here the old man paused and wiped his tears. 'At first I thought my grandson, being a careless youth, had just travelled onwards to Bhopal, although he was also obedient and respectful towards his elders, so I did not understand why he had not visited my brother. So I packed what provisions I had and travelled to Bhopal, although my old bones are not capable of such long journeys any more. But what else could I do, sahib?

'At Bhopal, I enquired about his whereabouts at the place and the locality where he was supposed to stay. They had not heard of him. Of Sukh Ram there was no trace. I went everywhere; I asked as much as I dared to. I became a vagabond, wandering the city hoping to see a sign of my grandson's face. I was abused and mistreated on the streets by the servants of the rich, men who, when I was younger and vigorous and in the army, would have never dared to look me in the eye. After days of living like this, I decided to retrace my steps. I realised that, in all likelihood, my grandson had never reached Pipariya. So I reached the next village between there and my own village, and asked if they had seen or heard of him.'

Reading the report in his own hand, Sleeman recalled once again his admiration for the old soldier. In the midst of his desperation, in his lonely search with almost no resources in the face of caste barriers, he had made a series of logical conclusions.

'I asked at each village. Finally, I reached Bina, which was smaller than my own village and in the middle of a valley.

The people of the village prior to them had said they did not remember seeing anyone who resembled my grandson. The people at Bina said they had seen my grandson, and that he had travelled west. But the speed with which they recalled my grandson made me think something was wrong. How could they remember him so well, sahib, and without prompting? Was he the young Maharaja of Ujjain? But I also felt that they wanted me to leave as soon as possible. So I went away. Afterwards I went to other villages. Some told me of men from their families who had been missing too.

'Sahib, I went home, and I locked myself in. It is possible that I had become mad sometime during those days and never realised it. It is possible. I do not know. People say many things about me in the village now. It is easy to say things about an old man who has nobody in the world, for now they know that my grandson will never come back. But I sat alone in the hut, and I thought about it, and a few days later I went back to Bina.'

Here the old man paused to cough, for his throat had become dry from talking, and Sleeman waited while he excused himself, went and drank some water from his caste's pot on the other side of the yard and staggered back.

'I still remembered how to march, sahib, and how to think on a campaign. The only difference was I was alone, and old, and the world was full of evil. I waited in the hills till it was evening, and then went down to take a look. I do not remember what I was expecting to find. It is just an ordinary village, with the houses in the middle of a few fields. It is not a prosperous place, not more or less than my own village, or any other in these parts, although the valley is parched. The only other difference was some distance from the houses, at the edge of the forest, where I could see a lot of crows and carrion birds land in the dusk. It was an offal pit, such as one would find in a village, where they bury animal carcasses. But this one was big, sahib, far bigger than it would have been for a village of that size, even if only Muslims or meat-eating jatis lived in it. And the mound looked like it had been freshly dug up several times.

'I could not find anything else. I decided to return home even though it was night by then. But as I was stepping up into the hills, I was struck from behind, and then beaten till I lost my senses.

'When I awoke I was tied hand and foot, in a cowshed, in the dark. There were men standing around me, their faces covered with the cloth of their turbans. They asked for my name, and the name of my village, and what I was doing prowling in the hills after dusk. They beat me regardless of whether I answered or not. But they were careful not to beat me so much that I lost consciousness again.

'I told them I was just a poor Brahmin, and that I did not want to have anything to do with them. The village meant nothing to me. All I wanted was to know where my grandson was. I just wanted him back. I said, if he is dead, at least give me his body so I will know, and so that I can perform his last rites. I kept saying that.

'At some point, the masked men were joined by other people, and they talked among themselves outside the cowshed. Then they returned and started asking questions again. They kept wanting to know what I did in the village. Was I really a garpagri? This I remember. They kept wanting to know that, and even asked me about the rituals and mantras. After some time, they stopped beating me and left.

'They returned after what seemed a long time, untied me and pushed me out of the cowshed. They pointed to a bundle on the ground and said, "Take him, and go." Sahib, I opened it, and saw my grandson's face in the torchlight. He had been buried for several weeks, but I could recognise him. They also threw some copper ornaments on the ground, which I remembered he had taken with him to sell if he could in Bhopal.

'They said, "Old man, take him and go. But do not breathe a word of this to anyone, or we shall claim you in his place. Your life shall be taken, just as we strangled him. The Goddess will not be denied if you betray us."

'Sahib, in the dark, I picked up my grandson's corpse and stumbled away. I did not dare look back, for I knew that if I were to even glance at those evil men, I would fall over and die. I carried him up the hill, and along the path, and sometime after dawn I reached my village, where I managed to conduct his last rites. Nobody came to help me, for news had spread by then.

'After that, I took his ashes to my house and locked myself in once more. I was in a daze. I did not know what I was doing, or what I would do. But after some time I remembered my duty, so I took his ashes to the Narmada to immerse them.'

At this point the army officer had interjected to tell Sleeman that the old man had quite lost his senses after reaching the Narmada, and had become a vagabond till the officer had come across him on the road and recognised the old sepoy. He had taken the man to his house and nursed him back to some extent, after which he had convinced the man to come to Sleeman, as the magistrate closest to the scene of the crime, to register a complaint.

'Sahib,' said the old man, 'I know I am already dead. I think I have been dead since that night, but my body has not realised it yet. I know they will find me, because I have spoken to you gentlemen, and they will claim me. But I have to tell you this. The Phansigars waylaid and killed my grandson, and they live in Bina, and there is not a soul in those parts who does not live in fear of them, as I was told. I thought I had seen the world, and could return home to a quiet life. I did not know that I would be destroyed by this evil next to my own home.'

And after this, the old man had left for his village. Sleeman had assured the officer that he would take steps, so he submitted a report to the Agent of Bhopal, because the area was just outside the jurisdiction of Sagar and Narmada and fell within the princely state of Bhopal. The agent's office had sent Sleeman a curt reply to the effect that the political department did not have the authority to make any inquiries in the territory of Bhopal on the request of a person of Sleeman's rank.

But there had been no talk of a restriction on his travel, so Sleeman decided not to reply to the agent. Instead, he had paid a visit to the old man's village. But when he reached there, he was met by residents who assured him that all was well in the neighbourhood. On being asked about the old man, the sarpanch had claimed that he had never returned from immersing his grandson's ashes, and that his hut had caught fire a few days earlier.

Sleeman had gone to the spot himself, and found nothing remained of the hut beyond some burnt thatch and twigs. The sarpanch had expressed some anguish at the situation, telling Sleeman that monsoon was nearly on them, and the village would have to find a new garpagri.

In the decades after the Mughal Empire retreated from the Deccan, leaving feuding satraps and insurrections in its wake, the region around the Satpuras and Vindhyas from the northwestern Deccan to the northern banks of the Mahanadi had hurtled into an endless cycle of conflict. The world whose systems and structures had once been forged and administered by the heirs of Timur had been broken again, leaving the people, the long-suffering peasants who were the soul of central India, to their own pitiable, insufficient devices. Of the armies that ranged through the region, the most dreaded were the Pindaris, once irregular infantry and light cavalry which used to follow Aurangzeb's army, and later the Peshwas. By the beginning of the nineteenth century, the Pindaris had become an autonomous force of destruction, known and feared across the land. It had taken a coalition of forces led by Warren Hastings' Bengal Army a year to destroy their last holdouts in a bitter campaign, beginning around the time when Sleeman, far from these events, had just begun his long road to recovery in Calcutta.

Of those terrible times few records remained, and the memory of the many crimes which were committed could be found only in the hearts of people or in half-remembered legends in the countryside. The Pindaris had not been the only horsemen of the apocalypse in a broken world, as Maratha noble fought nawab and raja for mastery over a city, or a trade route, or a trifle. Life had been cheaper than usual and the law a legend, its guardians a myth from some long-forgotten age of heroes.

Over his decade in the central provinces, Sleeman had heard tales of those times, of hardship and misery, of degradation and loss and of hopelessness. But of all these tales, none had left him despairing for humans as much as the story of the old man.

'I have often wondered why you were so affected by it, William,' said Amelie in the evening after he had told her of reading the account yet again. Of his small circle of intimates, Amelie alone understood the true nature of the horrors which had occurred in central India. From her father she had heard of what the family had suffered on their journey to exile during the Revolution, and what dark deeds had been committed in France in the months afterwards. The dismantling of empire and the collapse of absolute power is an apocalyptic process no less traumatic than the forging of an empire. Her father had come to terms with it through ghoulish masochism, by narrating to her the demise of French aristocracy. This had left her inured to most details of human excess. Her way of dealing with it had been to seek beauty, in art, literature and music, in the hope of drinking enough from these fountains to forget the despair in her father's voice. This was another reason why Calcutta had held few illusions for her.

Nevertheless, Sleeman could not explain to Amelie why the old man's story had made him feel the bleakness that nibbles around the edge of most human life. Perhaps he felt a former soldier of the Bengal Army who had served in the hill campaigns and endured much deserved better. But he knew of many others who had returned to civilian life and suffered much as well. Perhaps it was the congruence of the cruel and macabre; the image of a man stumbling through the dark, paralysed by fear, carrying the corpse of the last proof of his time on earth. Perhaps Sleeman had looked into the old man's eyes and seen the frightening landscape that lies at the end of all hope and all fond illusions. Or perhaps it was something else.

The sequence of events, the interrogation and beatings, the sudden decision to hand over the corpse, the assurance with which the threats were made, and in all likelihood, carried out, spoke of something else. For a moment, a veil had been lifted over the countryside, over a people quietly going about their daily lives, and the shadow of something sinister had revealed itself. For only a moment, and no more, for the old man's village had been a dead end and Sleeman had not heard of any such case about Phansigars in the years since; only stories, allegations and rumours, and a few men brought to trial on occasion. But in that story, lurking around the edge of the man's experience was a group of people, ruthless, organised, with systems and methods. Something more than a mere criminal enterprise. Something that functioned with the knowledge that there was no rival system or mechanism which could contest it. Perhaps that was the root of Sleeman's discontent. That he had chanced upon the barest hint of an elaborate system of rituals around the taking of lives and had not been able to do anything about it or the criminals who held such terrifying power over villagers. Yes, perhaps that had been the reason for the story haunting him over the years.

'I have never been able to think of that poor broken man without wondering what it speaks of us as a species. In the years afterwards, I have often imagined him: carrying his grandson's rotting carcass, stumbling in the dark over broken country, perhaps not even certain if he had not been lost, over mile after mile, driven only by his love and a sense of duty, or perhaps not even that. Maybe he too had died, and his body was just going through the motions without being aware of his demise. But that is too fanciful a notion. But I do think of him, utterly alone on the forest trail with the body, fleeing unnamed terrors, made all the worse by the fact that they were not supernatural, but just as human as you and I. A people should not have to live with such terrors.'

'You never told me what happened after you visited his village.'

'After speaking to the sarpanch and the patwari, I was convinced that they were hiding a great many things from me, perhaps out of fear of these Phansigars, or from sheer bloody minded obduracy, or because I was a white man. I never could tell the difference. Although I know that when one speaks to a villager in his dialect, or a close approximation of it, he does not hold the colour of your skin against you. But most of these villagers are secretive by nature, and will not speak even to blood relatives if they are so inclined.

'I walked around the village and saw what could be seen, which was hardly anything. There was not much I could do about the matter. The old man had disappeared, and of his house or possessions little remained. The brother he had mentioned lived in the lands of the Nawab Begum, and any matters of inheritance were to be overseen by the patwari, so I could not intervene with the excuse that I was a magistrate. I had been instructed by the Agent of Bhopal not to pursue the matter, so I returned to Narsinghpur much chastened.'

'But what do you think had happened?'

'Till our recent visit to Calcutta, I had thought that the grandson had been the victim of some robbers who had a village in their thrall, robbers who had a specific belief system which caused them to return the boy's corpse and exact their revenge on the old man afterwards. There was no other conclusion I could have drawn. I knew with certainty that the village was the key to the problem; if only I had been allowed to visit and inspect it. But as you can see from the report of the doctor in Madras, the Phansigars who killed the old man and his grandson, and who had such power over the village near the forest, were not an isolated band of dacoits. There are similarities between the old man's account and that of the doctor's, as if these crimes were rituals to be conducted in a specific manner, as if travellers are targeted in a planned manner. These are not ordinary crimes.'

And Amelie, the only one of his close friends who knew there was no such thing as an ordinary crime, and also understood his silences as much as his words, said, 'I shall be happy to assist in your investigation in any way, William. But I hope you will not exert yourself too much in this new task, particularly during the rains. And you will need to delegate some of the responsibility to Lieutenant Reynolds. I will not have you shouldering all of it yourself.'

Sleeman was waiting to discuss the matter with Reynolds, even though he did not think he would be required to delegate much of the work. Apart from travel to a few necessary places, the investigation would not be a complex affair beyond his capabilities.

But Reynolds' absence was beginning to vex Sleeman. The lieutenant had left Jabalpur a fortnight before the Sleemans had started for Calcutta. He had accompanied his wife to explore what he had termed an excellent opportunity in real estate. He had gone to Simla.

The place had been discovered a little more than a decade earlier. They used adjectives like excellent and salubrious for it. Two years earlier, Reynolds had bought a small plot in the valley and had not stopped talking about it since. The wealthy or the ambitious or both had bought the best plots already, he said, and urged Sleeman to buy land for his retirement too.

This time the lieutenant had made the long journey to make plans for a house and to develop the grounds.

Sleeman began to work on the investigations himself till one evening when Reynolds rode up to his residence and dismounted from a lathered horse. He had ridden in advance of his group with a small number of sepoys from Jhansi on receiving word during the return from Simla that he had to hurry. Sleeman greeted him in the study, and assured him that the matter could wait till the following morning, but Reynolds insisted on being given his instructions as early as possible. He had spent years with the political department, but was one of those people who never left the army. Brown of hair, medium of height and mild of eye, Reynolds carried himself with the suggestion of considerable physical strength and the kind of earnest self-righteousness that comes to people who have an honest, uncluttered view of the world.

Sleeman gave him a précis of his conversation with Bentinck and Macnaghten and mentioned the report from Madras, ending with the account of the old man and the village of Bina.

'I believe there are two distinct matters here, Reynolds, and we must bear that in mind always. The first is, the complaint about Phansigars is not, on the face of it, without basis, and there seem to be some similarities between such incidents in these provinces, and in Madras and Mysore. We, therefore, need to investigate all complaints about Phansigars. What do you know about them?'

'Only the few stories we have heard, sir, and some cases in a few of the provinces, including in Allahabad. There was a case in Dhuriaghat and another in Chitrakoot some months ago. I remember reading a report that after sepoys were said to have disappeared on their way home, the Company government had told them not to carry a lot of money while travelling alone.'

The disappearances had come down after those orders, but had not stopped. How the government expected sepoys to take their pay of several months back to their families, Sleeman did not know. Perhaps Government House had not thought of it either.

'I never paid much attention to the stories of the Phansigars, sir, or the poisoners that are called Dhaturias. There are some violent dacoits in the countryside. The princes send out soldiers when they hear of dacoits, if they think there should be a chase and capture. It might not be easy to find Phansigars unless we hear of a specific incident. We might have to chase a lot of hearsay and rumours, sir.'

'Yes, we might have to, but we should not be daunted by the task. The second problem is a little delicate, Reynolds. We will have to reassure the Scindia and the Nawab Begum that we are working to solve these depredations. We will have to visit their courts at some point. I shall begin by writing to the respective agents. But first we have to decide how we are to investigate the matter. We will use our district police, and those of any other province that we visit. I hope we will not have to visit the princely states, but we will if we have to. In which case, we will need assistance from the army. If we need to bring back some prisoners for interrogation, we will need to house them at the district jail.'

'Yes, sir. I shall start to make the arrangements.'

'We have to begin with the village, Reynolds. We must begin from there.'

The central provinces had been quiet for several months and the officers of Jabalpur Camp had left for Calcutta with their families. Brigadier General O'Halloran, who appeared to have no attraction for the big cities and was never to be found away from his station in Sagar, was prompt in his reply to Sleeman's request. The Bengal Army would be glad to assist, he wrote a few days later, and ordered the Jabalpur commandant to depute a hundred sepoys with ten sowars to accompany Sleeman in the princely states.

'The general says he will be sending a good man over to you, captain. He says we will not regret taking him in. It appears the general has taken a personal interest in our work and in this young man's future,' said Reynolds, reading the general's reply.

Accompanying the letter was a summary of the man's background, which Sleeman read with interest.

The district had other matters that needed Sleeman's attention. The diwani adalats, tasked with functioning as trial courts for the district, were never short of civil and criminal litigation, overseen by qazis and Hindu lawgivers. For some civil matters, local zamindars had been given powers to adjudicate over their tenants. But sometimes matters required Sleeman's intervention, such as a land dispute between two prominent zamindars who lived some distance outside Jabalpur. The claims were contested, the land not demarcated to the satisfaction of everyone, and no records existed older than a dozen years. Sleeman suspected the zamindars had little real interest in the disputed plot, and were litigious as a matter of course, or perhaps to keep themselves entertained.

He was trying to distract himself from the newest set of complaints by examining a survey map of the district when his munshi announced that a Second Lieutenant Moore was waiting outside.

John Moore was a slight, short man in his early twenties, with fair hair and an honest face which made him look like an older adolescent. He also had very tired eyes and walked with a limp.

'Good morning, captain. I was directed by Brigadier General O'Halloran to report to you,' said Moore, saluting.

Sleeman said there was no need to salute and that he could take a seat. Moore's service record was still lying on the desk. Sleeman had not read a report like that in a long time.

'You have an excellent record. It is rare to meet someone so young with such commendations. I trust you have recovered from both your injuries,' said Sleeman.

Moore said he had. Sleeman suspected there were other injuries which were not visible, or physical.

'I see you fought at Yangon and Danubyu.'

'Yes, sir.'

'We lost many officers and men there.'

'Yes, sir.'

'Quite a lot to malaria, from what I have been told. It was the same in the Terai with my regiment. And I understand the battles were quite difficult.'

Moore nodded.

The general staff had still not seen it fit to give the young man a promotion, despite his medals and service in Burma. Did the Bengal Army now expect its young officers to die in battle before they could be considered for promotion?

'I see that you requested to be transferred to Jabalpur rather than be posted in Assam.'

'Yes, sir. I did not want to see another monsoon in the swamps.'

Sleeman had read the doctor's report of Moore's headaches, deafness and disturbed sleep.

'You will find Jabalpur a quiet place. We are forming a unit to investigate some dacoits. The work will not tax you overmuch. I will not ask you to do much soldiering, Moore.'

'I do not mind the soldiering, sir.'

'I understand. But we will be doing a different kind of work, and you will, I think, be suitable for it.'

Moore saluted and left. Sleeman contemplated the

incredible bravery that some young people possess, and how rare it was to survive at the end of it. He doubted the tiredness in Moore's eyes would go away soon.

The district's work was wound up to the satisfaction of the agent, who was still recovering from his illness. There was no end to work around Jabalpur, but a day came at last when Sleeman could set out for the village near the forest. With him went Reynolds, Moore and the sepoys. Sleeman wanted Spilsbury to join them. He suspected he would require the surgeon's expertise in more ways than one, but Spilsbury had patients to attend to. The surgeon, who had shown considerable interest in the matter, had given some guidance on what to look for, and also deputed a native medical officer, carrying the implements of his profession. There were also six or seven leather workers from their settlement at Jabalpur, for the Brahmin and Thakur sepoys would not agree to dig up graves or exhume bodies if such an occasion arose.

Reynolds had also found a British officer with an interest in breeding game dogs, and who had several in his kennels which he claimed to have a keen sense of smell. Sleeman did not know much about the small and rather arcane world of dog breeders, and understood even less of their methods and objectives, but the officer vouched for four of the beasts, and they had joined the group, led by two handlers. If it had worked in Bangalore it should work here.

It was a quiet winter day. Sleeman and Reynolds led the group, followed by the sepoys on foot and the sowars led by Moore trotting behind.

'Do forgive me. I forgot to ask you how Simla was,' said Sleeman.

'It was a pleasant stay. I shall begin construction of the house next year. I also met a gentleman from Delhi who wants to grow apples on a stretch of land not far from mine. I might place some money in the orchard.'

'I find it difficult to imagine you as an apple farmer, Reynolds.'

'I shall not be growing them myself, sir. But he is certain the air and soil are good for our Pippins, and he seems to know a lot about them.'

'I see. Apples?'

'Yes, sir.'

They continued in silence for some time. Sleeman had nothing further to say, and Reynolds thought he did.

'Will you also consider purchasing a plot there, sir? I have heard that almost all the senior officers in Delhi and Ambala will build houses in Simla,' asked Reynolds.

'A more interesting question, Reynolds,' said Sleeman without glancing at the junior officer, 'is that why you would like to live there.'

'It has a pleasant climate. It is a wonderful place to spend the summer.'

'Reynolds, I can understand a person like the agent wishing to be carried uphill in a palanquin to escape the summer. I can understand summer being difficult for an Englishman from England, or for someone like Mr Hodgson, who has been in poor health for years. But you were born in Bombay, were you not? So were your parents and your grandmother, if I recall well. You have lived through thirty-five summers. From where does this need to avoid the heat emerge, then?'

'That may be so, sir, but Simla will be a pleasant place to live in, and I anticipate this with pleasure. Between the dry season and the monsoon, Mrs Reynolds would like us to have a house in a milder climate.'

Sleeman knew it was fruitless to argue with Reynolds'

convictions. In this case, he suspected the junior officer was merely in love with the idea of living in the hills like upper-class Englishmen who dreamt of home despite spending years in the tropics.

Early in the morning of the second day, after breaking camp at dawn, they marched off the stony road to Sagar and along a trail through the forest. The landscape became yet more broken and rock-strewn. The soil was no longer the fertile black layer of the region that gave such a rich harvest.

Sleeman's maps had not recorded this, nor had they prepared him for the village as he saw it on rounding a bend in the trail. It was built on a dusty ledge of rock, beyond which the ground fell away into a series of ravines. On the far side was a great mass of forest. There was a creek nearby which in monsoon might have a thin stream, but was dry then. It was land unsuitable for farming, and not intended for much else. Even the wild animals would not chance upon it while looking for a water hole, and it was doubtful that any game animals would venture over the rocks of the ravine, even during the dry season when desperation set in. Through a combination of wind patterns and geography, the place did not receive much rain during the monsoons. Either through bad luck, or poor judgment, or both, or a set of circumstances of which no record remained, the people who had settled in the village had assured themselves and their descendants a lifetime of poor harvest and empty stomachs. It had been seven years since that old soldier had crept into Bina looking for his missing grandson. Which meant little about life here would have changed. Time passed at a different pace in the countryside, and sometimes did not pass at all.

The arrival of Sleeman and the soldiers caused commotion. He had sent a detachment to circle around the settlement and keep watch from the other side, but he still had enough sepoys and sowars to cause considerable alarm among the people.

Sleeman and Reynolds dismounted and walked up to a group of men standing at the entrance with folded hands. Sleeman folded his hands and greeted them in turn.

'I would like to talk to the headman, if he is present,' said Sleeman, speaking in Bundeli. The villagers were surprised to hear him, but were silent.

An elderly man approached the group and introduced himself.

'Have you been the sarpanch for a long time?' asked Sleeman.

No, he had been chosen three years ago, after the previous headman had died. Sleeman had been hoping it would be the same person as when the incident had occurred.

'We would like to see the village and how you live.'

The headman and others looked at him with some disbelief, as if they were not used to anybody asking them about their problems.

'Perhaps you can guide me around your homes?' said Sleeman.

The sarpanch was reluctant but polite. It was not a large village, with about five hundred residents, none of who appeared wealthy or well-fed. They had no horses, and only a few livestock. On the outer edge of the settlement, where the land fell away into the ravines, was a patch of cleared ground. On the other end of the village, set some distance away at the foot of a small hill, was a tiny temple without a door. Sleeman could glance inside it without needing to peer in. It had a small statue of a goddess.

Moore, who had led the detachment to the other side of the ravines, sent a sepoy to inform Sleeman that they were watching the village, and nobody had left since their arrival.

Sleeman asked Reynolds to get the game dogs. The handlers led them through the village. The dogs seemed to have been trained well, and were obedient. They were quiet till they reached the clearing, where they began to whine and scratch the earth.

Sleeman looked at the sarpanch.

'This is where those who eat meat throw the offal and bones, sahib,' said the sarpanch.

Sleeman nodded and the dogs were taken away. The officers were invited to sit on a cot in the sun, and hookahs were produced for them. Sleeman and Reynolds declined the hookahs.

'We are not a rich village, sahib. We produce just enough to feed ourselves, and sometimes not even that. It is a wonder that we have survived for so long in this place.'

'How old is this village?'

'We do not know, sahib. It has been here since time immemorial. Since the days of my grandfather's father, at least.'

The idea of immemorial time was fluid. It could be a few generations or the previous week.

'And the temple?'

'It is of the Goddess, sahib. Of Bhawani. She is the deity of our village.'

'And the temple, too, has been here since time immemorial?'

'Yes, sahib.'

'What are you, headman?'

The elderly man drew himself up with pride. 'I am Rajput, kaptaan sahib, a Chauhan. My father had a horse.'

'There are many of your jati here?'

'Yes, there are. We also have some other Rajput jatis, but most are Chauhan.'

'Are there any Muslims?'

'Yes, sahib, there are five families of them.'

'I take it they eat meat?'

'Sometimes, sahib, on festive occasions or when they can.'

'Naturally, you do not.'

'No sahib, we of the Chauhan jati here do not eat meat. Only the Muslims do, and a few other jatis.'

Sleeman was quiet, listening to the silence of the village. Everyone, it seemed, was holding their breath.

'It is quite some distance from the road to Bhopal, is it not? Do people visit often?'

'Not at all, sahib. Travellers do not pass by, for there is no settlement beyond here. Only the forest. We are the last people.'

Sleeman nodded. The village held its breath. It was time to begin.

'Sarpanch sahib, I should very much like to know why there is such a large pit for dumping offal, if you have just a few families of meat eaters.'

'Sahib, there have been generations of them living here…'

'I shall be obliged if you arrange for a few men and dig up the pit. I have some men with me who will help.'

The sarpanch looked at Sleeman with entreaty in his eyes. Somewhere at the edge of the village, the dogs whined on their leash.

'Sahib, I do not understand. The pit has offal and bones. Unclean things. If the meat eaters have caused trouble, please tell us. We shall make amends.'

'Sarpanch, as you can see, we have travelled far. We too would like to set our minds at ease, and wish nothing but good fortune on your village and your people. We would like to see this offal pit for ourselves.'

The headman inched back up on his feet and called for a few villagers. They walked to the pit and, under the eyes of Sleeman and Reynolds, began to dig.

Three or four feet under the soil the ground turned to rock. At this point the diggers came across some bones and skulls, of goats and sheep. The stench of offal buried days earlier began to fill the air. The dogs started a low whine till Reynolds ordered the handlers to take them away.

Under this layer of offal was fresh soil which had been brought from elsewhere and laid.

'Please, keep digging,' said Sleeman, his voice terrible in its gentleness. The sarpanch looked back at him, his hands folded, trembling.

After another three feet, the diggers came upon the first pile of skeletons.

Two hours later, they had reached impenetrable rock. There was no water under the arid ground. Instead, the pit had yielded twenty-one distinctly different sets of skeletons of what appeared to be full-grown men. These had been brought up and placed in rows on the ground. The sepoys were talking among themselves. Reynolds had an unreadable expression on his face.

Sleeman was sitting on the cot which had been brought to the pit. His nose had stopped registering the stink. He was looking at the yawning mouth of the pit, and the basalt layer which lay at its bottom. He was thinking of how hard it had been to dig through the basalt at Bada Simla.

'Are these the only bodies here, sarpanch?' asked Sleeman, his voice still gentle.

The headman, his eyes shut and palms folded, was crouched on his haunches on the ground, silent.

'There are other offal pits nearby, are there not?'

The headman said nothing, but shook his head.

'You must understand what I am trying to tell you. Would you like us to search the ravine with the dogs?'

The headman got up and walked towards the ravine.

Sleeman and his men followed. The villager pointed to three other spots where the stones had been cleared away.

By evening, all three spots had been dug down to rock. Neither Sleeman nor his soldiers had eaten. The villagers had gathered in one mass at the other end of the settlement, silently watching the diggers, and being watched in turn by the cavalrymen. Nobody had moved, none had dared to leave. Even the cows in the sheds had been silent. The headman, mute, his limbs shaking, still crouched on his haunches, downcast.

Sleeman looked at the rows of corpses and skeletons which stretched to the ravine's lip. A great and crushing weariness had descended on him. At the moment, he was thinking of the old soldier, struggling through the night carrying the broken corpse of his grandson, not knowing what terrors stalked him in the dark.

The few corpses whose tissues had not decomposed in full had received the most attention. There was little Sleeman could tell about them, and wished Spilsbury had been present. The medical officer had made a v-shaped incision at the base of their throats, and confirmed what the surgeon had told Sleeman to look for. The captain looked at the cowering sarpanch.

'Old father, what have you done?'

There is no person as lonely as a traveller on an Indian road. This might appear unlikely considering the crowds around village haats, melas, river crossings, pilgrimage sites and elsewhere in the countryside, or on the approaches to cities. And yet a traveller is always aware of how isolated he is from everybody else. The upper caste traveller does not visit villages he passes, choosing instead to eat the food he carries with himself for reasons of ritual purity and culture, and if he has any valuables with him, for reasons of safety. He does not eat with his fellow-travellers, or share food with those he passes by, or visit an unfamiliar village, again for reasons of caste and purity. He passes through the countryside leaving not much more than a ripple in his wake. The oppressed castes do not visit unfamiliar villages, not knowing if they will be welcomed or driven away.

If the traveller meets anyone at all between the beginning and the end of his journey, it is someone he has known for years, or those related by blood and marriage. The village Bania has perfected these intricate meshes which support his commerce. Clan ties support the Bania, and he knows if his trade fails, his people will put together money to set him up in the business again. The village goldsmith, the sunar who is traditionally considered of humble rank and low varna, sits in his shop crafting gold into art. The jeweller does not create this, but he knows who to sell it to in a town or city far away, and thus he profits from the goldsmith's labour. The grain trader has the bullock carts or donkeys which carry the farmer's produce, and the journey multiplies his profits.

The village Bania, who travels often in small, quiet groups, carrying valuables of gold or grain as the case may be, is a suspicious man. Generations of making deals and cutting corners, generations of seeking advantage over his peers or peasants makes him trust nobody except those he knows as well as himself, or those who speak his arcane language and see the world the way he does.

Therefore the conundrum of the Bania: a man who travels much in the course of his business but returns home not a whit the wiser or more knowledgeable or compassionate, only better versed in the ways of his trade and the means of appropriating the wealth of the already poor. Therefore the conundrum of the Brahmin, sent out of home and village by the demands of infallible scripture and sacred geography on pilgrimages over vast distances. He returns still convinced of his purity and sacred calling, his unseeing eyes oblivious to the vast drama of existence playing in hovel and palace. Steeped in tradition and memorisation by rote, in seemingly profound questions about the soul and spirituality, he is unaware and unconcerned about the quiet desperation which is the normal state of existence of the Indian peasant, or the profligacy and meaningless extravagance of the princeling. Therefore the Muslim, separated from the Hindu castes by faith and from his own co-religionists by descent and clan, by ethnicity and class. Therefore the conundrum of the many nations that form India: a land connected by vast, sclerotic routes of commerce and exchange, faith and tradition, weddings and funerals, yatras and ziyarats but where people live near, and not with one another.

Sleeman knew this traveller and the intricate strands of jati, varna and biradari—oppressive, unequal, dense and multi-layered—which surrounded him. And yet, the earth had just given back the corpses of these travellers, who had vanished in the middle of going about their everyday trade, whose rules of exclusion had not saved them from harm at the hands of their fellowmen.

'Old father, what have you done?'

The sarpanch continued to cower and was mute. Reynolds walked back to the cot. His boots and trousers were caked with the white dust and black soil of the graves. Towards the afternoon he had grabbed a shovel and jumped into one of the pits to dig with the regimental labourers and villagers, cursing the latter with fury in every language he knew. Now he was just tired and sweat-stained. Sleeman gestured to him to sit on the cot and have a drink from the water pot nearby.

'You must tell us what you have done, father. How could you have allowed these dacoits to kill so many innocent men, and use your village as a graveyard? How could you have committed this sin, father? For sin it is, and as terrible a sin as if you had killed them yourself.'

The sarpanch wiped his face with his angucha and looked up at Sleeman, puzzled.

'I do not understand, sahib.'

'I am asking you to tell me where the dacoits are hiding, the Phansigars who killed these men. You need not fear them. You can see the soldiers I command.'

The sarpanch swallowed, and spoke through a dry throat.

'Sahib, they are of this village.'

Reynolds swore under his breath. Sleeman looked at him with disapproval and turned back to the sarpanch.

'When did they come to live with you? Or do they just visit you? Why did the panchayat not tell the tehsildar or the Nawab Begum's officers of this? What could you have to fear from them? Where was your pride?'

The sarpanch was silent. His expression was unreadable.

'They do not visit, sahib,' he said at length.

'What do you mean? Then how did these corpses get buried here?'

'Sahib, I mean the tehsildar, patwari or other people. Neither the Company Sarkar from Jabalpur nor the Nawab Begum's officials have ever visited us.'

'But that is impossible. They must visit once in a while. Who measures your land and calculates the revenue, then?'

'We do, sahib. But nobody collects the revenue. It has always been thus.'

And so, through questions and yet more questions, Sleeman managed to arrive by inches at the truth. The village did not exist, neither for the Nawab Begum of Bhopal, nor for the office of the Agent of Sagar and Narmada. It was so wretched and poor, so isolated, forgotten in the tumult of generations of warfare that nobody had bothered to collect revenue or administer it.

'How long has it been like this?'

'It has always been thus, sahib.'

Sleeman sighed. This was another complication. The Nawab Begum's court was not going to be happy with the revelation. Not because it was a substantial loss of revenue. The total taxes due in a year from a village as mean and parched as this would not be enough to buy a single one of the Nawab Begum's famed gold-embroidered cushions. But it was a matter of prestige. Border villages could not be allowed to vanish.

'When did these murderers arrive here?'

The sarpanch was silent again. Sleeman did not press him. At length he appeared to have arrived at a decision.

'Sahib, they did not come from elsewhere. They are of this village.'

'I see. And you have allowed them to murder strangers with impunity. What hold did they have over you? Do they give you a share of the loot?'

'Sahib, it is not like that.'

'Then explain to me, for I do not understand. And explain it well, or nobody from this village will be freed.'

'Sahib, you see how wretched we are. It is not just when the rains do not come. The land is poor, and we have very little to feed ourselves. Nor do people bring trade and wealth here, or pass through. We are the refuse of this region. Sometimes, when life becomes difficult, the men go out on journeys.'

'What kind of journeys? Which men are these? You will need to identify them by name.'

'There are different kinds of men, and they get together and leave in small groups. They are gone for several weeks at a stretch, for there is not much to be gained by staying at home and farming the dirt. They travel from Narsinghpur to Sagar and Itarsi, Bhopal, Gwalior and even Guna. They befriend travellers and pretend to be of their trade and clan. They lull the travellers into betraying confidences, and at a certain place they strangle them.'

'Are you saying that the men who strangle travellers live in this village?'

'Sahib, the men of this village go on journeys, find travellers, strangle and rob them.'

The distinction seemed to matter to the sarpanch. And then Sleeman understood. The gang of Phansigars had not come to stay at the village. The villagers were Phansigars.

'How many of the men in the village are stranglers?'

'Only a handful, sahib, for it is a difficult task…'

Reynolds muttered another oath and sprang up. Sleeman told him to go and make arrangements for their camp for the night.

'Continue, please.'

'Only a handful of the men are given the task of strangling the chosen victims, sahib. The others have different tasks, like striking up a conversation with them and making sure they do not become suspicious. Some hold the victims while those assigned to strangle them do the work.'

'How do they manage to lull their victims?'

'We know how different people talk. We know the words of their trade. We know which jati eats what kind of food and holds which kind of belief. It is not difficult to be as one of them.'

Sleeman imagined a gang as the sarpanch had described, befriending a group of traders or small merchants, perhaps farmers not unlike them. There was no bond more fraternal than jati identifiers, for those were the basis of a person's identity.

'Are they always strangled? Why so?'

'It has always been thus, sahib. It is the sacrifice we are asked to make.'

'Why do you say we?'

'My father was a strangler, sahib,' said the sarpanch, without a tremor.

The father. The Rajput, the Chauhan who once owned a horse. Sleeman paused for a moment to register this, and plunged on. 'And what about you, sarpanch? What noble task do you perform?'

'I have only been on a few journeys, and not for a long time. I have not been given many significant tasks, merely to strike up conversations with other Rajputs or Thakurs if we happen to find them, or to act as lookout.'

'How many journeys have you been on?'

'About fifteen in my life, since I was a very young man.'

'And where are the victims killed?'

'There are several places in the countryside, sahib. There are fixed spots where we rest and perform the sacrifice. There are spots nearby to hide the bodies.'

'And what of these men in the graves?'

'Not many people come to Bina. These were lured here by the villagers after assuring them of rest and shelter. It is a long journey to the nearest villages east and west. I know the Company Sarkar will hang me for this, sahib. I shall tell you all. But most people of the village are innocent of murder. I request you to show them mercy. We have nothing, and sometimes less than nothing. We would not have participated in this if we had not been forced to, by the will of the Goddess.'

'Who was the sarpanch here seven years ago?'

The headman told him the name.

'I want you to think before answering. Did you hear of an old man who came here once, back then, looking for his grandson?'

The sarpanch thought about this for a few moments, and then said, 'Yes, sahib. I remember. I was present.'

'You were in the village when the man came?'

'Yes. I was in the fields, so I did not see him when he first arrived. But I was present on the night he returned.'

'When they caught him.'

The sarpanch nodded.

'I remember that night. Nobody had ever come to the village to ask about a traveller. We thought we had driven the old man off. We did not know if he would return, but we were afraid somebody else would, so we were alert.'

'His grandson was killed here?'

'Yes, sahib. He was a very young man and did not know anything about the world. He was brought to the village and killed. We did not get much from his possessions. If we had known he was a lakra, we would not have gone through the trouble.'

'Why do you call him a stick?'

'Sahib, that is what we call somebody with no possessions, nothing valuable worth taking.'

'What language is this? I have never heard it before.'

'That is the language we use on our journeys.'

'Do stranglers from other villages know of this language?'

'Yes, sahib. We all know the words. It is thus that we recognise and aid one another on the road.'

'How is the loot divided?'

'It is divided according to rank, sahib. Those who are senior and experienced in the trade are given more, and so are the bhartotes, who do the strangling. Kantgars like me, who act as lookouts or lures, get a little. If we make a lot of loot, it is given out among the villagers.'

Sleeman was silent again as he let the import of this sink in.

'Sarpanch, are you saying that everybody in the village knows of what you have done?'

'Yes, sahib. We all know.'

They all knew. The specific tasks were just words. They all knew.

'The grandson was killed and buried in an offal pit, and nobody expected his family to seek him here.'

'What about his companion? I believe his name was Sukh Ram.'

'I do not remember his name. I did not know him. But I was told he talked a lot to our men who befriended them on the road.'

'What happened to him?'

The sarpanch pointed to the row of corpses. So Sukh Ram had not been involved in the murder after all.

'Tell me what happened that night, sarpanch. And be careful in the telling. Leave nothing out.'

'The old man came back, and was seen creeping around. He was caught by the guards and taken to a cowshed. He was beaten to an inch of his life, for the panchayat was angry and afraid. They did not know what to do with him. I too went to see him. We were afraid that others would come after him, but it turned out he had told nobody. He was just an old man, starving and half-dead, looking for his grandson. We asked him what he did and where he was from. He told us he was a garpagri in his village. That caused consternation, sahib.'

'Why would it trouble you? Surely you do not hesitate to kill a Brahmin?'

'No, sahib, we do not, for had we not strangled his grandson? But a garpagri was a different matter. It was the dry season, and we needed the rains to save our crops. Killing a garpagri in the dry season is an ill omen. We could not decide what to do. The panchayat conferred with the priest of the temple, sahib. We had to know the will of the Goddess. Without her will, we do not attempt such a thing. It was decided to give him back his grandson. To appease the Goddess, we told him not to speak a word to anybody, or we would claim him in the stead of the boy. We heard from one of our people in his village that he had spoken to an Englishman after immersing his grandson's ashes. We knew he would not stay quiet. So we sacrificed him.'

'You strangled him?'

'No, sahib. It was not a sacrifice for the Goddess. There had to be blood. We cut his throat.'

'Is he among them?' asked Sleeman, pointing to the rows of corpses.

'No, he could not be among them. The body was cremated.'

'Why do you call them sacrifice?'

'Each of these men is our sacrifice for the Goddess. Therefore, they are to be strangled and buried. It has always been thus.'

Sleeman recalled that the small temple outside the village

had neither rice nor vermillion offered to the idol. The offering was the lives of travellers.

'You will now tell me the names of all the people involved in this. Are they all present?'

'Yes. Nobody has left the village.'

'And you will tell me which of them are stranglers and who are like you. Tell me everything, and perhaps your life will be saved. So will the life of everyone else who tells me whatever they know. I cannot speak for all the bhartotes, but I will see what I can do for the rest of you.'

'I thank you for your kindness, sahib.'

'You will also tell me of all the people you know elsewhere who are involved in this.'

'I do not know of many of them. The others do.'

'We shall talk to them as well. We are just beginning our task here. You will also tell me the words of this language you use. Does it have a name?'

'We call it Ramasi.'

He had to take them back. There was no other place where he could keep them. A guard had to be posted at the village on the faint chance of other Phansigars visiting and being forewarned that secrets were being spilled. But those of the villagers who had confessed to the murders or to the abetting of them had to be taken back to Jabalpur.

Bound in shackles and stout ropes, led by sowars on all sides, went four dozen men including the sarpanch. Behind them went a cartload of corpses. Curious crowds would follow when they passed through villages, but Sleeman had ordered silence and the crowds, given a spectacle with no explanation, would stop following after a distance. They would not know that only a few of the one hundred and thirty seven bodies found in the village were being taken along.

Who were the captured men? Dacoits, said a rumour. Rebels, said another. But who had they rebelled against? The Nawab Begum left the people alone, and was liked because of her tragic life. Only a heartless qazi would rebel against her. Unrest against the Englishmen, then, for reasons which were of no concern to anybody else, for the taxes these villages paid were a thimbleful in the vast ocean of wealth that went to Calcutta. And so the countryside, woken out of its slumber, went back to the everyday round after the procession passed.

Where Reynolds fumed and talked of constructing gallows outside Jabalpur, Sleeman was exhausted by the time they reached the town and he had finished questioning the captives. The litany of crimes he had recorded over the past few days was exceeded in its horror only by the casual manner in which the arrested men had recounted it. There was a clinical approach to how they viewed their victims' fates, which was more horrifying than the murderous rampage of dacoits because of an absence of passion. Life existed, it was sacrificed and then it ceased to exist.

To strangle a human, leave alone a full-grown man in his prime, is a difficult task. The choice of implement is important, for it is only a man of immense strength who can throttle another man from behind, by himself, with his bare hands without giving the victim time and space to struggle. Too thin a ligature, and the outer edge of the strangler's palms gets abraded or even cut deep, if the ligature is of metal. Therefore a rope, or angucha, or turban, wrapped around the hands to brace against the bucking of the victim. Then it becomes a mere contest between the muscles of the forearm of the strangler and the fragile necklace of bone and tissue around the victim's throat.

But for all that, life does not end without a fight, even though other hands might weigh down the victim's limbs. In the last moments, when extinction is imminent and the comforting fictions of afterlife or reincarnation fade away, even the sick, the weak or the drugged summon secret reserves of muscular strength, lapsing into spasms as will drains away. The world is reduced to gasps, to red-rimmed breaths; all memory and thought is swept aside by pure instinct as the seconds stretch into eternity and then nothingness.

They talked to Sleeman of this. Nobody had ever asked them, nor had they shared their lives with anyone not privy to their lore. But he asked, and he listened, and wrote, and they talked. Some like the sarpanch of Bina talked because they wanted to be spared the noose, others because they were willing to turn approvers even though they had been stranglers themselves. Some, on being captured, became passive, submitting to what they thought was the will of their deity. Others, the more senior in rank, confided only what they had to. Yet others talked because they believed they had transgressed in not following the omens and rituals, and had been punished with capture.

For any of these reasons, faced with mounting evidence, with piles of corpses and eyewitness accounts, with articles of clothing and seized valuables, with their doom certain, they talked.

They spoke of the Phansigars they knew by name and reputation, of where they lived and what they had done. From the stranglers of that first village Sleeman was told about dozens of other expeditions, about scores of such groups spread across the district and beyond, of killings spread over years and generations. It became apparent that this was not a task to be accomplished with ease, or by himself as he had supposed at the beginning.

Sleeman and Reynolds began by writing in confidence to magistrates of districts administered directly by the government, informing them of Phansigars known to live or travel through their jurisdiction. The meagre resources of the police department, such as it was, had to be used. Sleeman and Reynolds were either away chasing every lead they could find, or questioning those of the arrested men who had some valuable nugget of information. And thus they talked, and the mists cleared a little more each day.

The Phansigars had names for every kind of role to be played in the drama of inveiglement, deception and sacrifice. They would greet one another on the road with 'Aulae bhai, Ram-Ram' in case the other was a Hindu, or 'Aulae khan, salaam' if he was a Muslim, aulae being their term of self-reference. The young and new to the trade they trusted with only the simplest of tasks. These were kotaks, and it was up to them to prove their worth during expeditions. Kautgars ventured alone or in pairs, scouting ahead of the group for potential victims. Accompanying them would be lughas, of humble rank because all they were fit for was to dig graves for the dead. Sometimes, if the size of the Phansigars' group was small, a man had to perform multiple tasks.

But even the most weak or vulnerable victim may fight, and it would not do to have a sacrifice with more struggle than necessary, and therefore there had to be a man to hold the feet of the victim while the bhartote did his work, and others to hold the hands and thrashing body.

'Thus it has been for ages, kaptaan sahib,' said one of the men arrested by a raiding party led by Reynolds, and brought back to Jabalpur. He was just a sotha, an inveigler whose task was to gain the confidence of the victims. He was old and had not been given a position of greater responsibility because he had not had the temperament for such work. Only a few became bhartotes, after demonstrating that they would not be unsettled by the act of killing, and would not, through an attack of nerves, betray the gang in the crucial moments before turning on the unsuspecting victims. Everyone began as a novice. But only a few became bhartotes, and fewer yet became chandus, of great respect, and sardars of expeditions.

'Thus it has been for ages, kaptaan sahib, and you will find us no matter where you travel in any direction from here, as I have seen. There are innumerable aulae on any road you may take. Even in the forest temples near Daulatabad you will see sculptures of sacrifices being strangled, while others hold the feet, and yet others prepare the graves. The temples are sacred to us, for we sometimes visit and pay our respects to these images of aulaes long gone,' said the sotha.

Amelie refused to believe this. As the evidence mounted, and the amount of material about the Phansigars and their lore increased, she started compiling the argot and the beliefs into a cohesive glossary. Sleeman was not certain if it would be proper for her to visit the jail during his interrogation of the prisoners. He mentioned her social standing, if not her sensibilities. Neither she nor Spilsbury would have any of it.

'Even the Phansigars seem to have women among their rank and file, William,' she said, and it was true, and thus the argument was settled.

Amelie, who accepted without incredulity accounts of murderous expeditions and details of appalling slaughter, drew the line at claims of sculptures depicting Phansigars. Neither Sleeman nor she had yet visited the temples of Ellora, and could not verify this from memory, but Sleeman resolved to write to the magistrate of Daulatabad asking if it was true. He doubted if the magistrate would make the thankless effort of examining the thousands of sculptures at the temple complex on his behalf.

'It might be just a coincidence, or minor sculptures which in a certain light may appear to resemble Phansigars. I understand temple sculptures have a great deal of variety, but no king would stoop so low as to commemorate Phansigars,' Amelie said.

Sleeman did not know what to believe anymore. The more he investigated, the more he was certain that the Phansigars could not have existed for so long without the complicity of some form of authority. Where a village or a patwari or even a zamindar could be coerced or bribed into cooperation, where a sarai keeper could become an informant for less than the price of a chicken, kings or governors could have a price too. The inveigler would not be the only one to claim Phansigars were commemorated in stone at Ellora.

Life existed, and then it ceased to exist. For Phansigars, the act of taking life was followed by the question of disposal of bodies, for which their lore and beliefs were extensive. Some buried the bodies whole; others believed in cutting them up before inhumation, so that a bloated body might not burst and betray the grave through stench or through settling of the grave soil. This would in turn keep scavengers like jackals away.

They had names for their implements, and even for the kind of graves they dug. Circular ones with a mound at the centre, which they believed kept wild animals away, were called gobba. The more common oblong graves were called karwa. Much thought had gone into these beliefs, combining superstitions for which neither Spilsbury nor Amelie could find a basis in known folk beliefs, with the practical requirements of a gang of seasonal murderers.

They even had a system of instruction for newcomers. The highest regarded bhartotes were proficient in the use of the ruhmal or kerchief, and each had a unique way of tying the knot, called the gur-ghont. A disciple of such a guru, being more proficient than someone who had not received this kind of proper education would keep the end of his kerchief tied in a similar manner. Such a trained disciple was called a gur-ponch.

'One may perhaps call them graduates,' said Amelie. Neither Sleeman nor Reynolds knew if she spoke in jest.

They had an elaborate lore, which in turn had subtle regional variations. Every aspect of their life was governed by rules and beliefs, which could not be broken. The sonoka was one such. It was the first murder committed during an expedition. The loot from the victim was immaterial. What mattered was the victim could not be a woman.

It was, said Amelie, considerate of them.

But the list of exceptions for a sonoka went beyond women. Neither a Brahmin nor a village official such as a kaet, a mendicant, a kumhar or an oil presser, carpenter, sunar, lohar, elephant driver or anybody herding livestock, or wearing gold jewellery in a conspicuous manner could be sacrificed. Nor could people carrying the ashes of their parents for immersion, musicians or dancers.

'We might never know how they came by this list. There is no connection among these jatis or professions. Under no circumstances will you find a Brahmin associating with an oil presser,' said Sleeman during one of their endless discussions about this belief system.

Superstitions played a role too. A dog barking or passing dung at the wrong time, such as in the moonlight; a hare crossing the road in either direction; or even a sneeze at the beginning of a journey. The donkey was of supreme importance. A donkey braying towards the left of a group at the beginning of an expedition, and another braying on the right shortly after, was the greatest good omen that could be sought, for it guaranteed success even if the expedition were to last several years. Meanwhile, a menstruating woman in the family of any of the expedition members was an ill omen. If the woman was in the family of the leader, the expedition would not begin.

'In that, at least, they are not different than the most pious Brahmin of Benares,' said Amelie to nobody in particular, while Sleeman and Reynolds pretended not to have heard her.

A second aspect of Ramasi was the peculiar words of code they employed. There were words of caution, as warning to fellow Phansigars, as signs that the right victim had been found. Thus a beetu, anybody not a Phansigar, had to be lulled into lowering his guard. 'Hukka bhar lao' was a common signal to begin strangling the victims. This special group of signals was called jhirni. 'Jurawan ho jao' was the signal to run away.

There were names for professions, such as 'thulla' for a policeman, or 'rangwa' for a redcoat, 'khorchi' for barber and 'kantju' for cutpurse. The words of Ramasi were borrowed from everyday Hindustani of the Doab, or common words in Bagheli and Bundeli. There were words which only the Deccan stranglers used, and others which were specific to Telangana or the Punjab, but of these Sleeman did not know except by hearsay.

Their relation to other criminals was complex. That it would be in the form of a hierarchy was inevitable. They had a considerable amount of contempt for Dhaturias, gangs not dissimilar to their own in terms of deception and geographical spread but whose principal method was to poison their victims, rendering them either unconscious or dead depending on the type or severity of poison used. After some of the Phansigars showed a willingness to reveal everything they knew about Dhaturias, Sleeman realised the poisoners constituted a distinct class of deceivers, no less dangerous because some of their victims, at least, had a chance of survival.

The Phansigars even had a revered patron saint, a long-dead bhartote to who they would offer libations while out on a journey. Dada Dheera they called him, and would visit his tomb with offerings and entreaties.

In Multan, they said, there was once a Phansigar called Jora Naik, who on expedition with just one assistant had come across a trader carrying an incredible amount of one lakh and sixty thousand rupees in jewels and gold. Jora Naik and his assistant had sent the fellow to the Goddess and returned home with the money, whereupon Jora Naik, his wife and assistant had called all the aulaes of their village and distributed the loot in equal amount to them. The fame of the trio spread across the land, and they became saints from then on for the Phansigars.

And behind and around these layers of lore and beliefs was the Goddess. Each village where they found Phansigars had a small shrine for her. She could be Kali, Durga or any of the other forms, appeased only by the sacrifice of the victims. Each expedition of the Phansigars had to have a sacred pickaxe, a kassi, with which to start digging the graves. There was no particular shrine to which all the aulaes went. It was a revelation for Sleeman when one of the captured men said the Dhakeshwari temple was revered above most others. The enormous spread of the Phansigars would have sounded incredible if he had not seen the evidence of it with his own eyes. There was no distinction between Hindus and Muslims within the lore either. On an expedition, everyone had their assigned roles, and everyone paid obeisance to the Goddess.

'It seems to be the only instance I have heard of where all the castes, all the Hindus and Muslims work as equals, at least during the expedition,' said Amelie, and it was true. Sleeman had not heard of such an occurrence either, and wondered how they would go back to their jati hierarchies on returning home. Perhaps that was why it was important for them to work with Phansigars from the same village.

Spilsbury's expertise was needed at every stage of the investigation, for Sleeman had resolved to present, at the trial of the murderers, as much forensic evidence as could be gathered. It was not much but the surgeon could point to one telltale of the Phansigars' handiwork, which had been verified at the first mass graves at Bina.

'The tongue bone of a victim of strangulation, captain, is found broken. There is no other circumstance, to my knowledge, in which this bone is broken, owing to its shape and location at the base of the throat. There is, however, a caveat,' Spilsbury had told Sleeman at the beginning of that first expedition.

The tongue bone became more dense and less flexible with age. In the case of a victim of strangulation in his thirties or older, the bone was certain to be broken. This was not the case with younger victims.

'What should we do then, doctor?' Sleeman had asked after returning from that first village to tell the surgeon what they had found.

'If you want to establish beyond doubt that the victims have been strangled, you must focus your attention on intact corpses or skeletons which have not lost the lesser bones, and among them you must examine older victims. I do not think you want to, or need to, establish cause of death of each body in a mass grave of this magnitude,' said Spilsbury.

Between the bodies, and the testimonies, the confessions and complaints of missing persons and valuables that Sleeman and Reynolds compiled, there was enough evidence to hang several of the men who had been captured. But the more he probed, the more he began to hear of a shadowy figure who knew all the lore of Ramasi, and who was a subedar, no less, of all the Phansigars of Gwalior and Bhopal. First one approver, and then another, in their confessions, began to talk of this man.

'William, this must be like Jora Naik. You will hear an elaborate legend, and somebody will tell you this man has been haunting the highways since time immemorial, or you will come upon a tomb in the countryside,' said Amelie, who was so immersed in Ramasi by then that she could speak the code just as well as the confessors.

Spilsbury was of the same view. Reynolds, prosaic and dutiful as ever, refused to venture an opinion, busy as he was in supervising the letters the clerks had to write to magistrates in other districts about captured Phansigars. He had neither the will nor inclination to speculate about legends.

But there was a legend, and the more Sleeman probed, the more the legend seemed to reveal itself, like a terrible truth that was in the process of being birthed.

'Kaptaan sahib, this happened many years ago. I know, for I heard of it from my own guru. There was once a zamindar in the employ of the Scindia Maharaja, who did not pay customs duty for some goods which had come to him. The king asked him to pay the duties, but he refused,' said a bhartote. This was how most of the legends began.

The Maharaja, they said, had asked the Bengal Army to help, and a British officer had led a regiment to the village of the offending zamindar. With horse and cannon they had assaulted the village, levelling it through a night's worth of carnage.

'The zamindar's family escaped with their lives and what little possessions they could take. His sister happened to be in confinement at her maternal home at that time, and in the shock and chaos of the battle, gave birth to a child in the forest that same night,' said another, an old inveigler.

Born in the middle of battle, in the ashes of his family's possessions, with little hope that he could survive the night, the child had somehow lived, and from then on carried an epithet which referred to the hated foreigners, the firangis who had destroyed the village. He was called 'Firangia'.

This, with minor variations, was the legend. What did not vary was the amount of customs which was levied to the uncle, which was said to be eighteen thousand rupees, or the name of the uncle, the zamindar brought low by the Bengal Army.

This was the origin of the subedar of Phansigars in central

India, keeper of the lore. A formidable figure, at once heroic and lofty, driven by rage, injustice and all the ingredients of folk theatre in the countryside. There was much of this theatricality in the deceptions of the Phansigars as well, and neither Sleeman nor Amelie were certain where folk customs ended and Phansigar lore began.

But there was a figure, that was certain, and perhaps it was a real figure. Sleeman could confirm that the numerous groups of Phansigars which lived and worked in different regions were in communication with one another, and their subedars knew each other by name at the least. He did not know anything else about them.

'Any one of them could lift the veil from the whole lot, Amelie. I just need to find this man, this subedar of whom they speak,' he said.

'Perhaps there is a real person, but he will be unlike anything the legends say. That is the nature of legends. The truth will be a diminished version of the story,' she said, aware that he was not convinced.

The Agent of Sagar and Narmada summoned Sleeman on a quiet day to his office, having recovered and resumed his responsibilities. The only interest he had shown in the investigations was to question the captain after the exhumations at Bina.

'I gather you have arrested a village, captain,' he had said.

Sleeman had explained the circumstances and discoveries to him, after which the veteran of the political department had decided to drop the matter and hope for the best.

On reaching his office, Sleeman found the agent contemplating a piece of parchment rolled into a cylinder. He recognised the seal of the governor-general's secretary. The agent was unhappy.

'Captain, I have called you here to inform you of this

communication I have received from Government House. Lord Bentinck will make a formal announcement at the meeting of the governing council this week, following which we are to announce it throughout the agency. This is Regulation XVII, under which, the secretary informs me, the practice of sati in all its manifestations has been prohibited. Violation of this law will invite exemplary punishment. You may read it if you please,' he said.

Sleeman read it. Bentinck had made his first move. He had started with sati.

'I need not tell you that this is a sensitive matter, and though I welcome the step taken by the government, we must prepare for possible repercussions. We must begin by holding discussions with prominent Hindus of the Agency. I have sent instructions to assistants in the other districts. You may proceed to take steps as required here,' said the agent.

Sleeman would have to convince the upper castes of his jurisdiction that the measure was not part of more interference in their culture or religion, but the redressal of a grievous wrong. There were some in the district, he knew, who would not hesitate to speak out in support of the practice. It would be a fraught situation.

'However, I do not think there will be much direct opposition to this here. It is not that the governor-general wants to allow widows to remarry, or grant married Hindu women the right to divorce,' said the agent.

Sleeman considered the consequences of such a law. He could not imagine it.

'How is the status of your investigation, captain? I understand you have assisted some magistrates in other provinces to begin trials?'

'Yes, sir. I have written to the magistrate of Allahabad, Mr McLeod, with corroborative evidence.'

'I believe you should now meet with the Maharaja at Ujjain and the Nawab Begum at Bhopal, to inform them of the progress you have made.'

The time had come to travel to the royal courts. The art of talking to monarchs was not Sleeman's natural ability, but he could steel himself to it. But it also meant returning to an estranged mother. That might yet be beyond him.

Sleeman and Reynolds arrived in Bhopal on the afternoon of a day when the wind was whipping down from the Vindhyas over the many lakes of the city. It blew away the awnings of shops, and straw from the stacks outside the great timbers and iron spikes of Dehli Darwaza, where merchants and travellers halted to feed their animals after a journey, and to pay tax for their cargo. The wind blew across Sleeman's face and the dust stung his eyes. It was not cold, for it is never cold in Bhopal, not even on the shores of the lakes in the dead of winter, but there was dust in the air, and Sleeman's eyes were red. His back was stiff and ached from being on horseback for more days than he cared to count, on difficult roads and terrain.

They had come down from Sagar after making some enquiries. Between Jabalpur and Sagar they had learnt much and little, and had arranged for the incarceration of some arrested men at the camp jail in Sagar, which did not yet have a civilian jail or enough police personnel or inspectors, known as najeebs, for the district.

They fought the wind to the city residence of the agent. The Bhopal Agency was one of those creations of Government House whose reach snaked into the dominions of neighbouring rulers both petty and important. The agent oversaw not only the extensive lands of the Nawabs, but also that of the three rajas of Narsinghgarh, Rajgarh and Khilchipur, small portions of the Scindia's domains and those of the wary Maharaja of Tonk. There were also minor principalities like Khurwai and Muhammadgarh, and landlords too numerous for Sleeman to be familiar with. Bhopal Agency was sought for, pursued and given as reward to aspirants whose reach was known, on occasion, to exceed their grasp, for what appeared to be certainties in Calcutta became complications on arrival in the princely states.

The current incumbent had travelled in the East on behalf of the Honourable Company and had made a considerable amount of wealth in the indigo and opium trades, before coming down with a severe case of political ambition, and had acquired the Agency some years prior to secretary Macnaghten's arrival in Calcutta. His haveli in that city was known to have a small fortune in valuable Chinese artefacts, but they were not in much evidence at his house in Bhopal.

It was larger than it should have been, filled with the kind of furniture Sleeman would not have been able to afford with his salary, and with objects which Amelie would not have liked to see in the morning. Also not in evidence was the agent, who had gone to the palace of the Nawab Begum, and awaited them there. Perhaps pressing matters had called him to the palace before Sleeman had arrived. Or perhaps he had been too embarrassed to chaperone them to the palace and therefore be expected to be answerable for their conduct. An agent had to step with care, for there were many interests he had to balance beginning with, in this case, his own.

Sleeman and Reynolds, who were not offered refreshments by the household staff, returned to their horses and rode another half a mile to the palace. It was not large but well-guarded and the morning crowd of petitioners had begun to thin, for the azaan was due to be sounded and official work would be put aside for the interim.

The two officers were admitted through the main entrance into a grand hall, where diwans sat with their assistants and petitioners assembled in front of them. Sleeman and Reynolds were led through this and via a small door to a passage open on one side. Cane curtains had been drawn across the openings, on account of the wind, which still howled outside.

They followed the guards down the passage to an anteroom, where European-style chairs with high backs had been placed. They were asked to wait here. Some time later a young bearded man in fine silk and followed by an assistant entered and greeted them. He introduced himself as a minister to the Nawab Begum.

'I thank the royal household for permitting this audience. I believe my last letter was delivered a week ago,' said Sleeman, after wishing peace on the minister.

The agent entered accompanied by his own assistant. The great man was bald, stout, sheathed in silk more expensive than the minister's and of a brighter colour. On his face was the professional smile of a merchant who had made his wealth from negotiations with courtiers from more complicated polities. Bhopal was a sinecure as far as level of political complexity was concerned.

'I see you are here, captain. Shall we proceed with the audience?' he said in English, which was incongruous with the kind of clothes he was wearing, if not with his face.

A man who had gone native in the worst possible way, which was the sign of a type of venal mind, might have behaved thus. But the agent was too well-connected in Calcutta to be accused of venality to his face, so Sleeman gave him the courtesy his rank deserved.

The agent saw in Sleeman a tall officer in uniform, browned by the sun, speaking in perfect Urdu with the minister. They observed this contrast in each other, and let it pass unremarked.

'I shall see if the Begum Sahiba is free now, huzoor,' said the minister and left through another door in the opposite wall. The visitors settled down to wait again.

'I was expecting you earlier in the day,' said the agent, for want of anything else to say. Sleeman did not know how to reply to this, because there had been no reason for the agent to expect him at a particular time.

'We went to your residence first, sir, expecting you to be there,' Sleeman said.

'I had to be present here. You look tired, captain. Are you well? I hope the rigours of your investigation have not begun to affect your health.'

The minister returned before Sleeman could think of a reply, or determine the tone in which the question had been asked. The minister gestured for them to follow him.

'Is it necessary for me to be present?' asked the agent, but he was looking at nobody, so it was not known to whom he had addressed this remark.

'If you are required elsewhere, sir, we shall not detain you,' said Sleeman. He was not sure what a political department veteran or a Government House diplomat would have said under these circumstances, but felt this was a safe statement. The agent hurried away, and the relief he felt lingered in the air. The minister could not have missed it, but did not indicate he had noticed anything.

Sleeman and Reynolds passed through the door into the audience chamber. It was lit through open windows, now covered against the wind, which caused a dappled light across the floor. In size it was moderate, as befitted a room where senior visitors could speak without raising their voices to a volume beyond the courteous. Along the walls were thick mattresses and pillows. At the end was a wooden platform. Some distance in front of it two comfortable chairs, made of burnished wood, had been placed for the European visitors. Sleeman noticed the two chairs first. Either the agent's absence had been anticipated, or Reynolds had been expected to stand. He suspected it was the former reason. The agent was predictable.

On the platform, seated on a mattress covered by a thick rug sat Qudsia, the Nawab Begum of Bhopal. She was twenty-eight, dressed in muted colours, her head covered but with the face visible. Sleeman had been told she no longer followed the purdah, but he had never met her during his previous visits, nor had he ever expected to.

She looked older than her age, but whether this was because of the austerity of her expression, or the natural lines and angles of her face, or the flickering sunlight through the curtains, Sleeman could not tell, nor did he wish to hazard a guess to himself.

Begum Qudsia had been married to the Nawab at sixteen, and widowed a little more than two years later, under circumstances which had haunted her ever since. Now she ruled, and her untrammelled powers were supported by Government House, where she had many admirers, for they were the kind of men who liked powerful women at a safe distance from the orbits of their own powers. What Sleeman knew, from his understanding of local politics, was she had no difficulty in dealing with lesser men like the agent.

Now she greeted the two officers with a courteous nod. The minister asked them to take a seat, and stood by their side while she finished dictating to a scribe. Then she dismissed her attendants and turned to Sleeman.

'I see that the Honourable Agent sahib could not be present. I was anticipating the pleasure of conferring with him as usual,' she said. Sleeman doubted that. One of the advantages of conversing in Urdu with a person of wit and a sense of irony was the manner in which some words, in particular adjectives, acquired complicated meanings by the choice of their usage. The Nawab Begum, in all likelihood, wanted to hear from the agent about his views on people and events, which she must have found amusing in the way she would have found a jester's words.

Sleeman repeated his gratitude for being granted an audience.

'You are polite, Captain Sleeman. I know the governor-general sahib himself has appointed you for this task, and I thank you for visiting. Also, your Urdu is…proper,' she said.

Sleeman murmured his thanks.

'I have read your letter, and about your findings at this village and subsequent investigations. It is unfortunate to hear of such things. My revenue officials were not aware of the existence of this village within our dominions,' said the Nawab Begum.

'Yes, of course, your highness. We discovered this after we had reached the village,' said Sleeman.

'But it still falls within our borders. I see from your letter that my local officials were not informed before you reached there.'

'We apologise, your highness, but we had to conduct our investigation without delay. It is the nature of this case, of these unique kinds of criminals, that we pursue information with speed. We meant no offence.'

'It is a small matter, captain. Now, I understand you have requested permission to speak to my ministers about the presence of these criminals within the boundaries of Bhopal. You would like us to share whatever we know of them. You believe these Phansigars are a bigger problem than we think?'

'I believe we have not scratched the surface of it, Begum Sahiba. We have amassed an enormous amount of information about their activities, including specific details about their crimes, from the confessions of arrested men. We will be happy to provide these details to your ministers, and hope we will then be guided on the right path.'

'Then you will be more fortunate than I, for I have received little guidance from them on any matter of late,' she said, again with the hint of amusement in her voice.

The Nawab Begum was silent for a few moments, and then instructed the young minister to assist the officers in their queries. Sleeman and Reynolds were about to get up and seek to be excused when she raised her hand.

'I would like a moment with the captain, if he will be so kind.'

Sleeman sat back down. Reynolds and the minister bowed and left. The Nawab Begum looked at Sleeman for a few moments in silence.

'Captain, the governor-general sahib must have shown you the yaddasht I had sent to him a year ago. This was after a letter I had written had not had any visible effect in Calcutta.'

'Begum sahiba, he did not show me the letter or yaddasht, but his secretary mentioned them. He also talked of a similar letter from the court in Ujjain.'

'Which must have been sent after I sent mine. Captain, the Maharaja is young, and rash, and rude to his mother, who suffers much. Do you have a son?'

'We have not been blessed with children, your highness.'

'Then you are fortunate, because they are a trial and a penance, whether one is queen or peasant. And the less said about in-laws, the better. Do you have pleasant relations with your mother-in-law, captain, if I may ask?'

'I regret to say that my wife's mother passed away before I met my wife.'

'Then, Captain Sleeman, you have been graced beyond measure by fate, and you should be thankful that you are not plagued by a large family. The only joy in my life at present is my daughter, and I have every intention of making her my successor. I shall live to see Government House salute her with cannon in Calcutta.'

He had not expected to exchange such insights about family life with her. The wind had begun to die down at last. The Nawab Begum listened to the growing silence.

'What I meant to say was, the Maharaja is a child, and misadvised by his large adopted family and by retainers who ought to know better. His mother's behaviour and absence of ethics do not help much either. But between the complaint from Ujjain and from my court, a lot may be lost by the time it reaches the ears of Government House. May I ask you, captain, what you saw on your way here?'

'I do not understand, your highness.'

'I mean, while passing through the streets on your way to the palace, what did you see? Or perhaps you did not see much, owing to the wind and the dust,' she said, and this time Sleeman was certain he could hear the amusement in her voice.

'I saw the usual street sights, your highness, that I see when I visit the city.'

'The usual street sights. Yes. Captain, my husband's ancestors, as you are sure to be aware, were governors here a hundred years ago, and then rulers. Now I rule. I am not as learned as I would have liked to be, but I do know that in these years, the streets have not changed much, nor has the surrounding countryside. Of course, we build some structures once in a while, like this palace. But change, such as it is, does not seem to happen too often.'

Sleeman waited in silence, because he knew there was more.

'When my husband was killed and I had to choose my fate, I had some trusted advisors to guide me with the task of governing. I cannot read or write, as you have noticed. I have to dictate my correspondence and trust my counsellors to know the nuances of your language. My father did not think I needed to have learning, for it was enough that I could bear healthy children. After I was widowed, my advisors at the court could only show me the process of kingship. There was nobody who could show me what I wanted to know, which was the nature of it. Do you understand what I mean, captain?'

Sleeman was not certain if he did, and said so.

'I have four hundred soldiers and an equal number of cavalrymen, trained and commanded by your able officers. Sometimes your friend the agent also tries to impress me with his knowledge of martial matters. It is entertaining, as you may imagine. In the days of my father-in-law's grandfather, this number would not have been enough for the royal guard, but this is how we are today. And we do not need more, I am told, for now that your people are here, there is no instability and no ambition among the native rulers. Therefore, too, there is nobody to contest my rule. In the olden days, I would have been assassinated days after ascending the throne, by a brother or a general. A woman anywhere outside her chamber was an…aberration. It is not so anymore in some places. For that, I suppose I must be grateful to the Company Sarkar.'

There was no bitterness in her voice, or if there was she masked it well.

'But what is the nature of kingship, captain? What is the task of a ruler? One might say the welfare of the people, but that means different things to different kinds of people, does it not? I have concluded that kingship means a particular kind of transaction with the people. Men allow other men to rule over them so long as the men who are ruled are in turn allowed to be monarchs of their home, of their wives and children and servants. The petty tyrants allow the greater tyrant to rule them. Even in these times, when tyranny is moderated, if I may say so, by Government House, a Nawab or a Maharaja is free to be eccentric, to write poor poetry and waste the treasury on fine beasts, on mahogany carriages and ugly weddings, and is even adored by the people as they starve. But only so long as we allow the people to believe they have some autonomy, that their beliefs, or even the ideas which oppress them, remain unchallenged. Now I think you might want to ask me to explain.'

Sleeman smiled, and was apologetic, but asked her to explain if she would be so kind.

'Your problem, captain, or rather the problem of men like Bentinck sahib, is they are not satisfied with being kings in this manner. They have to mould their people according to a vision in their heads, and at a time of their choosing. Therefore, he begins by trying to save our poor women from the funeral pyre—a noble quest, I assure you—but where will he end? I do not know. Do you? Or do you for a moment think the petty tyrant, sulking in his shabby home, will agree to let his daughter acquire learning, perhaps step out of purdah and speak to strangers? Do you see the Brahmin letting the cobbler's son drink from his well, or the Syed breaking bread with the Kunjra? Do you see a qazi ever accepting that the testimony of a woman is equal to that of a man? The mere mention of these acts will cause blood to be shed on my streets, and in my palace, or in the Scindia's. Calcutta or Bombay will be no better, although you might think so.

'Perhaps change happens. I do not believe it does, but

perhaps I am wrong. But we can't expect it to happen at the pace in which we seek it to. Therefore I see difficult times ahead, captain. This is neither a threat nor a warning. I am merely speaking my mind, which I know you understand. Take away too many fond delusions, too many petty privileges, remove too much of what is called customary or traditional, no matter how cruel, and the people turn on you. They will turn on Government House too. It will not be us, captain. The Maharajas and the Nawabs are content. And it will not be led by the farmers or the least in the land, for when have you heard of them leading anything? It will be the ulema and the temple priests, the sadhu and the fakir, the dispossessed ruler and the princeling. The Bengal Army has fought holy men before. It will happen again, and it will be much worse. It might even come from within the Bengal Army. And they will cloak it in scripture or love for the land, or vanished empires, but what they will be fighting for will be the right to domestic tyranny, the right of the highborn over the low, the right of the upper castes over the oppressed, of men over women. They will be fighting for all the numerous small and large cruelties that constitute our relations with one another.'

'Your highness, I understand the meaning of your words, even if I do not think there is an immediate cause for concern. I shall reflect on it.'

'Will you? I am grateful, for I fear I have spoken too much, and only because I see you have been trusted by Bentinck sahib, and therefore deserve my trust. Captain, I sent the letter and the yaddasht to Government House because I am convinced that the court of the Scindia or powerful people there encourage dacoits and all manner of criminals to prey on my people, and only Government House can intervene in this. I sent it to them because I wanted Government House to know that I am concerned about the rule of law in these lands and even, difficult as it might be for you to believe, in those provinces which are a part of Bhopal Agency but were under Gwalior. I knew neither of the existence of these graves, nor of the activities of people that you have mentioned in your letter. We might just be able to tell you how many households we have taxed in Bhopal. But we certainly can't tell you how many people live in this city, leave alone across our dominion. Much happens that we have never been expected to know of. Now I do not know where your enquiries will lead you.'

'Your highness, what did you expect of us when you sent the letter?'

'I do not know, huzoor. Perhaps a political response. Certainly not the prospect of your soldiers and horsemen crossing the countryside in pursuit of criminals. And I know the Scindia did not expect anything else either. We are both content to administer and tax, and let the people live the way they have done. You see, I am not much better than the petty tyrants I warned you about.

'I need your reassurance, captain, that your activities will not send a message to Government House that my rule is inadequate, and therefore I need to be replaced, or that the throne of the Nawabs is to be abolished. This prospect haunts me, as you may imagine. And more. What if you were to conclude that we are thus: that our villages hide unknown graves, that our people to a man are bloodthirsty savages, that our travellers hide murder in their hearts, that we are, in the final measure, unworthy of your idea of the law and deserving only of contempt?'

'Begum sahiba, I assure you, on my word of honour, that it is not my intention to destabilise your rule, or misreport it to Calcutta. And from what I understand, it is not the intention of Lord Bentinck or Mr Macnaghten to replace or abolish you. Our only concern is the apprehension of these murderers. I have nothing but sympathy for the law-abiding villager and the common trader going about his business.'

'I accept your word for it, captain. Although I am surprised at the pains that you appear to be taking for what is, according to me, the job of a mere kotwal or najeeb.'

'Please excuse me for saying this, your highness, but what if you were to find evidence of monstrous crimes, and mass graves, and an extensive network of murderers across the land? Would you not be filled with revulsion? Would you not make all the efforts in your power to pursue them?'

The Nawab Begum was silent again for a few moments.

'Captain, I have held you back from your duties for too long already. Permit me a little more time, for I must tell you about this. You are privy to the public details already. One afternoon eleven years ago at Islamnagar Fort, I heard the report of a musket in the garden. We had gone there for lunch. I found the Nawab sahib lying on the porch where he had been sitting. Our beloved daughter, Sikandar, not even sixteen months old, was on his lap, covered in his blood. I did not know she was unhurt and thought she had been shot, not as it turned out her father. But standing near them was Faujdar, the Nawab sahib's own aunt's son, with a smoking musket. He was just eight years old and such a polite child. It breaks my heart to remember the expression on his face. And yet, as I reached and found my dying husband and his blood on our daughter, the first thought that occurred to me was: could it be an accident? For the boys in the family are taught to shoot from an early age, and Faujdar knew how to handle a musket, or so they told me. Do you understand what I am trying to tell you, captain?'

Again, Sleeman was not certain if he did, and told the Nawab Begum so.

'We cannot be certain whether our own children have committed a crime by accident or design, or are pawns, because of the way we raise them. We give muskets to small boys and are proud of their prowess with firearms. The first reaction among royal families is to suspect everyone of treachery and malice. Can you imagine what horrors a poor villager's family has to endure every day? So, what is it about these Phansigars that has affected you? Is it the matter of violent death? It is commonplace wherever you look. I am sure the streets of London are not safer than those of Bhopal or Calcutta. Or is it the mass graves? You have seen deaths at large scale, have you not? Or is it these theatrical codes and superstition, or this zubaan of which you hint, but whose details you have not included, doubtless for good reasons?'

'Your highness,' said Sleeman, 'I have been given a task, and I intend to complete it to the fullest extent possible. But it is true that I have been affected. The impunity of it makes me angry. I have reason to believe that most of the murderers we have caught so far were driven to it by desperation, poverty, perhaps a drought or two or ill-fortune. There are very few men, in my experience, who find pleasure in taking lives. Most of the stranglers we have captured began as assistants or deceivers, and had to prove over years that their heart had been hardened to the deed before they were allowed to kill. Therefore, while their continued existence is an affront to me, I understand how someone may be driven to such acts. But above them sit the creators of this structure, and they have existed with impunity so far, with the complicity of petty village officials, revenue officials, zamindars, even governors and rich merchants who profit from the loot. I feel enraged at the scale of this.'

'Is it only murder that affects you thus? Captain, I have a request to make to you directly instead of writing to Government House and waiting for a reply which may never come. You have been travelling across the land, and have seen much. I request you also, in the course of your enquiries, to look into the kidnapping of children. For there are many such kidnappers abroad, travelling in many guises, as tinkers or mendicants, priests or merchants, who kidnap children who are never seen again. The girls might find their way into nautch houses in my own city or even in Calcutta. The boys too, or perhaps they are killed in tantric sacrifices or enslaved. The gruesome possibilities are too many to enumerate at this time before namaaz. I have been asked by the qazis to think pious thoughts for my own sake, but it is difficult when I think of these deceivers who steal our children. Are they not just as terrible as the deceivers you hunt, or the tricksters who poison people?'

Sleeman said he would begin enquiries about missing children as well. The Nawab Begum was silent again, perhaps wondering if she had spoken too much about too many things with a stranger, trusted or not. Sleeman was wondering about this too.

'You are an interesting man, captain, in your silences. I shall await your findings. But please remember: it is dangerous for the upholder of the law to be swayed by emotions, except the necessary one of mercy. And equally dangerous to expect people to change the way you would like them to at a time of your choosing.'

Sleeman thanked her, excused himself, rose and left. A courtier was waiting outside to lead him to the rooms of the minister. Sleeman found Reynolds discussing with the young man about the problem of Phansigars in the kingdom of Bhopal.

What was known was myth, legend, accusations, a few men caught without evidence, and little besides. The city had a kotwal and some najeebs, in addition to palace and city guards, but their main function was to regulate merchants entering or leaving the gates and to quell public disturbances. The countryside did not see much enforcement of the law beyond a few patrols by the Nawab Begum's cavalry. Records of people, let alone of criminal matters, did not exist. The sheher qazi, who administered sentences based on the Shariat, was a learned man with a prodigious memory, aided by a group of young hafizes whose task, by definition, was about memorisation. Therefore they did not forget much, but did not commit criminal matters to paper either.

The minister could recall one instance which had stayed in his memory owing to the circumstances. Three years earlier, a merchant had been travelling on the road to Khilchipur and had vanished along with his munshi, servants, cargo and some money. His brother in Khilchipur had complained to the Maharaja on the evening of the same day when the merchant was supposed to have arrived. The Maharaja was thirteen, the brothers were influential, and the court's response was therefore swift. A unit of horse was sent out the same evening. The details, the minister told Sleeman, were unclear, but sometime in the night the cavalrymen had come across a group of men in a desolate place. They were questioned, and on being searched, were found with pouches of gold coins, some of the missing cargo, and a silken waistcoat. The cavalry captain, who seemed to have some initiative, questioned the captives with some vigour and they led him to a clearing where they had interred the merchant and his men. The culprits had been taken back to Khilchipur and had confessed to strangling the victims after joining them en route, pretending to be fellow traders.

The stranglers and the men who had interred the bodies were found to be Muslims, so the Maharaja had sent them to the sheher qazi of Khilchipur. Some were from villages near Bhopal, so the sheher qazi had written to the qazi of the royal capital and conferred with him. Then he had pronounced the sentence of death on them. The sheher qazi of Khilchipur, a young follower of the Hanafi school, had declared the brother of the dead merchant had the right to qisas from the murderers, who were, therefore, strangled in a public square.

'And did anything come of it? Did the Maharaja order an investigation into the presence of Phansigars in his lands?' asked Sleeman.

'I do not think he did, huzoor. He was a child, and I suspect was happy the merchant's brother was satisfied with the justice that was handed out,' said the minister.

The two qazis had not thought it necessary to discuss this with the Nawab Begum. The minister told Sleeman the qazis of Bhopal and neighbouring principalities no longer looked up to the throne after Qudsia Begum's ascension. There had been some talk of British interference in Islamic tradition.

As for kidnappings of children, there were so many complaints, said the minister, that there could be no count. Some kidnappers were captured in the act or while trying to escape, and administered summary justice by the people unless the men of the kotwali rescued them from the fury of the mob.

'Such kidnappers are also counted among the deceivers here. If there are some who are better organised than most, I cannot tell,' said the minister. There were no laws, either Muslim, Hindu or British, which addressed this class of deceivers. Sunni lawgivers had diverging views on the punishment for kidnapping of free children.

A messenger entered and conferred with the minister.

'Begum sahiba has requested your presence at the dinner

she will have with the court this evening, if you will be so kind,' the minister said.

Sleeman wanted to excuse himself and leave Bhopal by the evening. He had to visit Ujjain after this.

'The agent will, of course, be present, and will be happy to find you there,' said the minister. There was no trace of humour in his voice.

'Then I shall be delighted to attend the dinner,' said Sleeman.

Qudsia Begum was a clever and perceptive woman.

'And now, since the namaaz-e-zuhr has been called, I shall take your leave. If you will be kind and wait here, I shall take you to the sheher kotwali, to see if we can help you in your inquiries in any other way,' said the young man, before bowing and leaving the room.

Dinner was pleasant. The Nawab Begum had frugal tastes, but the table was supplied well, and her cooks were talented. Sleeman had an informative conversation with some senior courtiers and the Nawab Begum, who apologised for talking about such grim matters earlier in the day and asked him about Amelie's interests in music, in which she appeared to have good taste. The day had not been productive, apart from warnings of discontent among clerics and of deceivers who kidnapped children. But the agent was dismayed on seeing Sleeman at the royal elbow, which also counted for something. The captain's back still hurt, and there was no end to travel by horseback, and ahead lay Ujjain, which carried much menace and pain, but not of the physical kind.

There are no travellers as lonely as those on an Indian country road. And of them, there could be none as lonely as the messengers of moneylenders involved in the opium trade.

The British monopoly over the trade, which extended in an arc of poppy fields from Khandesh through Malwa and Bundelkhand to Bihar and Bengal, had by the turn of the century created a by-product that in hindsight would appear the most natural of progressions. It had created a need for large sums of money. Growers, transporters and refiners of poppy into opium, and those who shipped them to China needed more and yet more money to carry out transactions in bulk. Not all such transactions were based on the staid old principles of deferred payment, on muddati or sahyog hundis, on the principle of trust between merchants who might have met just once when they were young, or not even that if the families had been trading for generations. It was a new world, a bolder world where creditors demanded the physical presence of money and where lineage or clan was not enough to supplement the idea of deferred payment. Therefore, a new class of moneylender had emerged, able to put together cash consignments for lending to merchants across provinces. And the corpuscles of this circulatory system for wealth were messengers of the creditors.

They were noted for their meekness, for their average stature and absence of mannerisms that might call attention to themselves. They went about in rags, as mendicants, as beggars and destitute, sometimes even as madmen, to avoid the attention of thieves, cutpurses and highwaymen. For an armed convoy could not be arranged for the convenience of a single messenger or even a small group. So heavy was the traffic in these consignments that the trade relied on swift passage at a pace at which the Indian merchant had never worked over the millennia. At any time, a lender or saraf could have several messengers on the road and thousands of rupees in circulation.

The messengers were known to be trustworthy and discreet, reliable and regular, even punctual as much as travel over the Indian countryside could allow. Without them, the inland poppy trade would have been crippled. They were intelligent and alert, devious and well-versed in the ways of deception and disinformation. It was not enough. The Phansigars set out for them with an unparalleled singularity of focus. They were no mere rabble of cutpurses or dacoits to be hoodwinked by the crafty messengers.

Sleeman had not yet compiled an exhaustive list of victims whose identities had been confirmed, but Reynolds and Amelie could have told him that it would include hundreds of the messengers, carrying lakhs of rupees in cash. From Kota to Indore and Chitrakoot to Kanpur, besides stories that arrested stranglers told of killings in Bengal, the messengers had fallen to a foe of greater guile and ruthlessness. But among all these accounts, Sleeman had yet to hear of a messenger betraying his oath to a moneylender, or being in league with the Phansigars. In that they had shown greater integrity than an average village official, and had paid for it with their lives. A moneylender's messenger would never be included in the list of prohibited castes for the sonoka.

Thus, Ujjain. Storied Ujjain, Benares of Malwa, site of legends for the mariners of Antiquity who skirted India's coasts and heard of how all roads led to this centre of commerce. Ozene the Fair, as the Greeks of Alexandria had called it. In the young Sleeman's imagination, before he had ever left Cornwall, Ujjain had been the light which drew him to the east. A few months after joining his regiment, on furlough in Bombay, Sleeman had travelled by horse and boat to Ujjain. The reality had been different, and he had turned away in embarrassment, a child reprimanded by the truth of the world and thus ashamed of his youthful fancies.

The pilgrimages were eternal, and the temples as grand as in myth. But the countryside had been given over to poppy under the tutelage of the Company, through which the zamindars and merchants of the city made enormous wealth. His people, and the people of his adopted land, had disappointed him with their greed and venality. Sleeman had returned to the city since, but only when ordered to.

Reynolds and he arrived at the Residence to find Major Stewart waiting. Sleeman was acquainted with the agent and had found him a capable man, one of those cavalry officers of integrity who were not impressed by the wealth of those with who they associated in the course of their duties.

'The Maharaja will see you today, as requested. He never turns down an audience with us. The Rajmata would not have seen you anyway, and I did not want to complicate your work by asking her,' said Stewart, as they sat in his office.

'I hope my visit does not cause problems for you, sir,' said Sleeman.

'I do not think it will. But you need not have come. There is nothing to be seen here regarding your dacoits, Sleeman. It is as incongruous as seeking a highwayman in the middle of a civil war. I do not say there will not be one, but what are the chances of catching him if he is?'

'It cannot be as bad as that, sir.'

'It is much worse than Government House thinks. You cannot imagine the acrobatics we have to perform to be on the pleasant side of everybody. Government House asked the Rajmata for a loan to finance the Burma campaign. She must have anticipated the request, for just two days before the letter arrived, she sent a note to me saying she was impecunious, and if we could advance her a loan.'

'I had heard rumours about this, but I found it rather difficult to believe, sir. She must be the richest woman in all of India.'

'She has more money than she herself knows, Sleeman. She is in business with two of the largest opium merchants in the Malwa, she's broken the Company's monopoly, she has her choice of Parsi ship-owners in Bombay. There is no pie in which she does not have a finger. She owns half of Benares, including the largest Indian bank there. And she does not like us.'

'I hope it is not personal, sir.'

'I do not think so. With her it is not personal. But she does not want the Maharaja to have complete power, and has been inciting the court and the Brahmins against us. She has been calling for more powers to the Peshwa, which the Brahmins were sure to support. I doubt she has become patriotic at this point in her life. I think she just hopes for more commerce if we were to leave the opium trade, or were forced to. At any rate, there are so many events happening at present that the taking of thieves, or murderers if you will, is not a concern for anyone.'

'I do not understand. You have seen the list of victims said to be from or near Gwalior. Most were messengers of moneylenders involved in the trade. The merchants here, including the Rajmata, must have lost dozens of couriers and lakhs of rupees over the years of which we might never be aware. It should be in her interest even more than the Maharaja's to stop the Phansigars.'

'Sleeman, do you know how much she earns in a single season? Or how many of these messengers are sent out every day by the sarafs? No matter how many have been killed by the gangs of stranglers, the loss would be so minute that it would not even matter to someone like her. What would matter more would be the wound to her pride if she were to seek our aid. As far as she is concerned, there are no missing messengers.'

They waited for an audience with the Maharaja in another ante chamber, and were ushered in a short while afterwards. The Maharaja was seated on an unadorned wooden platform, under a banner which showed two coiled snakes, hoods spread, facing a sun in the middle. A few courtiers were in attendance. He was dark of skin, thin with an angular face and looked older than his fourteen years. A certain force of character which shows on the faces of some monarchs was, Sleeman saw, absent, but the eyes were frank and honest, as far as they could be judged.

The Maharaja smiled and greeted the delegation, asking them to be seated. The courtiers remained.

'I must thank Government House for taking up my complaint, Captain Sleeman,' said the Maharaja in Urdu.

'I thank your highness for granting this audience to us,' said Sleeman, in the Sanskritised Hindustani preferred by the courts of Ujjain and Bithoor. The Maharaja appraised this and smiled again.

He had been born Mukut Rao, to a modest Maratha family with little prospects, distant relations of Daulat Rao, the Maharaja of Gwalior. Daulat Rao had died without an heir from any of his three wives and an adoption became necessary. The royal widow, Baiza Bai, now the regent to the throne, wanted to adopt someone from her side of the family, but was compelled to adopt from Daulat Rao's, and thus Mukut Rao became Jankoji Rao, the new Maharaja. Baiza Bai found her prospects of running the kingdom vanishing, and saddled with a son she did not want.

Baiza Bai was as committed in her opposition to the British as she was shrewd in her business dealings, and was locked in a feud with the supporters of the young Maharaja.

'Despite the interference of my mother, Captain Sleeman, we have attempted to rule with care, and try to make sure our subjects have safety and security. But the countryside is lawless after so many years of war. We receive complaints of vanished people, from merchants to children. Our subedars hear complaints of poisoners who will drug your food and disappear before you have realised you were drugged. It is an impossible situation, captain. Even the merchants with whom my mother is in business have lost countless messengers transporting money, in far-off places, although she will not admit it. I do not want to complain against my neighbouring monarchs, but we have heard of dacoits living in the forests of Bhopal, and stranglers in the villages there. If the governor-general sahib has tasked you with looking into the matter, I am overjoyed. As you know, a valuable gift, a horse which was being sent to me, vanished.'

'Yes, your highness, I was informed of your complaint.'

'It was sent by the household of a prominent Brahmin in Poona. It was a Marwari of high breeding. I had sent a trusted courtier with a unit of matchlock men to fetch it, along with some other less valuable gifts. I have not heard from them ever since.'

'There is no possibility, your highness, that this courtier might be involved in the disappearance?'

'There is none, I can assure you. Mirza Akhtar is from a respected family. His grandfather was a captain in the Peshwa's huzurat, and his father is in charge of an artillery unit here. Major Stewart has met him a few times. The family has fallen on hard times lately, but of their honesty I have no doubt. Mirza Akhtar was a strong and courageous man. I cannot imagine what must have happened to him. Not to mention, I had to explain to the Brahmin in Poona, and through him to the Peshwa, that we have not received the horse.'

Sleeman had thought of meeting the missing courtier's family, but realised there would not be any clues to be found there. This Mirza Akhtar would not be the only trustworthy messenger to vanish with invaluable cargo.

'I request you to pursue inquiries as you see necessary, Captain Sleeman. If in the course of them you are required to travel through our lands or visit any of our possessions, please do so with freedom. I understand you have some names of arrested men and wish to enquire about them. Our sheher kotwal would be happy to answer your questions.'

Sleeman thanked the Maharaja and took his leave. Here, at least, he was not expected to be present at any banquets. The court had other matters to occupy its interest. Stewart directed him to the sheher kotwal, who said he would ask about the men who had been named by arrested Phansigars, and would send word if they were captured or located.

Sleeman was beginning to understand that the Nawab Begum and the Maharaja had not been interested in uprooting the Phansigars as much as in proving their trust in Government House. Or perhaps where they had the will and the integrity, they were affected by the absence of mechanisms to uproot people like the Phansigars. This was turning into just another political department exercise: full of misdirection, scheming, and little in the way of results. But Sleeman was determined to forge his own path. He, at least, had no more illusions about Ujjain or the nature of trade in the Deccan.

Jabalpur baked under the summer sun. The monsoons were a glint in the eye of a distant god. The more sensitive Europeans had left for cooler places. Reynolds' wife had gone to Simla. Reynolds had accepted that he would have to stay on. He was in Bundelkhand following up on information about a large group of Phansigars on expedition.

The Sleemans did not leave in summer. Amelie did not want to travel all the way to Simla by herself, and her husband did not mind the summer. It was what came after that tested him every year. And now there was no question of abandoning the investigation.

Sleeman was trying to create a system to deal with organised crime of the type that he had found. He could not keep using sepoys and cavalrymen every time he stalked the stranglers. But the provincial police, such as they were, could not solve the problem if left to themselves. They owed their roots to the kotwali system of the Mughals: part watchmen, part medieval city militia, they had been designed to have an adversarial relationship with citizens, to control mobs or riots when needed. In the British-ruled provinces, poorly trained and equipped, they thought of themselves as soldiers but were still not much removed from the watchmen who patrolled the streets of princely cities. The idea that they represented the people and were not an occupying force would not have occurred to them, or to the Company's officers who oversaw them. The chances of somebody volunteering information about criminals to such a group of men, for the larger welfare of the people, were minute. Until the police could be induced to act as representatives of the people, and not the rulers, until they were taught to look beyond the hierarchies of caste and biradari, Sleeman did not expect an improvement in the situation, and was aware that organised gangs like the Phansigars and Dhaturias knew this as well. And he knew how fruitless it was to expect caste to disappear from any aspect of public life or administration.

The problem, as Dr Wilson had told Sleeman, was whose peace were the provincial police supposed to keep, and whose law they were supposed to enforce. The interests of the prince, the Company, the political department and the many divisions of the people never coincided, nor did their ideas of justice and fairness.

Magistrate McLeod from Allahabad sent word of the first trials of arrested Phansigars. Some had turned approvers and had been providing testimonies and evidence. The mass of information about Phansigars had been mounting, but so had the evidence of the kinds of people who had benefitted from them.

Inured as Sleeman thought he had become to atrocity, humans could still surprise him. The dry season, as the saying went, makes beasts of men, but some are worse than beasts to begin with. McLeod wrote of sarai keepers who had been arrested for being informants for parties of stranglers. They sometimes even permitted murders to be committed on the premises, provided no witnesses escaped and the bodies were disposed of. No less complicit were some zamindars, who were aware of their tenants who went on expedition, and from who they exacted a tithe of the loot at the end of it, in exchange for protection, or as morka, the part due to a sardar or subedar of stranglers.

The leader of an expedition, otherwise a marginal farmer,

was arrested and brought to trial. His zamindar, a Brahmin to whom he owed considerable money, now removed his protection from the man's family. The zamindar went to the tenant's cottage, violated his wife and threw her out along with her children. She was found wandering on a public road, dazed and out of her mind, by a minor district official who put the facts together and took her to McLeod. The zamindar had not expected to be arrested or charged, but found that he was. Now McLeod was besieged by powerful people in Allahabad, Indian and British alike, who advised him to temper his idea of justice with mercy. He was a capable man, and a hardworking magistrate, but admitted in his letter to Sleeman that sometimes his work exhausted his spirit.

Sleeman had to capture the subedar of Phansigars, the keeper of their lore, the man who was many men, who knew the heads of the other regions and how to find them. But beyond legends and vague sightings, beyond descriptions of great physical beauty and charisma, beyond origin stories centred around the Bengal Army's atrocities and of sightings during Phansigar expeditions, there was nothing substantial yet. Two bhartotes even said they had heard the man had been present at the killing of a nobleman, and had ridden away on a beautiful horse. The rumour was too specific to be false but too vague to be of any help. The man was some kind of totem, appearing to some and seeming familiar with every place.

The district's work stuttered on. A delegation arrived on an evening seeking audience with Sleeman. They had travelled north for five days from the large village of Seoni, on the advice of a farmer who owned a few bighas of good land and was a well-regarded mahajan there. He had earlier served as a jamadar in Sleeman's regiment and had been a capable man, as jamadars had to be. A problem that such a man felt unequal to solving must be a difficult one indeed, so Sleeman gave them a hearing.

The dry season had been more harsh than usual for Seoni and its surrounding villages. The wells had dried early and the streams which flowed to the Wainganga River had become mere trickles.

'We started digging deeper wells, but the ground is drier than I have ever seen,' said one of the villagers. They were sitting on the verandah of the court, fanning themselves. Dusk was some distance away, and there was no wind.

The land was fertile but many from Seoni and its neighbouring villages also herded cattle. Fodder was one of the first farm stock to be affected by the drought, and herders began taking cattle and goats deeper into the jungle, or into the rocky terrain at the base of Mahadeo Hills. That was when the attacks began.

'About a month ago, a farmer awoke on hearing the cries of cattle in their pen. He found four or five cows and bulls with deep claw marks on them, and a calf dead. He had never seen or heard of this before,' said a villager.

The attacks continued. Goats vanished from pens, dogs disappeared, grazing cattle were attacked near the edge of forests. Calves would be found dead and partly eaten.

'It was not like an animal hunting, sahib, but more like slaughter. Sometimes it seemed the animals were wounded for the sake of it.'

The villagers were worried, then angry. The mahajan led a few men to find the culprits in the forest, but it was difficult to track them over dry ground. It was broken country, in the foothills of the Mahadeo Hills which separate the Wainganga from the Narmada to the north. The hills rose in steep inclines north of Seoni, and the ravines and gulches were treacherous when the streams were dry. It was the perfect place for a predator waiting for wandering cattle. Watches were kept on wooden platforms, beats were organised, but still the livestock continued to be slaughtered.

'Sahib, our cattle and goats are already dying under the sun. We have not heard of leopards or tigers doing this to our livestock in the past. Between the mysterious creatures and the summer, we will be driven to destitution,' they said.

The answer, the mahajan had suggested, was a beat led by a lot of well-trained men on horseback with guns.

'The day is not far when the people will be attacked, and we have little to defend ourselves, sahib. We cannot stay locked inside our homes. We have to go out to save our crops and livestock, or starve.'

The dry season created desperate men in the Satpuras, and the villagers were being pushed into a corner. In which case, the ex-jamadar had taken the right decision. This was a task for soldiers.

Sleeman summoned Second Lieutenant Moore and told him to take thirty sowars to Seoni, as soon as he had arranged for their equipment and supplies.

'The area around Mahadeo Hills is not horse country, so you may need to conduct some of your searches on the dismount. Organise a beat and flush out these predators. I shall not venture a guess about the identity of the beasts responsible. If you feel more men will be required, we shall send them,' said Sleeman.

Moore nodded. They were looking at a survey map of Seoni and its surroundings.

'Also, Moore, please remember that the dry season is difficult for all creatures. Whatever the culprits are, if you can show mercy to them, do it.'

Moore left with his sowars the next day, followed by their

porters and the villagers on foot. He told Sleeman he would send word in case he needed assistance, or if the matter became more difficult than they had thought it would.

Ten days passed. The sun continued to beat down on the town, and even proverbial mad dogs were not to be seen on the streets, leave alone Englishmen. Sleeman laboured through another hearing in the case of the litigious landlords. Both had hired, at some expense, formidable mridhas who raided and harassed the other's tenants, or so they claimed. The landlords themselves were present during the hearing, and took pains to reassure Sleeman that they were pacifists at heart, and had only been oppressed by the other. Sleeman had the ominous feeling that he would be hearing their case for the rest of his natural life.

Spilsbury received a joyous piece of news. A potter of his acquaintance in Narsinghpur had come across some large stones buried in the earth, which he thought might be of interest to the doctor. Spilsbury had hurried over and discovered that they were massive petrified trees of a type that he had never seen before in the region.

'I find it difficult to believe, captain, but I suspect they are remains of a variety of palm,' he said, when he had returned to Jabalpur after making arrangements for the safekeeping of the finds. He returned to Narsinghpur, his bags packed for a few days, and wrote a detailed study of the objects, which were each the length of a grown man and of almost the same diameter.

'Mr Prinsep or Mr Hodgson could shed light on this, I am certain,' he said, and sent the report to the office of the Society.

Sleeman examined cases of kidnapping of children in the province. Some were crimes of retribution, the result of clan quarrels. But there was evidence of organised gangs at work in Sagar and smaller towns. Deception and occasional violence were their stock in trade. These, too, were a class of deceivers who sold their victims at big cities, he concluded, and wrote of them in his monthly report to Calcutta. He did not have the resources to investigate this class of criminal. Only someone like Macnaghten could help him.

On a quiet afternoon, Sleeman was dozing in his study at home after lunch when Moore returned. The captain awoke to commotion and voices, and hurried outside. He found that a large crowd of Jabalpur's citizens, including its urchins and louts, had entered the courtyard. Amelie was trying to tell them to stop jeering and making noise. Sleeman's appearance made them quiet, although they continued to murmur among themselves. Those at the back, certain that Sleeman could neither see nor recognise them, continued to jeer.

Sleeman could see sepoys down the street, heading for the house. The crowd parted, and he saw the reason for the commotion.

At its centre was a wooden cage, not more than six feet by six, made in haste and lashed together with rope. It had been carried in by porters. Moore was standing next to them, and four other sowars had also dismounted, awaiting orders. The crowd had forgotten the rifles on the sowars' backs, for everyone was staring at the cage.

Inside was a huddled figure. Sleeman walked closer and saw it was a human, or perhaps an anthropoid figure, of small stature. Then it moved, and Sleeman was looking into a human face—thin, pinched, the cheekbones jutting out, the mouth open in a snarl, the teeth black and yellow. The eyes looked unnaturally white in a face darkened by the sun, and the hair was long and filthy. It was a boy, perhaps not older than ten, but he looked smaller due to a poor diet. His ribs jutted out, and while the legs looked sinewy, the heels, from what Sleeman could see of them, were cracked and scarred much more than even a farmer's, while calluses covered the elbows and kneecaps.

The boy was naked, crouched on all fours, staring at the crowd. The more he snarled, the more the urchins jeered. Sleeman could hear Amelie's fruitless entreaties to them over the din.

'That is enough, I should think,' said Sleeman. 'I request you all to please leave the premises. I believe you have had enough entertainment for the day.'

By then the sepoys had entered the courtyard and formed up. The crowd left with reluctance, muttering and laughing. Amelie was asking the household's groom to see to the sowars' horses. Sleeman turned to Moore.

'There must be an explanation for this, Moore. Am I to take it that you have captured the culprit behind the slaughtered livestock at Seoni? He must be a desperate fellow, to be caged like this.'

Moore looked at the crouching figure, and back at Sleeman.

'It is a little more complicated than that, sir. I request permission to present my report,' he said.

Sleeman led Moore inside and to his study. Moore looked fresh and alert, in the way that young people can manage to be even after hours in the saddle. Sleeman remembered a time when he had been like that.

'We reached Seoni in two days without incident, sir. The drought has indeed been severe in the region, and not a village that we passed had been unaffected. We first met the panchayat of Seoni, and the mahajan who served with you. He welcomed us and told us about a few other details which the delegation had not mentioned.'

'There was great fear in the neighbouring villages. Some had already begun talking of supernatural elements abroad, and of the drought being a curse on the land. The mahajan told me that we had to find the culprits soon before people began turning their suspicions and fears on one another. "The dry season," he said…'

'"…makes beasts of men". I know.'

'Yes, sir. So we spent the first day and part of the next visiting the affected villages and looking at the places where the livestock had been slaughtered. There was not much to see. The terrain was difficult, and Mahadeo Hills are unclimbable if one is not familiar with the lay of the land. But we began by riding around all the water holes in the forests nearby that we could find. Most were dry as bone.

'Two days after we reached Seoni, a herd of goats was attacked and several taken away. We rode to the village as soon as we were informed of this, and searched the area. We found some animal tracks, and blood. There was no human presence for miles inside the forest. The mahajan said he would provide us with a tracker, but it would be difficult, and their dogs are not trained to follow old game scents.

'We decided to beat the area anyway, and organised a group from all the surrounding villages. It was not easy on foot. The land is broken into steep ravines, and all the gulches are dry. We came across what had till recently been a lair of dholes. Quite a large group, from the appearance of it. Perhaps thirty members. We saw no sign of them.'

'I would be surprised if they had stayed. Dholes are notoriously shy around humans,' said Sleeman.

'Yes, sir, but the tracker said it looked like the dholes had fled some days earlier.

We were about to take our horses across and pick up the trail when we heard cries from the flanks, and turned in that direction. We came across the dholes cornered in a ravine, where they had dragged the goats. We opened fire on them, and managed to hit some, while the others escaped through the line of beaters. We examined the ravine, and the older lair. It appears that the dholes had arrived there around a month earlier.'

'When the slaughter started.'

'Yes, sir. As far as we understood, the pack lived somewhere in the Mahadeo Hills and was forced to the plains by the drought, and the scent of easy livestock.'

'So why did the pack abandon the first lair?'

'I was going to tell you. Just as we were examining the ravine, the beaters hailed us. Some distance away, we saw a pack of wolves running single file along the lip of another ravine. They had been flushed out of a rocky stretch by the last group of beaters and were trying to escape. The last wolf was loping along in an odd manner. We rushed at them, and it was only when we came close that we realised the last wolf was a human. I ordered the men to fire in the air. I did not wish to harm the beasts, since we had found the killers already. The pack scattered, and I ordered the men to corner the boy. He nearly slipped through, for he was walking on all fours and was agile in a way that I found difficult to believe. It took several men to catch him and wrestle him to the ground. He was a sight. He nearly bit off a finger of one of the sowars. It might yet be infected. You saw his teeth. We tied him and took him back to Seoni. It seems the wolf pack has been living in the deep jungle for a long time. When the dhole arrived, the wolves had to fight for territory, and drove them out of the first lair.

'We talked to the panchayat at Seoni, and posted watchmen on trees at the Wainganga ford, to see if the dhole returned. Late in the evening we got word from across the river that they had still not been spotted. We were exhausted from the day's drive, but somebody had spread a rumour that the boy had lived among the wolves and had been a cannibal. You know what people think of wolves. They would not believe that we had found the bones of livestock in the dhole lair. By the evening a crowd had gathered with implements and wanted to lynch the boy. The mahajan and panchayat tried to stop them. I do not think I could have prevented them from it on my own.'

'We decided to leave Seoni as quickly as possible before some other rumour started. That night, we heard the wolves howl in the forests nearby. The mahajan said it was unusual for them to come so close to the edge of the jungle. It might be fanciful of me, sir, but I think they were howling for him.'

'We made the cage by the morning, put the boy in it and crossed the Wainganga, camping on the other side. We organised another beat the following day on horseback, but didn't find the dhole. There were no reports of any person or livestock having been attacked. The mahajan thought the remainder of the pack had scattered or returned to Mahadeo Hills.'

'A remarkable account. One does not often hear of dhole attacking livestock and committing indiscriminate slaughter. It has been a difficult season indeed. What happened afterwards?'

'We decided to return to Jabalpur after another two days had passed. The villagers are not much happier than when we went there, but at least they know it was not the work of bandits, tigers or demons.'

'But they have not stopped believing the wolves were behind it.'

'No sir, they have not. There was no sign of the wolf pack either.'

'What shall be done about the boy?'

'I do not know, sir. I thought he would be safer here than at Seoni. He is quite wild, as you can see.'

They went back to the courtyard. Amelie was standing in front of the cage. The boy was lying curled up and still in a corner inside.

'What did the mahajan have to say?'

'The wolves live in that part of the jungle. The villagers know of them, but do not see them often, for that is deep inside the jungle where people do not go with no cause. The wolves do not come out even in the dry season, for there are some deep streams which survive most drought, if not one as severe as this year. There had been some rumours about a child who lived with wolves, but the mahajan had thought those were just rumours. One hears of them all the time.'

Stories of feral children were common, and often apocryphal. Sleeman himself had heard of several, particularly in the terai when he had served there. Most of these stories involved children raised by wolves, and in one instance by monkeys. Perhaps because these were social animals, among whom an abandoned or lost human infant could have some chance, however remote, of surviving. And a pliable, supple mind might even, when forced by necessity, be able to learn to live among them. Stranger things had been known to happen.

'But the child must have come from somewhere. What of his family or parents?'

'We made enquiries. Some said they had heard of a child which had gone missing from a village nearby, but nobody knew which village, or when.'

'Does he speak at all?' asked Amelie.

'Not a word, ma'am. Only snarls and grunts. He does not like being touched, but does not attack unless you approach him within a certain distance.'

'You would not call him dangerous, would you, lieutenant?'

'I doubt he has enough strength to be a danger to anybody,

ma'am. He has not eaten much since we caught him, except some strips of raw meat I thought he would like. If he has lived like an animal, which he has, he is not a danger to us any more than any other wild creature. Perhaps much less, for a wolf is born with its own weapons.'

'If he is completely mute, it means he has been living with the wolves since he was very small. They would never accept an older child who could speak or who smelt of the village,' she said.

Which in turn meant the child had had no human contact for more than eight years. Who could tell the circumstances which had led to him falling in with the pack, or how he had been abandoned by his people and had survived? For survive he had, in a place where the death of a thin-skinned animal would have occurred without a murmur. Sleeman doubted he would have, at any stage of his life, been able to live on raw meat for years on end and sleep exposed to the elements, without the most basic forms of hygiene. The child had nothing left to prove.

And yet, it must have been a precarious existence. Food for wolf packs, as far as he knew, was always difficult to come by, and there would be the constant peril of being hunted by humans if the pack happened to bring down livestock. Life would be doubly difficult in the dry season, with no water in the drinking holes and competition with other predators. It was almost impossible to imagine how difficult it would be for a human child to survive such conditions, for the pack would not be expected to slow down for him, or make allowance for his lack of fang, claw or instinct. There appeared to be scabs and healed wounds on the boy's exposed back, and a scar on the shoulder. Living in the midst of nature, or the raw version of nature which was the only true version, was a different proposition than some might imagine it to be.

Still, the boy needed care and nutrition, and might be persuaded, eventually, to join the ranks of humans, if he desired. The wolves had howled for him around the village on the night of his capture. A debt was owed to the wolves of Seoni, and Sleeman decided to honour it.

'Moore, you did well, both in finding the dhole and rescuing this boy. You may return to the barracks with the sowars and take a few days' furlough if you wish. There is some work that needs to be done in the matter of our Phansigar investigations, but it can wait.'

Moore saluted and led his horse out of the courtyard, followed by the sowars. Sleeman continued to stare at the boy, now curled tightly around himself and apparently sleeping.

'Do they have names, I wonder,' he thought aloud.

'His wolf pack? I doubt it. These are human affectations. They would have more immediate concerns. What shall we do, William?'

'First, we need to feed him, and I doubt he knows what cooked food is. Or the taste of vegetables. The logical solution is not what our friends would call civilised, but it can't be helped.'

The Sleemans would be buying a lot more meat from the cantonment abattoir than they had been.

'He has a family somewhere, I am sure of it. But finding them will be a difficult task,' said Amelie.

'And not many would want to take him in, if they were to see him like this. And even if he were a talking, well-mannered child, nobody would take him in unless they knew his caste. Under the current circumstances, they would not even touch him. Orphanages are out of the question. I would not like to throw him at the mercy of churchmen, and English families will not take him in either. Just because they do not have castes it does not mean they can be any less cruel.'

'William, we are not going to send him to an orphanage or a mission. He shall stay here with us.'

'I would not have it otherwise, Amelie.'

The boy slept on.

This river was more than a river, and less. Its name was from a classical word for leather. An unclean word for a society that needed carcasses removed, but would not accommodate those who removed them. The water was said to have run red in the far dawn of the world, in the age of heroes, from the skin and leather of animals which were dried along its banks. Cursed by a great queen, flowing through the land of an amoral king whose prowess at dice led a dynasty to civil war, the river became less than what it could have been, occupying a position of impurity between two water bodies of great merit. Sleeman's beloved Ujjain stood on the banks of one of its tributaries, and the river itself flowed into the Yamuna.

But this river was forgotten. Farmers would not plant crops along its banks. The dead would not be cremated or ashes immersed here. No festival wound its way from the hinterland to these waters, bringing pilgrims, mendicants and merchants. No great temple complexes crowded its meandering path.

The river became less than what it could have been, with its ravines and rock cliffs, perfect sites for outlaws, outcasts and fugitives, for ousted princes nursing dreams of reconquest and ghazis betrayed by their own men. But it also became more, for protected from the pilgrims and the corpses, from the effluents of cities and commerce, the river and its original residents still thrived, even in the dry season. But there were crossings, like this one.

There was little to distinguish this river bank from the rest of the immediate countryside, which was flat and given to jungle cork and kikar, ascending to deep ravines further downstream. A small shed roofed with thatch stood some fifty feet from the bank, on elevated ground. The river would rise during the rains, therefore the precaution.

But, for now the river was quiet, even dull. Not a ripple disturbed its surface. The reptiles so famed along this stretch and its tributaries were away elsewhere.

A small stone temple stood by the road leading away from the shed. Inside was an idol of a goddess on a makara. It was unusual to find such an idol along this river, for the form is a representation of the Yamuna, and sometimes of the Narmada, but not this river. The people who had built it and those who prayed here every day were unlettered, and did not know of these conventions. The river was cursed, but the crossing needed divine intervention.

The makara takes as many forms as the drapes on the Goddess, depending on the temple, the king or the people who have made it, but here it was a crocodile, if larger in relative size than its less divine cousins in the water. The idol was old, for it had been brought from elsewhere by a merchant from Kota and installed here with the appropriate prayers and rituals. The temple was new. It was newer than the shed on the bank, which was fifty years old, although people had forgotten about this and would say that the temple had always been there. Facing the small wooden door of the temple, on an elevated platform, was another makara, even larger than the first, also built on the decree of the merchant, who was a cautious man and an Agarwal. The makara is a guardian of doorways, portals and entry points. The shed and the path leading to it from the river was a portal which had to be guarded, and its supernatural guardian appeased.

Between the shed and the temple was a large tract of dusty land, beaten with the hooves of livestock, the wheels of wooden carts, hand-carried litters, palanquins, the pegs of cotton tents and the familiar indents of metal tripods on which travellers hung their cooking pots. It was a place where they waited for permission to pass, or to meet other caravans, or transfer their loads.

It was an early hour. Inside the shed, which had three mud walls, a British officer, unkempt, with stubble on his cheeks slept on a cot. He had been posted here for three years. Twice a year he would travel from Shivpuri to oversee the beginning of the caravan season, issue instructions to his troops and civilians, and return to his more comfortable quarters. He was young, and grateful for the uneventful nature of the posting. A fortnight after some energetic days at Shivpuri during Holi, he was content to let his small world follow its routine.

The second Englishman in the shed, also an officer, was not asleep, and had not slept for days. He sat on a rude stool, his eyes on the river and the path which left the other bank and disappeared to the west. An euhemerist, as Horace Wilson once was, would have been at the temple contemplating the meaning of the makara and the dry river. The officer was not Wilson, nor had ever wanted to be. Therefore, the stone crocodile and the officer kept a separate watch.

Across the path from the shed were faded grey tents, which housed ten sepoys on an average day. This not being an average day, four larger tents had been put up, in which had been quartered thirty sepoys and ten sowars, with a separate tent for the jamadar, who could not be expected to share space with the men he commanded. Their horses stood under the kikar trees at the edge of the clearing, where the shrubs held some moisture.

Due east, at some distance, was a town near a lake. The long-forgotten seth who had built the temple had also constructed a house there, large and comfortable by the town's standards. His only living son had not been the man the seth had expected, and both the family's business and the mansion had fallen into disrepair, and a portion of it now housed another complement of sepoys. The makara, foremost of vahanas though it may be, cannot compensate for the inadequacies of offspring.

The crossing at this shallow point on the river, the shed, the path and the town were part of the often disregarded, invisible arteries of India. Across the land, connecting cities ancient and new, villages significant and inconsequential, ports wealthy and in decline, settlements which only produced and others which consumed with ferocity, these arteries brought caravans, raw material, finished goods, produce and wealth. Much has been written, and yet more discovered, by those who have visited India and marvelled at the trade which sustains its wealth. But not much ink has been expended on humble crossings like these, or on the commerce which flowed through the invisible towns of the subcontinent which themselves produced little but acted as conduits. The only effort expended on their behalf has been on taxing this commerce.

The shed was the first customs post east of Kota. The second was at the town, where the transit documents and proof of payment would be verified. This was the shortest crossing to central India and to Kanpur and Allahabad, if a merchant were travelling from Kota, Udaipur or even as far as Saurashtra. There were numerous others, if one travelled north from Kota to Jaipur, and then to Delhi, or east to Agra.

From Delhi to Agra and then to Allahabad stretched the Inland Customs Line, and as much thought had been expended on its composition as on any strategic maneouvre on the frontier, or against the Maratha armies. At about the time when the customs shed was being planted on the cursed river, larger, more intimidating checkposts and chowkis were being set up at regular intervals on the road from Delhi to Allahabad, with supporting posts some miles to their east. Now the line was extending, like a creature coming awake with glacial inevitability, from Allahabad to Kanpur.

Far to the south, the humble shed near the forgotten town had been assured it was not a priority. The commerce that flowed through it was not to be dismissed, but would not be taxed with such sternness, or so it had seemed. Yet, now there was a contingent of sowars on patrol along the banks, led by a grizzled jamadar who could not speak below a growl and an English officer who did not seem to sleep, and had not been seen eating for two days. Which was sure to be an exaggeration, for officers manning customs check posts are not known to lose their appetites.

The new officer was a lieutenant unlike the sleeping officer, who was a second lieutenant. It was true that the former had not slept for days, for he had been on the march from Shivpuri, but he had been eating the indifferent fare which outpost cooks had been making for him for weeks. Now he just sat on the stool, massaging his left shoulder, which was sore, and looking at the riverbank.

A sepoy entered the shed with a brass tumbler of cold buffalo milk. The lieutenant took it and thanked the sepoy, but did not take his eyes away from the river. It was two hours after dawn, the comfortable time just before the heat began rising.

‘Leftan sahib, they will come, for this is their time. I have been here five years, and there has not been a time when the caravan has been late after Holi and Diwali,’ said the sepoy, who had greying hair and beard.

'Yes, that is what I have been told,' said the lieutenant. The sleeping officer shifted his weight on the cot and it creaked.

'They might be early or late by a few days, but they have always passed through to the town two weeks after Holi. Always,' said the sepoy.

The lieutenant nodded and the sepoy went away.

At this time of the year, caravans could wade across the river at some crossings, depending on the cargo they were carrying, but not here. For fragile goods, three large, square rafts with four polemen each made the crossing, for a nominal price. The earliest caravans left Kota at dawn, secure in the knowledge that the raja's watchmen patrolled the first few miles of open country. There had not been dacoits along the cursed river in recent times, and there was only the memory of a skirmish with a band of Pindaris, so long ago that people disagreed about the details.

The customs clerk arrived from a village nearby, his routine governed by instinct, for he was the oldest official of the Company government in those parts. He was followed by three young assistants, village youths supplementing the household income with whatever payment the clerk kept aside for them. Two were carrying a wooden desk and the third a bundle which contained official parchment, metal tokens, wooden customs stamps and ink.

The start of the caravan season after Holi was important, for in volume it equalled, if not exceeded, the trade that happened from the end of the monsoons till the beginning of winter.

The clerk passed by the shed after a brief greeting directed at the British lieutenant, and waited for the youths to unroll a dhurri under a kikar tree some distance away. They set the desk down, and he took his place for the day. It was unusual to see so many sepoys, not to mention cavalry. The clerk had been overseeing the post for nearly twelve years, and there had never been a need for so many uniforms. What kind of an army was this lieutenant expecting to fight, then? But the doings of officers were their own business, and the clerk had other duties to attend to.

The first of the traders appeared on the western bank. Wheat and vegetable sellers from villages not far away, on their way to the town. The vegetable sellers were too unimportant for the clerk, but the wheat sellers had to pay a nominal amount, not much more or less than what they would have paid to the Kota raja's officials had they gone west.

There trickled by the usual assortment of goods and people, jeweller and herdsman, farmer and potter, and the lieutenant still sat on the stool and kept his eye on the far bank. The younger officer awoke, apologetic at showing such slackness, but the lieutenant barely glanced at him as he went off to do his ablutions.

And then at last the far horizon began to stir. Through the haze and dust, the lieutenant caught his first sight of the vanguard of the army for which he had been waiting.

They advanced down the far path, all six hundred of them, to the water's edge. There was no question of wading through the river. The rafts were poled near, and the first batch walked on to them and was ferried across. And on and on it went, the rafts going back and forth at the same pace to the same spot on either bank, the slowest and largest metronome the lieutenant had ever seen. On the near side, the passengers did not even have to cross the entire breadth of the river. They just got off the rafts, walked over a sandbank and then up the incline to the path. The clerk's assistants stood on the side, guiding them to the open field.

On and on they came; patient, silent, all muscle and sinew and steady unblinking eye. Six hundred of the hardest working creatures in India, and yet also the most reviled in story, song and idiom: the domestic donkey.

They were led by their drivers, five to a man, and like all armies were followed by a small moving village of camp followers in the form of servants and forage stores on the backs of other donkeys, because such a large group could not hope for forage at just any village they passed. At the head of this army rode a man on a healthy young pony, followed by assistants and servants of his own.

At once the meaning of the customs shed, and the reason for its existence just there, would have become clear to a newcomer. On the back of each donkey were two maunds of salt. This was the first great salt caravan to the east sent by the owner of one of the largest salt pans in Kutch, for the dry season, meant for the stores of princes and great men in central India. This was the reason for the customs post's existence.

The posts of the Inland Customs Line in the Ganga-Yamuna Doab, or to the west in Multan and northern Sindh, and backwaters crossings like this one were meant to levy tax on salt. The sepoy outposts were to catch smugglers taking the commodity east. Each maund would fetch a duty of three rupees and four annas, to be paid in whatever currency was accepted by the customs clerk, for there was no uniform coinage across the continent's worth of land between Kutch and wherever the caravans' final destination lay. In this case, the Company government would be richer by three thousand nine hundred rupees, a princely sum, and from only a single caravan. The salt pan owner would add this to the price of the product at journey's end. The only people suffering from this transaction would be the unfortunates who needed salt.

The customs clerk had stood up at the arrival of the caravan, for he had to attend to such an important event himself. The young man on the pony got off and advanced to meet the clerk. They knew each other because the caravan passed this way four times a year, in either direction. The customs clerk accepted the piece of parchment the young man carried as proof of ownership, and was about to walk towards the field of donkeys when he noticed the lieutenant had risen and was looking at him.

'Please continue with your inspection of the cargo. I would like to have a word with this gentleman,' said the lieutenant.

The young man, with the confidence born of inherited wealth and experience at talking to British officers, smiled and greeted the lieutenant.

'This way, please,' said the lieutenant, returning to his stool in the shed and pointing to the now empty cot. The young man sat on its edge.

'If you find this unusual, please be assured that there is no problem, nor are you in any kind of trouble. I just have a few questions I would like to ask you, and I hope you will give me the answers with some thought. My name is Lieutenant Reynolds, and I am posted at Jabalpur. I should like to know your name.'

The young man introduced himself. The name was unfamiliar to Reynolds.

'The goods you are carrying...'

'Salt, leftan sahib, we trade only in salt, at least this far from home. We have brought one thousand two hundred maunds, the first consignment of the dry season.'

'Yes. And they are from the salt pans owned by...'

'The owner is my father. I oversee the transport of some of the cargo, and the rest are overseen by two of my brothers or my father's trusted men. Is there a problem, leftan sahib? We have always paid our dues. Our measures are accurate, and we have never been accused of breaking the law.'

'I am sure you have not been. How many such caravans does your father send?'

'We are travelling to Gwalior and then to Kanpur. There are four that come along this route. There are six others that go to Jaipur, Delhi and Agra, and four that go to Multan and Sindh.'

'And yours is the first of the four that come here?'

'Yes, leftan sahib. The next one should have started a week after ours.'

'And that is how it is done?'

'Yes, sahib, that is how my father does it, and all the other salt pan owners, and their fathers before them.'

Reynolds reflected for a few moments on the amount of thought that had gone into planning the caravans, which had been travelling through central India for generations. Only customs duties changed, and rulers, and sometimes temples. The caravans were eternal.

Reynolds knew enough about animals to observe that the laden beasts were not the ghudkhars that ranged across Kutch, but were common donkeys found elsewhere.

'Yes, of course. Now I want you to pay attention to what I ask. I want you to think carefully about all the men in your caravan. You must be familiar with all of them. Tell me, have any men joined you on this journey, on some pretext or the other? Are there any strangers travelling with you?'

The seth's son smiled.

'Leftan sahib, you have not met my father. He is a most suspicious man, and difficult to please, whether one is a son or a servant. He has specifically warned all of us not to trust anybody on the way, whether during this leg of the journey or during our return. For on this leg the salt is precious and can be looted and sold, while on our return we carry money or valuables with us. We are aware of the dangers on the way. We trust no one we do not know.'

Reynolds thought of how much grief people could be spared if they cared for their lives as much as the young man's father cared about his salt.

'We know of people who might inveigle themselves into our company, and of poisoners who might drug and rob us. We travel armed, although we are grateful to the Company Sarkar for the absence of robbers on this route.'

'I am sure the raja also deserves some praise for this,' said Reynolds, and the young man agreed.

'So if I understand you correctly, everyone travelling with you is known to you,' said Reynolds.

'Yes, everyone.'

'And there have been no newcomers among the servants and guards?'

'None at all. In fact the newest members of the caravan are some of the donkeys.'

'I was going to ask you about the animals.'

'There isn't anything strange about them. Most are from my father's flock. But last year, during the dry season, some died on the way from Agra to Allahabad. Not a very large number, perhaps a dozen. My brother was in that caravan. On the return journey, he purchased a hundred of them from one of the livestock owners at Agra, finding them healthy and in good condition, and took them home, and here they are.'

'I see,' said Reynolds, but what he was asking himself was whether there was something he had not noticed. And he was beginning to understand.

'The donkeys and their drivers have been with us ever since,' said the young man.

And Reynolds understood. So he had to confirm his information had been correct.

'What do you mean, their drivers?' he said.

'Leftan sahib, you asked me to think with care before replying. I request permission to speak freely.'

'Of course, please do.'

'When a large number of strange donkeys join another herd, chaos happens. They attack and bite one another, and even humans. Some become untameable. A herd of that size is of little worth without its drivers. So when my brother bought the herd, he also employed the drivers, for they knew a lot about animals, and have worked hard ever since. We have had no complaints.'

Reynolds stifled a yawn and nodded. Through the fog in his brain, he was beginning to see what had happened.

There were no strangers who had inveigled themselves on this journey. The prize was too precious, too rare. A caravan which would pay nearly four thousand rupees in customs duty alone would be worth an enormous amount at journey's end, on the way back, in addition to other valuables and the personal belongings of the travellers.

They had waited a year for this, journeying west with their donkeys and working in the nameless salt pans for the seth.

'Thank you, young man. You have been helpful, and I shall not forget. Now please do what I ask you to. Summon these men here, and make sure all of them are present. And please wait nearby, but take care not to talk to anybody about what we have discussed till I call you again.'

The second lieutenant returned from whichever mysterious place he had gone for his ablutions. Reynolds told him there might be a slight delay in allowing the other travellers to pass the check point. The junior officer kept his questions to himself, knowing the lieutenant would not talk, and knowing Brigadier General O'Halloran had ordered his regiment to cooperate in any way possible.

The merchant's son returned with the drivers. They were too many to fit in the shed, so Reynolds stepped outside. His jamadar was already standing at attention to the side. A small crowd was beginning to gather as people continued to cross the river and reach the customs post.

Reynolds looked at the twenty men who stood in a loose group in front of him. It would have been too much to expect them to stand in a line. For the lieutenant, there was no other way for a group of men to stand.

He was tired. He had been away from home for a while. He had started the journey from Gwalior, where he had found nothing definite, but some names and the location of a village near Jhansi. Here, a dạk rider had caught up with him, with instructions from Sleeman and some more information, which had led him to Shivpuri, where he had caught ten men, all bhartotes, who had just left their homes after Holi on a long expedition south. At each place, he heard fragments of a rumour, about a great prize, a chisa ripe for the taking, and some names, of an expedition which had lasted for months and travelled far. Of these, five names had been mentioned several times. They could have been real, or assumed. Reynolds was not certain if some bhartotes were better known by assumed names. But that was all he had, and the mention of a salt caravan at this crossing after Holi. So he had ridden overnight to this place, and waited for days.

'All right. I am looking for these five men,' said Reynolds, and announced the names he had been given. All five were present. He had the names of their fathers and their villages. All five were from near Agra. The information was verified.

Reynolds' sepoys and cavalrymen, in uniform, carrying guns, now stood behind the twenty donkey drivers. Reynolds ordered his jamadar to search them. The find was meagre: a few coins, some odds and ends, and a pouch of dried powder. Reynolds sniffed it, and thought it could be a drug favoured by the Dhaturias. He could arrest the man from whom the pouch had been found on suspicion of being a poisoner, but mere possession of such extracts was not incriminating by itself. If it were, half of the travellers on any Indian country road would be in jail, and quite a lot of Englishmen.

Reynolds had the accounts of confessed bhartotes connecting these men to other killings, the circumstantial evidence he could gather from the account of the merchant's son, and very little else. He was certain a great massacre had been averted, although how these twenty unremarkable men, some getting on in years, would have strangled an entire caravan worth of healthy working men he would have to determine. At some point on the road, others were waiting to follow them and join in the killing at some secluded spot decided in advance. He would have to question these twenty and find the whereabouts of the rest before they scattered.

For the five men, at least, Reynolds had corroborative accounts placing them at the scene of seven killings, in total. He would have to check the number of victims. In two cases, he had overseen the exhumation of the victims' bodies. All three requirements that Sleeman had specified for a trial had been met. As for the others, he would have to find their presence or role in other crimes. Of one thing he was certain. All twenty were bhartotes. An inexperienced aulae, who might not be trusted to carry out a sacrifice, would not have been trusted to travel all the way to Kutch and work as a labourer for months before the killing. And the Phansigars of Agra would not have sought such a prize without thinking it through.

'I am taking all of you into custody. Anything you have to tell me, and I know you do, you can tell me when we reach the town. I know enough, whether you believe me or not. I have your names and those of your villages, and what you have done. I have accounts of your fellow aulaes and bhartotes, and I have seen the bodies. I have dug some up myself. If you talk, if you are honest with me, you can expect the court to be lenient. But do not think for a moment that you will escape the law. The Goddess no longer watches over you,' said Reynolds.

This dramatic concoction was of his own devising. He thought it would be useful to induce some fear among the more hardened Phansigars by letting them know he was familiar with their lore, and fluent in Ramasi. That in turn would make them wonder what else he knew, and might loosen their tongues. It had worked a few times, and he expected it to work again. Their lore and code was sacred for them.

At the town, guarded by the rest of his men at the rundown haveli of the long-dead seth, were the Phansigars he had arrested from Shivpuri and Jhansi. The first order of business would be to verify the identity of the twenty he had picked up here and get their detailed statements. It would be some time before he could return to Jabalpur.

'We are leaving, for now. I cannot say if we will return or not. I thank your men and you for your cooperation. Do keep an eye on suspicious caravans for us,' he told the second lieutenant.

The merchant's son was waiting with his servants near the customs clerk's desk. The clerk was unhappy at the crowd and at his work being held up, but there wasn't much he could do about it.

'I am taking your men with me. It is going to cause you inconvenience for the rest of your journey, but that can't be helped. I am sure you have questions. Please come with me to the town and you might get some answers,' Reynolds told the merchant's son.

'Leftan sahib, I will come along. I must get the customs papers and will follow shortly,' the young man replied.

'I am sure you will, but your father's trusted men can do that work in your absence. I would like you to come with me. I insist,' said Reynolds.

At the town, Reynolds would take the caravan's owner to the patwari and get a signed statement that the young man was known to residents of the town in good standing. His father, family and village would be verified and set down in the records. It was not that Reynolds was suspicious or wanted to harass the young fellow, who after all was only following his father's orders. It was just that the lieutenant had reached a point where he was not certain if anybody was who they said they were. In the entire tableau that had been enacted at the river crossing that morning, the only parties above suspicion, he reflected, were the beasts which had trudged with their load from the salt pans of Kutch.

Reynolds trotted out on his horse along the path, crossing the clearing where the donkeys had been herded, and the small temple. The stone makara crouched outside, indifferent to the soldiers and stranglers who went past, and the first of the small traders and peasants with their offerings, seeking safe passage.

The summer had become one of the driest Sleeman had seen since his arrival in central India. Not even two arid seasons at Narsinghpur could compare. A small stream which ran past his house to the Narmada went dry early in the season, for the first time in many years, according to his munshi, who had lived here before the town was renamed. The part of town northeast of Sleeman's house suffered a lot, for they had few wells and no stream large enough to support them. South and west, where the town and cantonment reached down to the Narmada, people at least had flowing water to drink close at hand.

But they still had to go out into the sun, which was without mercy. The children of the town, Indian and British, suffered a lot. Those of the British who had left for the hills were safe, but the children of junior officers and serving men and of Jabalpur natives had nowhere to go. They had no recourse but to spend the days in the shade, under the punkha, keeping out of reach of the dreaded hot winds which swept down from the barren hills around town. Amelie and her friends had their hands full assisting the camp surgeons, Spilsbury and his staff with those struck by heat-sickness.

Amelie had made many attempts at communicating with the boy from Seoni. From Colonel Menzies the dog enthusiast and his wife, she had received some guidance and a small monograph on understanding the behaviour of dog breeds. She had begun with the idea of replicating words, signs and gestures which worked with dogs to see if she could talk to the boy. This achieved little success, with both Amelie and the boy confused by the end of it. Mrs Menzies thought the absence of a tail and hackles were hampering communication. Amelie was not certain if Mrs Menzies was jesting or not. It was difficult for her to understand the peculiar humour of dog fanciers.

Neither Amelie, Sleeman nor anybody of their acquaintance had any knowledge or insight to offer on the behaviour and psyche of wolves. Sleeman consulted some old notes he had kept since his days in the terai, but most of these consisted of half-remembered and passed-on tales about feral children and the attempts at reintegrating them into society. Nobody had made a scientific study of this, and the wolf had remained the subject of much myth and little substance, besides an enduring image of cruelty, greed and avarice, human traits which even Sleeman knew were not fair when applied to wild creatures.

Sleeman's munshi's cousin, who was employed at the camp, suggested that the stench of the pack was still on the boy, and as long as it remained the attractions of human society would not work on him. Only a succession of thorough baths would aid the process of bringing him back to civilisation. Amelie dismissed this outright. She thought it was another symptom of ritual purity and cleansing through water by which the upper castes, like the Kayastha munshi, set so much store. She said this in so many words to Sleeman. This time he was not certain if she jested or not.

The household servants had indeed thrown a few buckets of water on the boy in the first few days after his arrival, until Amelie discovered they had been more enthusiastic than gentle while doing this and warned them not to harass the poor fellow. A barber had been called, and on the request of Sleeman had agreed, with reluctance, to do something about the boy's long and tangled mop of hair. The servants had pounced on the boy and held him while he struggled, and the barber had snipped off the hair with haste and had given it some kind of order.

Left alone, the boy would not let anyone approach him at the beginning, and would snarl and lie flat on the ground facing the threat. Amelie tried to coax him to let her put some ointment on some of the sores on his body, but this proved impossible to do, although she resolved to keep trying.

The cage was too small and Amelie could not bear to see him confined in it for hours on end. But he could not be allowed to roam free within the grounds either. For one, his agility was extraordinary and he was sure to bound over the gates or walls and escape into the forest if he had a mind to. For another, the neighbouring children, Indian and British alike, would gather every morning and evening or whenever it was cool enough out of doors and hurl multiple taunts, jeers and clods of earth at him till they were berated by Amelie, towards who they held no fear, knowing she was incapable of punishing or complaining about them. If the boy were to escape and land among them, the consequences were not difficult to imagine. Nobody had quite come around to filing off the broken and pitted nails on his fingers and toes.

Amelie and Sleeman reached a compromise by letting the child out of the cage when there were no guests in the house, and letting him move around the large backyard at the end of a stout rope tied to his ankle. He got used to the rope after some time, and did not try to bound away to the end of the yard where his tormentors would be gathered.

Amelie, despite her misgivings, had known that the boy would not eat cooked food, at least at the beginning. Nor would he be used to any other kind of food except raw meat. So she would place some chunks of goat and buffalo meat on the bone under a tree near the cage, and a shallow pail of water. After throwing some berries to him by accident, she also discovered that he was used to eating them. This was un-wolflike as far as she knew, but perhaps he had eaten other kinds of food in the jungle as well. In her journal, she wrote that the affinity for fruits, for somebody growing up among a completely carnivorous species, indicated humans inherited omnivorous tendencies as instinct. Sleeman agreed that this might be the case.

As the dry season grew worse, the boy stopped eating much and instead began to drink enormous quantities of water in great gulps, morning, noon and evening. So much would he drink that his stomach, already prominent in contrast to the ribs, would bloat and distend. Sated, he would crawl to the shade of a jamun tree in a corner of the grounds and fall into a deep sleep. This happened day after day, and he appeared to weather the season well with no apparent sickness. Amelie noted this as well, and thought it was a way perfected by the wolves to survive the dry season and scarcity of prey.

Some relatives of the agent were passing through Jabalpur on their way to Agra before the monsoons arrived and wanted to see the sights. Sleeman's excavation sites at Bada Simla and Lameta Ghat were of no interest for them. News came that the great Dhuandhar Falls had been reduced to a trickle, an event which had not occurred in the living memory of anybody in Jabalpur. The agent's family wanted to see this for themselves, and to visit a small fair at Bhedhaghat on the banks of the Narmada. On a dawn, Sleeman and Amelie accompanied the distinguished group on horseback and open carriages along the riverbank.

The day was already beginning to get warm. The visitors passed a group of Indian women carrying water pots from the river.

'The women in these parts seem to be rather forward, do they not? I see that they do not cover their knees while in public,' said a lady with a disapproving sniff.

There was a murmur of agreement.

'They hitch their skirts up to gather water from the river, my lady,' said Sleeman. 'Besides, for them it is European women who appear to be forward, because you do not cover your heads.'

'Why, that is an absurd idea,' exclaimed the lady.

'I believe it is a matter of perspective,' said Sleeman and noticed Amelie looking at him, so he decided not to make further comments.

'You have a rather curious way of looking at matters,' said a younger lady, to which Sleeman smiled and made a deprecating remark, hoping the conversation would be steered to other topics, which it eventually was.

Dhuandhar had indeed been reduced to a trickle, and its famed roar, heard a long distance away on the paths along the riverbank, had been muted. The villages along the route had been suffering numerous privations. Even those farmlands which had irrigation channels cut from the river had suffered, for the channels had been among the first to run dry. Sleeman discovered that several of the worst-affected villages fell under the bounds of the two litigious zamindars, and resolved to ask them what steps they had taken to ease the farmers' distress, or whether they had continued to feud as earlier with no concern for the tenants.

Sleeman found himself working longer hours at the office, and late into the night with the agent in trying to prevent the drought that was taking over the countryside. Whatever time he could spare, he spent in trying to understand the extent of the Phansigars' reach. Reynolds was still away, sending news of one capture after another. The days melted into one another, marked by incremental progress. And still there was no sign of the man who was many men.

Late one night, a horseman rode into Sleeman's courtyard. He had been sent by a tehsildar from a village not fifteen miles away. A certain prominent Brahmin of the village, a landlord to scores of tenants, a noted figure in those parts, had died earlier in the day. The tehsildar had been informed that his widow was to commit sati on the following day, after the people had paid their respects to the dead man. The tehsildar had objected to it, but did not have the resources to prevent it from being carried out, and had sent the rider with haste, seeking Sleeman's aid.

The captain put on his army uniform with the vague idea that a red coat might help in the countryside, and started out with twenty sowars summoned from the cantonment, and a body of his new district policemen on foot with matchlocks. They reached the village much before dawn the following day and tried to get their bearings.

The tehsildar greeted them at the entrance to the village. He was accompanied by his revenue assistants and the village sarpanch, who was reluctant to be involved in a matter which had escalated thus. The deceased Brahmin commanded an enormous amount of respect, said the tehsildar, and his family was not accustomed to being thwarted in their wishes. Sleeman knew the kind of people he was talking about.

The Brahmin was only a few years older than Sleeman and had been in good health. He had taken ill and passed away within a mere two days. The tehsildar thought it had been hastened by the heat. The family and most of the villagers had been gathered at the house, where the last rites were to begin in a few hours.

'There is no question of allowing the sati to be carried out, of course. If they proceed to make such an attempt, we shall have to arrest all of them and prosecute them according to Regulation XVII. I hope you have made it clear to the family,' said Sleeman.

The tehsildar, looking unhappy at the situation, nodded. The family, he said, had refused to listen to him.

'In that case, I should like to confer with them. From what I gather, they are people of learning, and we should be able to reason with them,' said Sleeman, and even he realised how naïve he sounded at that hour.

The house was large and had been built some generations earlier. As Sleeman and his party approached, they found most of the villagers gathered in the courtyard and out on the street, singing a bhajan. Lamps had been lit on the windows and thresholds. The people looked up, solemn but with anticipation, as the horsemen came up the road.

The dead man's sons and other male relatives came out and stood in a row in the courtyard, their upper torsos bare, heads shaved. Sleeman dismounted and approached them, followed by his men. The family members were polite in their greetings, but there was concern on their faces.

Sleeman expressed his commiserations and apologised for intruding into their grief. He asked them if there was a place where they could confer in private. He did not want to place them in an awkward position in front of their tenants and other villagers.

The sons—there were four to who he was introduced—led him inside the house and to a far wing, where he was ushered into a room which must have been the dead man's study, for it was lined with books, scrolls and several rows of parchment and palm leaf manuscripts. It was a large collection even by the standards of pious Brahmin landlords of central India. Sleeman tried to remember if he had met the man at any point, or heard of him. It was clear that he had been a scholar.

'We thank you for arriving here in the night from Jabalpur, and for showing this concern for us. We are in a difficult situation, and it would not have done for the villagers to see us being held as suspicious in the eyes of the law,' said the eldest son, a mild-looking fellow with an austere, even gentle face.

'My concern is about upholding the law, panditji. But I am happy to hear that you think you are in a difficult position, for you can resolve it now if that were the case. Please proceed with the last rites. All I request is you not consider this heinous act of forcing your mother to commit sati. Surely you will agree that it is an act which no son can wish upon his mother,' said Sleeman.

There was a moment of silence as the young men glanced at one another and fidgeted.

'Sahib, we could not make it clear to the tehsildar, knowing he would have summoned you in any case. The truth is we do not wish our mother to cast herself into the fire,' said another son.

'I do not understand. Why did the tehsildar report that a sati was going to be committed, if this were not the case?' asked Sleeman.

'Sahib, it is not us, but our mother herself who seeks to commit sati,' said the eldest son.

Sleeman was taken aback. On second thoughts, this was a situation he should have anticipated, but had not considered possible. Nor had he prepared for it in the months after receiving news of Regulation XVII. Most women who were reported to have committed sati were forced into the act by avaricious or hidebound male relatives for who their lives had held no meaning independent of their husbands. There had been occasional reports of young widows who had neither the wit nor will to contest the aura of holiness attached to the act, and who volunteered for it themselves. But even they would quail at the final moments, faced with the blazing pyre. But it was unexpected for a woman with grown sons to insist on such an end, against their wishes. The only explanation for this was piety, an area which Sleeman would have preferred to avoid. There were countless pitfalls for an officer who locked horns with the pious in this land.

'I find this difficult to believe, young man. Even if you are all respectable and honourable children, as I am certain you are, I find it difficult to believe that your mother has taken this decision on her own against your requests,' he said.

'I know you would think this, sahib. Nevertheless, it is true. We are helpless,' said the son.

'There has been no coercion from you? What about her brothers, or your father's relatives? How am I to believe that the men of your family have not browbeaten or threatened her to accept this?' asked Sleeman.

'Please believe us, sahib. We would never think of coercing our mother, for that is not how we were brought up. Nor would we participate in such a crime,' they said.

Sleeman and the sons appeared to have reached an impasse.

'I am afraid there is nothing that can be done about this. I cannot allow it to proceed. As you can see, I have arrived here at the head of a force to prevent this from being carried out, and I am authorised to use any means necessary to accomplish this,' said Sleeman.

'Yes, sir. We accept that. With your permission, we would like to inform our mother of your arrival. She had anticipated that you would come. Only your sowars and you can stop her from doing this, if there is any force in the land which can,' said one of the sons. They joined their palms together and departed, leaving him sitting alone on a mattress in the room full of books. Their mother must be a formidable woman if they thought the only way to stop her from carrying out her will was a unit of armed cavalrymen.

A short while later, one of the sons returned.

'Sahib, with your permission, my mother has said that she would like to speak to you,' he said.

This was the second unexpected occurrence of the day. In Sleeman's experience, there were not many wealthy Brahmin widows who would seek conversation with a British officer of his rank and powers.

'Please tell her that I shall be happy to speak with her,' he replied. The son withdrew.

A few minutes later, the woman walked in. She was a little taller than the average Indian woman but just as thin, dressed in white with her head and face covered and her feet bare. She was unaccompanied, which too was unusual. She greeted Sleeman, to which he replied by standing up, folding his palms together and responding in Hindustani. If his accent surprised her, he could not tell. She gestured to him to be seated, and herself sat cross-legged on the bare floor opposite him. Straight of back, hands folded on her lap, Sleeman could tell she was not used to making requests of strangers not of her jati.

'I know a few words of English, but not many, for which I apologise,' she said in English. Sleeman guessed she said it to let him know that they both had a faculty for each other's native tongues.

'I shall be happy to speak to you in Hindustani, ma'am,' he said. She inclined her head to accept this.

'I understand why you had to come all the way from Jabalpur, captain, but you will have to understand that my mind is made up. I request you not to think that my family members, least of all my sons, are responsible for this. They are dutiful young children, and have given me great joy. But become accustomed to making additional efforts on behalf of the Hindu upper castes and for upper class Muslims. He could not remember when he had become a part of this process, aware though he had always been of the insidious nature of caste and class. He knew how Englishmen were content to be introduced to India through the eyes of Brahmins and Muslim nobility alone, not through the millions who toiled at the bottom or outside the caste and class hierarchies. Even in his pursuit of the Phansigars, most of the men he had arrested had been of the oppressed castes. Very few of the merchants, administrators and zamindars who benefitted from the depredations of the stranglers had yet been caught. How much was he to blame for this? How much of his blindness was wilful?

'The governor-general and his advisors have issued this order about sati, hoping perhaps to save the lives of us poor Hindu women. I am certain that the reformers of Bengal have our best interests at heart, or what they consider our best interests to be. But what of the women afterwards, captain? Does your government have anything in mind for them, or do you plan to extricate them from the funeral pyre and abandon them somewhere in the cremation grounds, your task accomplished? What does your Lord Bentinck want for us?'

'Ma'am, from what I know, there will be efforts to encourage education for women,' said Sleeman.

She laughed. It was an unexpected, bitter sound. Sleeman had never heard an upper caste woman laugh in his presence. It was not much different from Amelie during her sarcastic moments.

'I too have heard of reformers in Calcutta and Bombay who wish to teach women, to have schools and colleges for them. My own husband, may his soul find peace, wanted the this is my decision, and they should not be held accountable or punished for this,' she said.

'It is my duty to enforce the regulation, and under its provisions, I am in a difficult situation, ma'am. If you were to attempt to proceed with the unfortunate act you have in mind, I shall be compelled to prosecute your family as well as you. It would be regrettable, but necessary,' he said.

'And I believe you are accustomed to doing the necessary, no matter how regrettable, captain,' she said.

Sleeman did not know if this was a statement or a question, so he waited for her to continue. It was an unequal conversation. She could read his expressions. He could see nothing at all except the part of the sari that covered her head. That he was being scrutinised he could tell. He could also tell that he was not presenting a forceful, authoritative figure, but was reluctant to appear rude.

'I am accustomed to following the law, ma'am. And I believe this is a heinous, cruel practice, created by men to assert control over helpless women, perhaps to usurp their property, or otherwise force them to die,' he said.

'An interesting choice of words, captain. "A heinous, cruel practice created by men." And a law to prevent it, also created by men. Tell me, who drafted this regulation?'

'The advisors of the governor-general, ma'am.'

'British gentlemen in Calcutta?'

'Yes, I believe, and some learned men of Bengal who would like society to be rid of such cruel practices.'

'Of course. Do you find it difficult to believe that a widow would immolate herself on her husband's funeral pyre of her own volition, with nobody else, male or female, coercing her or otherwise influencing her feeble, feminine mind? That she might have other reasons for this and not just belief in scriptures or myth and custom?'

'I find it impossible to believe, ma'am. In my experience, most cruelties committed on women have been devised by men for their profit or pleasure, and no woman would participate in it of her own or after knowledge of this fact.'

'That is quite considerate of you. If you were among the jatis and, God forbid, were to die, would your wife ever contemplate sati, captain?'

Sleeman thought of this. He tried to imagine Amelie, heartbroken, preparing to jump into his funeral pyre, abandoning her life, her studies and interests.

'Under no circumstances do I see that happening, ma'am. My wife is too full of life to contemplate its end, even after my demise. She would mourn and seek solace in life itself.'

The widow was silent for a while as she thought of this.

'What about your children, captain? Would they want their mother to join you in the afterlife?'

'Alas, ma'am, we have no children of our own.'

'I see. I do not wish to impose on you, but the people here believe in the healing powers of a certain dargah near the river, downstream from here. Childless couples have been known to be blessed with offspring on visiting it.'

Sleeman acknowledged the advice with grace.

'But I see you will think of it as mere superstition, so I will not press you further about it,' she added.

Sleeman assured her that he had not been offended by the suggestion. Churchmen had given him similar advice about the healing power of prayer. The only offensive part of it was they had given this advice to Amelie as well.

'Captain, I need not tell a man of the world, and such a polite man as yourself, that you cannot hope to understand the life that I have led. I was married to my late husband when I was twelve, and had our first child when I was fifteen. It was a daughter, but so weak was I that she did not survive women of the family to learn the scriptures at the very least. It was he who taught me Sanskrit and the little English that I know, and for these many years, I have studied the books and manuscripts you see behind you. Tell me about your wife, captain. Is she educated?'

'She has received the best of European education, ma'am, and is far more learned than I.'

The woman glanced around the room at the books, and was silent for a while before continuing.

'I might be different from Brahmin women you have heard of, and I need not tell you that I make men of the village, and the other zamindars of the region, uncomfortable. They do not quite know how to treat me, whether to ignore or fear me. But what then, captain? What does my knowledge avail me? Can I conduct rituals in the stead of men? Can I oversee the priests of the village temple? Can your wife, with the best of European education, hope to be given the position that you have been? Or is this the best she can expect, to be the wife of an assistant to the agent in Jabalpur town? What do you want of us? We were told to die for our husbands, and we did for ages. Now we are told we will not be permitted to die for our husbands. What are we to do? Would you like me to travel to Mathura and there live on a bowl of rice and some gruel for the next few decades till I waste away and die, forgotten by my sons and their families? Or would you like me to retire in seclusion to a corner of this house while my sons administer the lands after their father? Do you know that I had been overseeing the family's finances for years while my husband spent his time reading the scriptures? Can my daughters inherit a part of the property, or own it themselves? How different is any of this from being cast into a fire, screaming and struggling, or bleeding to death on a birthing bed?'

'Surely there is more to life, ma'am. You can still pursue knowledge, and learning. You can still read books and gain wisdom.'

'Captain, you have done me the courtesy of listening without condescension. I request you not to begin showing me discourtesy now. I decided to end my life on my own terms. You have to understand this. It is not that I do not love life. I did, on the other hand, also love my husband, for he was a reasonable man and a kind one, after his fashion. I could have had a much worse one. I could have had a much worse life. I could have had only daughters, and could have been cast out on the road, perhaps, to fend for myself. But he was kind and cared about me. However, I do not think I love him so much that I would willingly cast myself into his funeral pyre, now that you have come with your brave regulation to save me. That is not why I have decided thus.'

'Then why do you insist on being a sati, ma'am?'

She was silent again, her head lowered, contemplating. Then she raised her head and adjusted her cover, lowering it further.

'I am tired, captain. I am tired of only continuing to live as an act of protest. I am tired of being saved by men, like my husband or your governor-general. I would like to end my life on my own terms. And if I have to end it while upholding such a cruel custom, then so be it. I shall commit it not as custom, but as parody of custom. I shall die cursing this custom, and the men who dictate terms to our bodies and our lives. And they shall think that I honoured them. I shall die laughing at their conceit. I do not expect you to understand this, although perhaps you think you do.'

'As difficult as it might be for you to believe me, ma'am, I assure you that I understand. At least this part of what you have said.'

'Perhaps you do, captain.'

'Nevertheless, I cannot permit you to carry this out in violation of the laws. Not to mention the fact that I cannot allow you to walk into the flames and die in such a horrible manner.'

'I had guessed that you would say that. Therefore, here is what I shall do. I have obtained a very lethal poison made of a particular mix of herbs. It is known, I assure you, to act instantaneously. I shall drink it just before stepping into the pyre. I shall not suffer, if that is your chief concern.'

'I cannot let you proceed with this, ma'am.'

'Then I shall end my life here, in this house. Before or after the funeral. At least before the day is over. If you take me into preventive custody, I shall return home afterwards and still carry it out. I shall do it. I know you can hear it in my voice.'

Sleeman could hear her absolute conviction as she said it.

'The best you can do is allow me to carry out this charade of sati, so that my sons, who are blameless if not giants of intellect, acquire some merit in the eyes of the people and perhaps some respect.'

'It will not help the cause of reform for women, ma'am. We will not be able to enforce the prohibition if we allow such exceptions to take place.'

'I doubt you will find such problems in these parts, captain. People follow orders here. I can reassure you that I present a unique problem. As for how Lord Bentinck intends to reform society and drag people into the modern world, I do not care much for such pious intentions. I do not have many illusions left and do not intend to humour our gallant champions of women or persuade them to continue to harbour their comforting notions about themselves. You have no options left, and I suggest you permit me to continue with what I intend.'

She arose, said namaskar and left the room. Sleeman sat in the gathering dawn as the sunlight filtered into the room and touched the books and manuscripts. A sheaf of papers, a quill and inkstand stood on a beautiful wooden desk on the floor. It might have been the late man's or his redoubtable widow's.

Sleeman closed his eyes. He was tired, and his head throbbed with pain. But he could not be as tired as the woman had been. For hers was an exhaustion with life itself. He passed his hands over his face and found that he had begun to sweat.

It was not enough to expect a piece of legislation or law to change society. Everything else had to change with it, and for that to happen in India would take time, like a gargantuan ship changing course in the middle of the sea. It would always be thus. Regulation XVII was meaningless if the lives of women were as wretched as they had always been. The arrests of hundreds of Phansigars would be meaningless if the provinces did not address the reasons which drove ordinary men to murder. Every aspect of life was connected, and it was futile to believe a small administrative action here or an order there had any significance on its own. And all he was in the end was an executor of orders from powerful men far away. He had neither the vision nor the means to address the roots of the problems he could see. He was just as futile as the laws he represented, and just as removed from the people he loved as the mighty men of Calcutta were from him.

He sat there for some time, defeated. Outside he could hear the villagers singing another of their interminable bhajans. Funeral rituals had an inevitability of their own, regardless of religion. A certain cadence and flow. He strained his ears, trying to catch the lyrics of the bhajan. His wife would know of it.

Sleeman stood up, gathered his hat and walked out of the room and down the passage to the entrance of the house. The sons were waiting there. He expressed his commiserations to them once again, but would not say more. They stared at him in consternation.

'Your mother shall be permitted to continue with what she has in mind,' he said. They stared at him and then at one another, but did not speak.

Sleeman told the tehsildar to leave the village with his men and assemble at the cremation ground. The revenue official was puzzled but did not question Sleeman. The matter was out of his hands and his relief was palpable.

Sleeman rode back in the afternoon with his sowars, and spent the day at his office. In the evening a messenger arrived from the agent, asking him to present himself at the latter's office as early as possible the following day.

He went home. The house was quiet as he approached and dismounted in the courtyard. He walked in and found a maid in one of the rooms. He asked her where Amelie was. The maid said her ladyship was in one of her rooms. It was locked. Sleeman knocked and waited. There was no reply.

'Amelie, can I please have a word with you?'

There was silence, and then the sound of approaching steps on the other side of the door.

'William, I request you to leave me to myself for some time. I am afraid I am not well-disposed at present, and will not make good company.'

'Amelie, will you please permit me to explain the circumstances…'

'I am not the agent, William. You are not required to give me any explanation or justification. I shall not write you a note of censure, as the agent is writing at the moment. You are not required to explain anything to me at all, even if I was disposed to hear one from you.'

He stood near the door in silence. The footsteps receded. He continued to stand. She returned to the door and opened it. There was no anger in her face, which made it worse. She was disappointed in him.

'Were you present for the funeral, at least, or could you not bear to see it?'

He could not bear to see it, but had stayed. It was the most cruel act he had ever participated in.

'How could you, William? How could you be a part of it?'

He explained the circumstances to her.

'Did you think of what would happen now? Every other Brahmin, Rajput or Bania would say: see, Sleeman sahib permits sati to take place. Nothing would have been accomplished by the regulation. Not to mention the suffering the poor woman must have gone through.'

Sleeman tried to mention the manner of the woman's self-administered death.

'Are the mere specifics of her death so important, William? Is that all that matters to you, that she died without pain? How could you permit this to happen?'

He asked her what he could have done to prevent it.

'I do not know. But is that not what an administrator is expected to do? Could you not find a solution to it? The men of Government House have reduced women to laws and statutes, to be saved or used in political contests as required. Is that all we are to you? How do you expect me to feel, William?'

He stood in silence because he had no answers.

'Please excuse me for the evening. I would like to be left alone,' she said and shut her door. He heard her footsteps recede to the other side of the room. He waited for some time, and then walked out of the house. He was not sure if the agent would see him in the evening, or whether he should go somewhere else.

All roads led to Guna, and along all of them came hooves and feet, in the scores and hundreds. The great Vaishakh cattle fair of Guna drew dairy farmers, horse breeders, camel and goat herders from across the land. Every year, livestock owners would travel from far-off cities and villages to buy or sell as they chose, animals for stock, for the field and, in case of the old and infirm, meat. Representatives of the nobility from all the princely states for hundreds of miles would be present, as would procurers and stable overseers of British garrisons from Agra to Ujjain.

They said the Vaishakh fair was started by a great Sultan from Delhi out on campaign and travelling to the Deccan, or perhaps to Gujarat and the coast. The Sultan's cavalry was stricken on the march, and he had ordered a halt at Guna, then a small village of little account on the Parbati River. To all directions of the compass he had sent his emissaries, asking the local rajas to bring their best horses to his battle camp. A fair had begun from the horses and livestock left behind when the Sultan had departed, and a tradition had been established.

On the identity of the Sultan whose command had birthed the fair, local legends are divided. Some say it was Ala-al-Din of the house of Khilji, who had marched nearly five centuries and a half before Bentinck from Delhi to Gujarat. This may be true, although the Sultan's chroniclers themselves said he had travelled through the deserts of Rajputana to the west. Yet others say it was the Sultan Muhammad bin Tughluq nearly half a century after Ala-al-Din, who had taken his capital and its hapless people en masse nine hundred miles from Delhi and settled them in Daulatabad in the Deccan. But that migration, and all of the Sultan's Deccan campaigns, had also passed through Kota in Rajputana. Precisely which Sultan had graced Guna with his battle camp might perhaps never be known, and matters not at all either to the people who travel to the fair or to the livestock they drive to it, for legends matter more than history in India.

Amanullah and his fellow livestock traders had trudged a long distance, day after day, in the blazing sun. They had gathered on the outskirts of Agra with their chosen stock of horses, buffaloes and cows. Amanullah's family bred horses and although some were meant for draft, the family was also known to provide hardy ponies and the occasional warhorse to the princes, and even to the British. Amanullah knew horses, and the traders who came to Guna knew and trusted his family.

In early winter, he would bring his livestock to the famed Bateshwar Mela, the animal fair which coincided with a religious festival at the little village of the same name not fifty miles from Agra. Bateshwar was greater by far than the mela at Guna, but two fairs were better than one, and the latter was the only chance to sell his livestock at a reasonable price before the rains made crossing the rivers difficult for the next few months.

Amanullah and his companions herded their stock due south from the former imperial capital till they reached the banks of the Chambal and then travelled east to the crossing near Dholpur, for even in the dry season parts of the river were deep and treacherous, with crocodiles lying hidden in the murky waters. Dholpur was the easiest crossing if one wanted to keep all the livestock intact, or as many as could survive under the sun during the long march.

Amanullah and his men passed through Gwalior, where he sold three horses at what he felt was a bargain, and bought numerous buffaloes which he knew would find buyers in Guna. Horse buyers fell into a few categories in his experience. The connoisseurs knew as much if not more than he did and would buy only the best, although if they were convinced of quality they would not bargain, believing that was a sign of nobility. The hardy ponies would find buyers wherever he took them, for the Deccan was pony country. Milch cows were always in demand, but dairy farmers were notorious for being stingy and willing to haggle the whole day for a few heads. Only buyers of buffaloes would make purchases in bulk, ask or expect little beyond the general health of the beasts, and would pay after the barest minimum of haggling, just enough to satisfy their consciences.

Jhansi, where they camped for four days, was disappointing. The Rao of the city, Ramachandra, was attempting fiscal prudence—with good cause—and had barred his nobles from buying luxuries. Therefore they were unwilling to pay profitable sums to Amanullah for his ponies, and in the few well-bred horses he had brought, they showed not the slightest interest. Nobody from the British garrison had dropped by either. Amanullah had little knowledge of or interest in the British and their doings apart from their cavalry units. His elder brother had arranged supplies for the procurer at the Agra camp and knew them better. Amanullah knew of the units at Sagar, but he did not have the creative mind and broad horizons which his brother had, and which helped him understand the British. It was enough that he could trade with them and had yet not been cheated by one of them, to his knowledge.

By the second day of the fair, after unavoidable delays, Amanullah and the farmers of Agra were in Guna, where they made a tidy profit in a few days and decided to continue southward for a stretch before beginning the journey home. Amanullah had spent little on the journey and had no vices worth the name. For the duration of the stay at Guna, he had not ventured beyond the livestock pens. He had little knowledge and almost no curiosity about the world and was content to trudge from Agra to Guna and back, plying his trade and following the rules, but was willing to listen to suggestions from the others, for no journey could be planned down to the last details. Sooner or later, the world intruded with the unexpected.

A few hours after starting out from the fair grounds, they came across a group of traders walking along the road.

'Aulae bhai, Ram-Ram,' called out Amanullah, for he saw that they were Hindus.

'Ram-Ram, bhai,' came the reply. Whether Amanullah was happy or not at the greeting, he did not show it. His was not an expressive face.

The second group, Yadavs to a man, had sold a large herd of valuable milch cows, and were returning to a village whose name Amanullah forgot as soon as he heard it. What mattered was they were shrewd traders who knew cattle and how to make a profit from them. About horses, alas, they knew little.

By the evening, the group had met and taken in several others along the road. Some he knew by face, while others were strangers. With each he called out 'Aulae bhai, Ram-Ram', or 'Aulae khan, salaam', as the case might be, and they replied after their custom, for livestock traders talk little as a rule, and are courteous people known to travel in mixed company.

By the evening, after they had taken in a group of seven cattle herders, it was suggested by a new face that they could stop at a pleasant meadow ahead and rest for the night. Amanullah, whose feet were aching, was inclined to agree, although he knew of a shaded grove not far ahead which could be more pleasant after the dust of the road. But he could not hope to direct the will of such a large group, so the decision was taken to stop at the meadow.

They had settled down in the field and begun to open their bundles of food when they heard the distant thunder of hooves.

'Rangwe,' said a voice near Amanullah, with contempt.

A group of sowars came into view, riding through the dust, and they stopped by the traders and dismounted. All of them, numbering nearly fifty, were armed. Their red coats were caked with dust, for they had been riding for several hours.

The British officer commanding the sowars called out to some of the traders, and they scurried to him, bowing deeply. Amanullah and his friends from Agra looked at one another. Perhaps some overconfident dairy farmer had sold substandard stock or meat to a cantonment along the way, and had to be brought to book. Although it was unusual for sowars commanded by an Englishman to accost some erring traders over such a minor matter.

The traders were conferring with the officer, who seemed to be querying them at length and on occasion referring to a small piece of paper in his hands. They were murmuring in low voices, and the traders were shaking their heads or gesticulating.

Somebody touched Amanullah on his shoulder, and he turned to find one of his Agra neighbours pointing down the road. In a few minutes, it became clearer: a squad of sepoys was marching up to the meadow, rifles at the ready.

Amanullah was beginning to get worried. Had a war

started somewhere? He hoped he would be able to reach Agra soon. He should not have come south from Guna, he thought. Still, it was a little late for recriminations. The signs had been good, even if neither good nor bad omens had been sighted at the beginning of their journey. With so many heads of livestock to dispose first, his group and he had not even carried out the sonoka. He would just have to wait for the soldiers to leave before setting off.

Now the English officer was conferring with his soldiers before walking out to where the dairy farmers stood in small, uneasy knots. The traders he had been talking to walked a few paces in front of him. When they reached the rest of the group, they separated. Each of them now walked through the crowd, pointing at some men at random.

And then Amanullah realised it was not random at all. Each of the men called out had been those who, to the cry of 'Aulae bhai, Ram-Ram' had replied 'Ram-Ram, aulae bhai'. Each of them was known to him. Each of them, on being pointed out, was caught and dragged away by the sepoys.

Amanullah was towards the rear of the crowd. His remaining horses were in a group, tied to stakes in a corner of the meadow not far away. If he ran, perhaps he could make it to one of them, hop on the saddle and escape. After that, it was one horse versus another, and he had a chance. All he had to do was make it past the groves down the road and into the jungle nearby. No sowar or sepoy could keep up with him through the broken country there.

Then he caught the eye of one of his men, who pointed with his head behind them. Amanullah turned around. Another group of sowars was coming up the road, blocking the exit. The horses seemed to be in excellent condition. They were the kind that his brother would have sold to the camps. Amanullah realised he might not be returning to Agra for some time.

One of the men who Amanullah had known for years, and who he thought was from Itarsi, came to stand near him and pointed him out. The sepoys caught Amanullah by the wrists and elbows and dragged him to where the rest of the captives stood.

The British officer had gone back to talking with the informers, for informers they must be, thought Amanullah. Too late, he realised he should have paid attention to his brother warning him of mysterious disappearances, captures and betrayals. He should have queried the men from the other groups before letting them join him, but he had thought, with so many beetus on the road, they needed a large group when the time came for the sacrifice.

The officer was checking his list and now looked up. He cast a long glance at Amanullah and ordered the sepoys to bring him over.

'Your name is Amanullah?'

'Yes, sahib. I do not understand. Is there a problem? I can explain.'

'I should like to know who you are.'

'Sahib, I am a trader in horses and ponies, from Agra. I had travelled to the Guna mela, and left it only this morning, with these men. My horses and livestock are over there.'

'I have no doubt that they are, Amanullah.'

'Sahib, what has happened? We are just small traders. If there is a problem, we can explain. I have proof of sale of some of our livestock at the fair.'

'We know that you do. We have also come from the mela ourselves.'

Amanullah did not know how to respond to this.

'Aulae khan, salaam,' said the officer and Amanullah realised, for the first time, the gravity of the situation. He was not being interrogated by the officer. He was being asked questions to which the man already had answers.

The group and their livestock were taken some distance down the road to the nearest village, where Amanullah found that a small camp had been set up while they were being captured and interrogated. The men were placed in an enclosure under guard. The captives spent the night in silence, for there was no purpose in loose talk at this point. It was the others, who had not been identified by the informants, who set up loud wails of anguish and complaint, till the British officer came among them and told them to bear with the privations for the night. The sepoys kept a close watch on everybody, as if they suspected that the captives would turn on the detainees in their rage. These fears were groundless, however, and dawn found the men tired from sleeplessness and worry.

The British officer returned from a villager's house where he had been put up for the night, and set about talking to each of the captives alone. When it was Amanullah's turn, the officer asked for his name, profession and city of origin. It seemed almost perfunctory.

The other detainees were also questioned. Some were quaking with fear, some fell at the officer's feet with loud cries, the typical theatricality of the small trader on facing officialdom. One even tried to bribe him with money, or so it seemed, for an enraged jamadar turned on the trader and cuffed him about the head mercilessly till the officer told him to stop. After a lot of protestations, further wails and cries of anguish, the round of interrogations was declared to have ended to the satisfaction of the officer. All the proofs of purchase, including a few rolls of parchment and metal discs or coins, were produced and examined with great care by a representative from a revenue shed in Guna and pronounced genuine. It would not do to have a cattle smuggler roaming the countryside when the Bengal army was on the trail of a different class of criminal.

The officer conferred with the revenue representative and the jamadars, and at last pronounced the detainees free to go. They departed with loud cries of joy and many blessings for the officer, who appeared to be immune to flattery or any of the more human frailties. Whether this was because he was made of stern material, or because he was exhausted, it was not clear. This was around the afternoon. Amanullah, although younger than the officer by far and much stronger in physique, was famished. The officer called for food to be given to the remaining detainees, who numbered about forty-five. It was meagre fare: a thin gruel of lentils and naan as dessicated as old parchment, but Amanullah ate it without complaint. The officer watched him in silence, and waited for him to finish and wash his hands and mouth before continuing with the questions.

'My name,' said the officer, 'is Reynolds. I am a lieutenant from Jabalpur. Have you heard of me, Amanullah?'

'No, sahib, I have not, begging your forgiveness.'

'There is nothing to forgive. I am neither prince nor fakir, and there is no reason for you to know of me by reputation. I work for a man who wants us to follow the rules in everything we do, and follow the rules I shall, for I respect and obey this man in all ways. You have the assurance that I shall obey the law in my dealings with you. If there has been a delay in providing the food, it is because we did not expect to find so many of you.'

'Sahib, I am ashamed to hear your apology, which you need not provide to such as us. But I do not understand what you mean by "so many of us".'

'Amanullah, I am sure by now you would have understood that we did not pick you up on suspicion or on some flimsy ground. I might be a beetu, and a rangwa at that, but I am not a simpleton. I hope you will understand that.'

Amanullah's head jerked back. He could not believe he was hearing Ramasi being spoken by a white man. It was blasphemy. If possible, it was even worse than to hear Ramasi being spoken by an Indian beetu. The Goddess would rain down destruction on all, man and livestock alike, for this.

'Sahib, I have been travelling down to Guna for years. My family is known for its horses. We even supply to the camp at Agra, to your brother officers. I have never broken the law in Agra, nor has my family been known for anything except honesty. Surely there has been a mistake.'

'We do know the standing in which your family is held in Agra, Amanullah. But I do not think there has been a mistake. Your fellow aulae have told us all. We caught them from various places in the weeks before the mela, and they have been on the road ever since, with our knowledge. They have told us of the group which comes from Agra every year, for livestock and the wealthy merchants that trade in them. They have told us of all the places where the sacrifices have been done. We know of the aulae you host from elsewhere during Bateshwar, and how they bring news of all the beetus who have travelled with them. We know of the places and the sacrifices where you were present. You will not believe the number of men who have confirmed this for us. We even caught the group of bhartotes your brother sent to the house of the salt merchant in Kutch. Did you know that? They told us everything, about how important your family is among the clan of aulae from your city. There is very little, Amanullah of Agra, that we do not know.'

Amanullah was silent. The officer's words sounded too loud to be natural, for they had the ring of a death sentence.

'We knew that a large group of you would converge at Guna, and we wanted to be present to greet you... appropriately. But we were delayed, so by the time we received word of your presence and rode to Guna, you had already left. But your friends, who have turned approvers for us, joined you on the road, and they have told us how you gathered in all the merchants going home. Tell me, did you know the chisas would be on the road, or did you happen to come upon them by accident?'

Amanullah's heart pounded within his chest on hearing another word in Ramasi. The certainties of his small world had begun to come crashing down around him. He closed his eyes and wondered what he should do. Perhaps he could survive by understanding what the officer already knew, and offering not a whit more of information. Of one thing he was certain. He would never betray his clan. Very few in Agra knew where they lived, and they might yet be safe from this British officer's reach.

'Sahib, you know all. Therefore, I shall not attempt to hide things from you anymore.'

'A wise decision, Amanullah.'

'Sahib, we knew some of the traders would be headed south after the mela. They had made a lot of profits and would be in a hurry to return to their villages. We also knew they would like the idea of travelling in a large group, for safety. Yadavs and other jatis do not mind travelling with Muslims, for much binds us, including our knowledge of animals. It has always been so. Therefore, we decided to catch up with them on the road as soon as we had sold our prime livestock and made our own profits. It was a good year at Guna, and we thought the sacrifices would also be good.'

'And yet here we are,' said Reynolds. 'If I had my way, I would erect a gallows in this village this afternoon. I do not care what the governor of Isagarh or the Scindia Maharaja on his throne would say. I would erect a gallows and hang all of you, and leave your corpses swaying in the wind for the vultures, so that all the aulae who ever travel this road would know: this is what happens when you treat people like cattle. I would bring such a flame of justice that your like would wither away like standing wheat. But I obey my commander, therefore I shall talk to you. Lie to me, and I shall know. So speak, and tell me only the truth, and nothing else besides. You shall take me to all the places where you have buried the sacrifices. All of them, for I know already. You shall tell me what happened, and leave no detail from your story. And you shall tell me about your family, and of the subedars of Agra. For it is them I seek. Do this, and I shall spare your life when you are tried in court. I shall say: this man Amanullah is an approver of the government, and has aided us, therefore he shall not be hanged for his monstrous crimes, but shall only be imprisoned or exiled.'

And after delivering these words in as theatrical a manner as he could, Reynolds waited, hoping his captives would thus be induced to cooperate. He was being truthful when he said he knew a lot already about each of them. About the imprecations and his wish to leave them hanging from the gallows, he was not certain if he wanted this or was just voicing the residual embers of his outrage at the Phansigars' deeds. He had seen far more of their burial groves lately than Sleeman had.

Amanullah was silent. Even at this stage he would not speak of the subedars of Agra, out of respect for his clan or the Goddess. Or because such an act of betrayal was unthinkable for him. For were not the Agariyas among the most honourable of aulaes?

But there were things of which he could make a clean breast.

'I shall take you to the groves, sahib,' he said, choosing his words with care.

All the people of villages and towns along the route

gathered to watch the curious procession walk past. For many it was as if a myth, remembered from some dim part of childhood stories and vague nightmares had come to life, for here were the Phansigars themselves. News had raced out from the first village where Amanullah and his gang had been quartered for the night. Many of the people who waited for the procession were just curious, but some were waiting to follow the captives and seek some answers. These were the broken ones, the children of long-vanished parents, and the fathers and mothers and grandparents of people who had never returned from journeys short and long. Not a trace had remained of these countless travellers, except a whisper of nameless horrors which stalked those who took the roads through the countryside.

And so they waited for this mythical procession to walk past. At the head came a British officer in a dusty red coat and riding breeches, stubble on his cheeks and his eyes red and tired. Those who knew of British armies whispered that he was a lieutenant, a leftan of sowars, with sabre and rifle slung from the saddle of a sinewy pony. Beside him on their ponies were two jamadars with beards so bushy and fierce that children hid behind their mothers on seeing them. And behind them rode a squad of twenty sowars, scabbards gleaming in the morning sun, lances at rest on the saddles. From each saddle extended thick knotted ropes of hemp, at the end of which were two or three men each, their wrists tied to the ropes and the feet manacled. They followed the sowars, their feet clanking on the dusty road. Behind them came row upon row of sepoys with rifles slung from their backs and swords on their sides. And behind them rode yet more sowars. At the end of the procession came the revenue official from Guna with his assistants, and porters with food and provisions for the soldiers, and labourers with pickaxes and shovels.

Some of the witnesses to this sight cowered in fear, but only because they were old enough to remember the great campaigns of the Marathas and their opponents in generations past. It was never a good portent when armed men rode through the countryside at dawn. Yet others smiled, and joined the growing crowd which walked slowly behind this procession.

Shortly after midday, Amanullah asked for a halt. He was brought forward to Reynolds and the rope was tied to the lieutenant's saddle. He gestured with his bound hands to the side of the road, to where a thick stretch of jungle extended. Reynolds led the procession off the road and into the trees. After a short distance, the ground became broken and pitted, and the undergrowth dense. Reynolds dismounted. A squad of sepoys came forward and surrounded Amanullah.

'How much farther?' asked Reynolds.

'It is along this way, sahib.'

Amanullah led the soldiers along an overgrown trail. A person unfamiliar with the route would have never come across it by accident. He stopped at a large clearing surrounded by tall trees. The uneven colour of the sod indicated it had been dug and filled over several times, over many years.

'Here, leftan sahib,' said Amanullah, pointing to a spot to his left. 'This was three years ago. We fell in with a seth who had sold several hundred heads of fine cattle at Guna, and was returning to Indore. His wife, boy, servants and herdsmen were with him. He told us of many hard bargains he had driven, and of the quality of the milch cows of his herd. We offered fifteen souls to the Goddess that night. They are buried here.'

'A child, Amanullah? Why did you not think of saving him?'

'He was of the age of awareness, sahib. He was too old to be taken by us and brought into the lore. It was too late for him, so he had to be sacrificed.'

Reynolds muttered an oath and ordered the labourers to start digging.

Amanullah pointed to another spot, which had been dug up five or perhaps six years previously.

'We met four young men going north some distance from here. They were farm boys travelling to a zamindar's household for the harvest. They had little on them, not much more than the clothes on their backs, so we buried them without taking anything.'

And so it went. There were five separate spots in the clearing, one which had seen two burials in two seasons.

Reynolds was sitting on a dhurri spread by the porters. His eyes burned. He could not say if it was because of the heat during the day's march, which had been more oppressive than usual, or something else. A great sense of exhaustion had settled on him as the digs continued and the bones were brought out. They had to be careful with most, for only the bones remained. The jamadars were dictating the position and condition of the remains to the revenue official and his clerks, and trying to confirm, where they could, evidence of strangulation. The tongue bone was so constituted that it decomposed faster than the thicker bones of the body, like the spine or femur, according to Spilsbury. Inventory was also being made of belongings, clothes and any objects of metal which had been found in the graves.

A sepoy walked up to Reynolds and saluted. The lieutenant looked up.

'Janaab, some villagers here would like to talk to you.'

Reynolds looked towards the villagers, who were clustered at the edge of the clearing and looking at him with expectation. He gestured to the sepoys to let them come up to him.

They were a mixed group of men, some elderly, and one who looked not more than a teenager. They came up and saluted him with deep namaskars, to which he responded, and asked them to sit nearby. This presented a problem, for he was already sitting on the ground, and they had to assume an equal station by sitting beside him on the grass, but it could not be helped. It was known that some Englishmen did not understand the significance of stations, or understood and did not care. Which was worse one could not tell.

'Leftan sahib, we greet you in the name of the people of our villages, which are some kos down the road. We saw you pass, and heard you had caught some Phansigars, and therefore we came after, with some women as well,' said an elderly man who seemed to have been put forward as a representative. Reynolds glanced back at the edge of the clearing and saw some women standing in a group, veiled, among the curious crowd.

'We thank you for capturing these Phansigars, sahib. We do not know them, nor can we recognise them, but many are the tales we have heard of their like, and of the terrible things they do. We are told that some can change shape into hideous demons on moonless nights, and consume the bodies of the slain, bones and all,' said the elderly man, who seemed to have a long-winded way of expressing himself.

'If that were the case, old man, we would not be digging for these bones here. I have come to know much about them, but I doubt they are demons, at least not of the kind that your mother or mine told us about,' replied Reynolds.

'You are right, leftan sahib. We have only heard of these tales. But we would not like to interrupt your work or intrude upon you. We have just one request. All of us here have people from our families who have been missing, some for many years. My son has been gone for four years now, and we have heard nothing of him. He was just a farmer and an obedient child, with no vices. He was as dependable as the morning, and would not have run away on a whim when he had gone to a weekly market some villages away. This boy here was young when his father disappeared. There is a woman over there whose husband was told by a visiting trader of a job as a sharecropper at a zamindar's lands near Guna, but he too never came back.'

Reynolds nodded. He had heard countless such stories over the past few months, and before that.

'Sahib, one of the women, not a year ago, said goodbye to her husband and young son, just a child, who were going to a mela to buy a cow. She still awaits their return, and has lost her mind, if I may tell you of it. We do not know who to ask, or where to go. Whenever a kotwal or a daroga from Guna passes through, we try to meet him, and we have mentioned this to the revenue official many times. But we are nobody, and therefore we had no recourse, till today. We request you to let us examine the bodies to see if we can recognise our own, if they happen to be there. At least we will know their fate.'

There was little with which to identify the bodies, except clothing and some possessions, but they could at least have the satisfaction of trying. Reynolds nodded and told them to ask the jamadars before they took a look at the bodies. They thanked him several times and stood up to take their leave. Reynolds called after them, and they turned.

'There is the body of a child from that pit over there. I have reason to believe that he was the son of a merchant from far away, but we have found some clothes, and you could ask the mother to take a look, if you think she can.'

The villagers went away. Reynolds stared into the distance for some time, his mind empty. The noise of the soldiers in the clearing, and the low murmur of the watching villagers, faded into the background. He lay back on the dhurri and closed his eyes.

The man who was many men arrived in Benares on a dry and dusty evening. The heat of midday still hung on the narrow lanes which led to Assi Ghat along the Ganga. A short distance away, Kashi Naresh Udit Narayan was building his new palace. They said he had been advised by the great astrologers of the city to name it after the river, but they said many things about him. King of Benares only in name because his lands had been taken away by the Company not two years earlier, and master of a palace which could no more rule the people than it could rule the Ganga. Udit Narayan had been called many things by the Company, but a good, or even fiscally prudent ruler, was not one of them.

The man who was many men neither knew the Kashi Naresh nor was concerned about the fate of his dynasty. He was dressed in rich silk and was carried into Benares on a tasteful palanquin. For the pilgrims on the streets and the ghats, he was an important and wealthy man, but not unique in being so. Brahmins from Poona, travel-worn and dusty, Maratha noblemen from as far away as Indore and Ujjain, seers and astrologers sent by the hill rajas from Rishikesh and Haridwar were making way for one another. Princelings from the desert, with their wives hidden in palanquins and guarded by horsemen, marched down the lanes. Merchants from Marwar and landlords from Bengal with their families and household priests clamoured to pay for additional rituals to wash away sins real and imagined. Peasants with flowers, bel leaves and small measures of rice, who would not be allowed into some of the temples, as they were barred from the homes of Brahmins, princelings and merchants, huddled in corners, patient, waiting for the great men to pass.

It was evening of the second day of the waxing moon, in the month of Jyestha. There was little more than a week to Ganga Dashami, the culmination of the ten most sacred days for worshipping the river. The Ganga, which had once flowed through the heavens, had descended to earth on the tenth day to cleanse the sins of humans, as the scriptures said. A pilgrimage to Benares on Ganga Dashami was equal to ten such on any other day. He knew of this, and the festival was the reason he was here. This was the only occasion during the year when he could hope to meet all the people he had come to meet. It was not as if he had been summoned. Nor could it be said that he had summoned them. They were all equals, and had felt it was necessary to meet.

He had stayed the previous night at the house of a friend on the outskirts of the city, and had been fed and entertained well. His servants were carrying his food, provided by the friend. He had been travelling for a fortnight, and was beginning to miss the fine food of his home. But that could not be helped. Perhaps the people he was going to meet would entertain him well too.

The palanquin stopped at a crossroads for a company of sowars, led by an Englishman, to pass. He knew of a barracks nearby where the cavalrymen had been stationed for the past few months. Perhaps the Company suspected disgruntled loyalists of the Kashi Naresh would incite riots. If they did, the man in the palanquin could have told the British not to worry. From Bengal to Awadh, there was no king or princeling who would raise a hand against the British. Not yet.

The palanquin bearers brought him down the steps of

a small ghat and placed it on the ground. He descended, and the mace-bearer who walked in front of the palanquin to clear his route saluted. Small children and mendicants glanced at the great man with curiosity. Today he was dressed as a nobleman in the Awadhi style, his religion indeterminate. He could have been a Shia courtier from Lucknow, or a Kayastha bureaucrat from the Residence in Kanpur. It was difficult to tell in these times. But he was beautiful, and he was magnificent, and his presence at the shabby little ghat improved its appearance at an instant. He took in the commotion along the ferry landing and smiled. He liked travelling down the river, and the evening was sure to be more pleasant than the day had been.

A merchant and his two grown sons, accompanied by family priests, had arrived at the landing before him, and were trying to understand the ferry rates from the long-distance boats moored there. The merchant was surrounded by half-a-dozen boat owners seeking his custom. It was understood that they would charge more from him than they would have from less wealthy passengers.

The merchant settled the price to his satisfaction with the owner of the largest ferry moored there. Labourers and servants carried the belongings of the family and the priests on board and placed them in a small hold at the fore of the vessel. The family was placed in narrow compartments along the hull. It was cramped, but even people not accustomed to river journeys could travel overnight or for a few days on these boats.

The owner of the ferry, pleased with the bargain, turned towards the Kayastha bureaucrat with a smile.

'A thousand pardons, sahib. It is the beginning of the pilgrimage season, and such a custom could not have been ignored.'

'I understand, Manik. If you do not strike a bargain with merchants now, when will you? I hope there is still space for me on your boat. I have been travelling since the morning and I am tired.'

Manik bowed and said of course, there was always space on his vessel for sahib. It could not be otherwise.

The newcomer did not have many belongings with him, and was accommodated without delay, along with a single servant. The palanquin bearers returned to the house of his friend. The boat took in some more passengers, including a small trader with a consignment of betel leaves bound for Ghazipur, and cast off into the middle of the river, the oars creaking in the locks as the boatmen fore and aft strained with the effort. It was easier to reach the deep currents midstream in the dry season, after which the oarsmen settled into a quicker rhythm and the vessel glided east in the dusk. The flickering lights of the city and lamps of the aarati on the ghats were hidden by a bend in the river. On the south bank, the forests came down to the water's edge.

He settled into the cushions. His servant lit a hookah and placed it in front of him. The moon shone down on the river. It was a beautiful night to travel downstream.

The servant returned in a while and laid out warmed chapatis and vegetables on a brass platter. There was a knock on the sliding wooden partition. The owner appeared at the door.

'Sahib, I hope you are comfortable.'

'I am always comfortable on your boats, Manik. You need not have worried. I am happy whenever I travel down the river, as you know.'

Manik tried to say something and hesitated.

'You are worried about something, Manik. Would you like to tell me what it is?'

'Sahib, my father is concerned. I can see that. I do not know all the details, but he is troubled.'

'If he is, Manik, I am certain we can set his mind at rest.'

'Yes, sahib. I apologise for the absence of better food on board during the Dashami period. We try to observe the restrictions during this time.'

'I did not expect it at all, Manik. I know you fast during Dashami.'

Manik was apologising for things which he should have known the man had expected. The boatowner seemed to have other things on his mind, which made him speak of these trifles. He hesitated again before continuing.

'I hope the noise will not bother you, sahib.'

'Thank you for telling me. Will there be some noise before I sleep?'

'There might be, sahib, although the men are experienced.'

'I shall be comfortable, Manik. You are as polite as your father.'

'Is there anything you would like, as a gift for gracing us with your presence?'

He considered it. He gave it a lot of thought.

'Manik, I would like some betel leaves. They will not compare with the produce from your groves in Dhaka, but I shall take them as a mark of your affection anyway.'

'They are yours, sahib. I wish you a pleasant night, and the blessings of the goddess.'

'And to you, Manik.'

The panel of wood slid shut. The oarsmen continued their efforts. The boat groaned and splashed through the currents. Sometimes a plank or two, under the weight of footsteps or cargo, settled and shifted. He looked out of the windows at the night sky.

Late in the night, some of the crew came down into

the passenger compartments. There was no music, or noise, or drama to distract or lull. They simply entered the compartments and strangled the merchant, his sons, the priests and their servants. The trader and his assistants, huddled in the other, cheaper compartments were strangled thereafter, with precision and little noise. Life was, and then it was not. The windows were eased open to their full extent, and the bodies, weighted with iron, thrown overboard after being stripped of valuable cloth. The windows were shut and the men returned upstairs. It had taken only a few minutes from beginning to end.

What a polite young man Manik had become, he thought, and fell asleep sometime later.

He was woken up by the servant in the early morning. It was pleasant in the middle of the river, with the breeze coming in from forests on both banks. He had not felt a better breeze on waking up in several months, ever since the summer had begun.

His servant brought him warm milk and almonds for breakfast. The ferry must have stopped earlier in the morning at a village on the banks to pick up milk.

He went up on the foredeck. Along both banks stretched farmland and forest as far as he could see, with the occasional village. They were still some distance west of Ghazipur, which was the next landing for the payment of revenue if one was transporting cargo down the river, and more revenue if one was taking salt to Buxar. Smuggling salt was not one of the crimes that he thought Manik would stoop to. The lad had standards.

A little more than an hour later, the ferry glided to a landing on a sloping meadow with a few trees growing at the water's edge. The morning was still pleasant, and birds called out from the trees. The man deboarded and his servant set about taking his belongings out on the landing.

Manik came out holding a small parcel wrapped in palm leaves.

'Sahib, I am happy to have brought you here. The betel leaves do not appear to be of the quality I would have preferred, but I present them to you as morka.'

'Manik, you are kind, and I know they will taste well. Shall I be meeting you at your father's?'

'I shall return in two days, sahib. The festival is a busy time for us. I hope you will stay till then.'

Manik saluted, told the men waiting at the landing to take good care of the guest, and got back on board the boat. The men grunted and pushed it back towards the middle of the river, and the oarsmen took up their task once more. It would be more difficult now, because they would be rowing against the current and upstream, and the journey would be slower.

The Kayastha bureaucrat, or perhaps Shia courtier, walked up the incline to the top of the rise, where a palanquin was waiting. He wished his host had sent a horse instead. It was such a beautiful morning and a pleasant part of the country. He would have liked to go for a ride. But Manik's father was a descendant of boat and ship owners, zamindars who preferred to recline on journeys and be carried by men and beasts rather than choose the more arduous backs of horses on which to ride upright.

The palanquin, followed by servants carrying his belongings and some goods, moved at a rocking, rhythmic pace through the fields, around a pond which shone like a polished mirror, to a haveli set amid a beautiful lawn. At the corner of the lawn was a temple. An edge of the lawn sloped gently to the bank of the river. The view was beautiful.

Manik's father, Banshidhar, was standing near the large doors at the entrance. He had aged in the year since the guest had seen him last, but smiled to see the man arrive, for his happiness was genuine.

'Sahib, welcome to my house. I hope Manik treated you well on the journey from Benares.'

'He is a polite child, Banshidhar seth, and I am well. I know this is a busy time for you because of the festival, and I shall try not to get in the way.'

'Sahib, you never interrupt anything when you visit. My house is yours. Please follow me. Your rooms have been prepared.'

The guest, refreshed and wearing silk, descended from his quarters on the first floor to the dining area on the ground floor, facing the river. Banshidhar was overseeing preparations for serving lunch.

A large wooden table with carved legs stood to the left of the entrance. Carved chairs had been placed around them.

'Some weeks ago I had this made by a carpenter who has been building them for English families at Buxar. It is meant for eating in their manner. What do you think of it?'

The guest said it looked like the work of a master craftsman, and expressed admiration for the quality of the timber.

'I have been foolish. I forget that you are familiar with how they eat. Perhaps you could show me how to get used to it?' said Banshidhar.

'It is just a matter of habit. But I am not sure if our friends will be comfortable dining in this manner, if you intend to have the feast here.'

'You are right. I will eat at this table on some other occasion.'

They therefore ate in the customary fashion, reclining on carpets laid on the floor, supported by large cushions.

'I hope the food is to your liking, sahib. I cannot eat

certain kinds of food during the festival, but our Awadhi cooks were happy to make your meals in the way you prefer,' said Banshidhar.

The food was indeed excellent, as were the sweets served to the guest afterwards.

'Manik mentioned that you were worried, Banshidhar seth,' he said, towards the end of the meal.

'I will not say that I am not, sahib. I do not know if it is age, or this season, or the world. There are far too many changes that occur, and I do not know if I am losing my wits, or these Englishmen are beyond understanding.'

'It cannot be that bad.'

'Perhaps it is not. Manik tells me that it is not, and he is a reasonable young man. For instance, the Kashi Naresh was dethroned, and it made not the slightest difference to my land, or my tenants, my boat and trade. Or to the chisas who strike such hard bargains to be my passengers for a night or two. I am the same seth that I was two years ago. And yet, sometimes I wake up in the middle of the night. I am fearful. I am anxious, and I do not know of what.'

'Perhaps that is just it, seth. You are concerned because there is nothing you can see that could concern you.'

'My friend, I would have agreed with you a year ago, or even three months previously. But after I received news of Amanullah, I have been disturbed. I have waited for this visit by our friends and you to set my mind at ease. I had never expected this problem to arise.'

'I can understand your concern, seth. It does look bad, and there have been problems, but it is nothing that we can't solve. It is not as bad as losing your land and tenants, or even losing a ferry boat. That which bothers us is just a man, and just a small lesion on our skin. Unexpected, worrying, but temporary.'

'I have prayed to the Goddess to hear these words from you. I do not know if I can ever understand the English the way your father did or you do. Neither their soldiers nor the officials of the Company Sarkar. No matter how long I know them.'

'The English are not too difficult to understand, seth ji. In their greed and avarice, they are not different from a Nawab or Maharaja. But in the way they see themselves, they could not be more dissimilar.'

Banshidhar was surprised, and wanted to press his guest further on this cryptic remark, but they were interrupted by the entry of a servant, who announced that the musicians had arrived. Banshidhar led the guest to the rear of the mansion, where they reclined on the floor, facing the tree-lined riverbank. The seth had summoned local musicians to play for his eminent guest. The two men listened to the musicians—who were not classically trained but played folk ballads whose lyrics were not always suitable for mixed company—and ate some of the betel leaves gifted by Manik, until the guest felt drowsy in the warm afternoon. He excused himself and went upstairs, where he fell asleep.

He awoke in the early evening to find the house had started filling with servants and guests. Banshidhar was in the backyard, standing outside his temple, overseeing preparations for the aarati.

This worship of the Ganga, organised in the evening along the river from its origin high in the Himalayas to where it met the sea, was the highlight of the ten days of Ganga Dussehra. Ganga aarati at Banshidhar seth's haveli was famed, and was attended by all the important people along both banks of the river for miles, on every one of the ten days, particularly the tenth. Banshidhar's family priest would preside over the rituals, and the seth's three sons would participate, although Manik was absent today.

The guest was walking down the staircase when he was hailed by a group of men standing in the main hall of the haveli. Three were Muslim and two Hindu, dressed in fine silk and cotton, attended by servants.

'Aulae sahib, Ram-Ram,' they said when he had descended and approached them close enough for a quiet greeting.

The people he had travelled there to meet had begun to arrive. But there were many other guests of Banshidhar who were not like these men, and in whose presence not much conversation was possible, so the special guests bided their time.

The aarati was followed by rituals invoking the river, while the notables and their families lit earthen lamps along the riverbank in the gathering dusk. This was followed by a reading from the Bhagavata Purana. This was the third consecutive day of the reading, and on the tenth would culminate in the account of the descent of the divine river to earth, and the fate of the dynasty which caused this descent. Banshidhar, who had an interest in genealogies and saw himself as a son of the river, was annually affected very much by this reading and found all manner of meaning and symbolism in the verses. He had even arranged for a junior priest to read out some of the verses multiple times so that he would memorise them, although his faculty for Sanskrit was, alas, not as great as his eye for commerce and the frailties of chisas.

The evening drew to a close and the guests departed, carrying prasad with them, gram and slices of coconut. Banshidhar's grandfather had come upriver from Bengal, and they still had family and property in Dhaka, and some traditions, like the ingredients of prasad, were inherited from their Bengali forebears.

Banshidhar greeted each of his special guests again, gave

instructions to his family for the rest of the evening like the patriarch he wanted to be, and led the men to a wing of the haveli which had been lit with large candles and by the moonlight through open windows.

The man who was many men sat in a corner and watched the others take their places. There were eleven in total. Together they comprised not the heads of all the clans that existed, but represented most of the important subahs. Six were Muslim. There was a soft-spoken man dressed as a prosperous merchant from Marwar, although he spoke with the accent of a native of Kota and was actually from Malwa. The head of the Biswas family from Dhaka was also present. Between Banshidhar and Biswas, they owned a large proportion of boats and ferries on the Ganga and the lower Meghna, from Dhaka to Calcutta and upstream to Delhi, and commanded all the Bungus, who were Phansigars on the river and its tributaries.

'I thank you for being present here today, and for participating in the aarati,' said Banshidhar. He said this whenever they met here during Ganga Dussehra.

'Banshidhar seth, we are honoured to be present on such a holy occasion, and to meet all of you,' said Sahib Khan, a young man who was representing his father and the clan from Telangana. Of them, he had travelled the farthest, but their clan combined business with their journey north at this time of the year. He had brought a hundred of his men, fluent in Hindustani and many dialects, with him on the journey so they could ply their trade, which was metalworking. The other clans expected their arrival and sometimes accompanied them in small bands through the countryside. It was the closest the clans had ever come to having a pilgrimage, although in many ways each expedition by even the most mean and humble group of Phansigars was a sacrifice and pilgrimage on its own.

'We salute our brothers and seek the blessings of the Goddess on all of us, so that our sacrifices will be pleasing for her, and all the omens be good,' intoned Baz Khan, the head of the Agra clan, among the most senior and well-peopled. So numerous were the Agariyas that they had spread from Gwalior to the Punjab and had prospered over generations of strife and lawlessness in those lands. Now Punjab was peaceful under the Khalsa Empire, but the Phansigars had spread deep roots and endured, from Lahore to Multan.

'And we salute our respected friend and his clan. We know their guidance and counsel shall continue to be invaluable for us,' said the Marwari. The man who was many men accepted the praise with grace.

'My brothers, we are present on an auspicious day, for which I am grateful. But I must tell you that I am troubled and cannot hide it. For generations we have served the will of the Goddess and offered sacrifices to her without fail. But now we seem to have an unexpected problem and it grows bigger every day. Near Guna, not a few weeks ago, a capable young aulae, Amanullah, was captured by the British. I am still not certain about how this happened, although I have heard different accounts of it. I am sure you shall enlighten me,' said Banshidhar.

Baz Khan informed them of how Amanullah had been captured, for the gang had been Agariya, and the clan had felt the blow the most. Now Amanullah's brother was on the run, fearful that the rangwas would come for him.

'I agree that it has troubled me. Amanullah's brother is a senior sardar, leader of many expeditions, and the only aulae from Agra who knows my real name and where I live. Never in all our generations have we experienced this. We have several here who are more familiar with our lore and the account of our people than I can ever hope to be, and we can ask them if this has ever happened,' said Baz Khan.

The subedars each shook their heads and assured Baz Khan that such a problem had never arisen.

'We have sometimes had an ambitious watchman in a city, or a najeeb, or an army commander, who might have caught a few of our fellows, it is true. Sometimes, due to the disfavour of the Goddess, or because they ignored the omens, some have been caught even while offering sacrifices. Then there are the greedy revenue officials of today, who sometimes catch us and make threats without knowing who they persecute. But these come and go,' said Biswas.

'I was telling the same thing to Baz Khan huzoor, when I met him earlier today. From what I have heard ever since we crossed Nagpur, this bilha is unlike any our people have ever faced before,' said Sahib Khan, uttering a dreaded word that had not been heard in their councils for years.

Sometimes, by the peculiar nature of the world, Phansigars would be forced to contend with an enemy sworn to bring them to justice, an enemy who could not be bought, coerced or otherwise tamed. But such a man, a bilha, was rare, and rarer still in these times.

'Over these months, I have heard of our aulae being captured from many places. They have been arrested in numbers too large and too often. I do not know how many, but enough to make me worried,' said the man from Kota.

'Why is this Englishman so successful? How much does he know? Even more important, who *is* he?' asked Banshidhar.

'I do not know how much he has found out, Banshidhar seth. I do know that Amanullah will not reveal whatever secrets he knows. He will never betray his brother,' said the man who was many men.

'I thank you for trusting Amanullah. But even if he betrays us, he does not know enough to tell this Englishman,' said Baz Khan.

'What do we know of this Englishman? He is in your territory, is he not?' said Biswas.

'Biswas seth,' said the man who had once called himself Ameer Ali, 'I had not known of him till a few months ago, and had not thought him worthy of being known. He is just an assistant to the agent, and was once in the army. He is otherwise of little account.'

'Is he from a worthy family? At the very least, he must be like us.'

'No, Baz Khan sahib, he is a nobody. But I would like to speak my mind here. At first I thought he was a zealous Englishman who happened to capture some of our men. It was a setback, and unusual, but I was willing to let it pass. But in the months afterwards, this man has been capturing our aulaes from the north and the west too. Sometimes his officers travel far looking for specific people. Sometimes they advise other magistrates or princes about which aulaes to look for. They collect bodies, loot and even find witnesses for their courts. They study Ramasi and know the words; they know of our beliefs and our rituals. This Englishman is a bigger problem than I had thought. He is not a mere watchman chasing a dacoit in the dark. I must therefore ask you to decide to have him removed,' said the man.

'I agree with sahib. The loss of Amanullah wounds me. It is better if this Englishman does not continue with his work, and we should decide with speed before he causes some more trouble for us,' said Baz Khan.

'Very well, but if I understand the lore, no bilha may ever be sacrificed to the Goddess,' said Sahib Khan.

'She would never accept an unclean sacrifice like this man. It would be a calamity,' said the man from Kota.

'I do not speak of a sacrifice, brothers. I say that he be executed, in the manner of them executing one they think of as a criminal. I would not like any of us to return to our homes in fear that the rangwas and their police will come for us,' said the man.

'That is proper. But we can't expect to hang him in public view. What can be done, therefore?' said Banshidhar seth.

'If I may make a suggestion. There are two clans of Dhaturias in those parts. One in Sagar, I believe, also works around Jabalpur. Perhaps you could request one of them to administer a poison of their preference to this Englishman. If they want, they can administer something which will make his death resemble one from natural causes. That will not be beyond their abilities, even if they have shortcomings in other areas,' said Baz Khan.

'Khan sahib, with respect, I find the idea of asking Dhaturias for a favour offensive. Surely we have not been driven to such extremes that we have to ask for their help? My pride would be hurt. I can only imagine what sahib would feel,' said the subedar from Kota.

'I will abide by the decision taken here. If you feel that we should talk to the Dhaturias, I shall meet the subedar of the Sagar clan. But whichever means we choose, dispatch this Englishman we must, and soon,' said the man.

'You are familiar with the English in Sagar and Jabalpur. What do you propose we do?' asked Baz Khan.

'Since the sacrifice of a bilha is not permitted in the lore, I think the simplest solution is the best. We should send one of our own bhartotes, but somebody proficient in blade-craft, to kill him by drawing blood. It might not be easy to approach this Englishman, if he is crafty and suspicious, but I am certain that we have many capable bhartotes with such talents, and one can be sent as soon as possible,' said the man.

There were murmurs of discussion by the subedars

with their neighbours. Biswas cleared his throat. Everyone stopped speaking and turned to look at him. Biswas was the oldest of them, and carried the additional prestige of being from Dhaka, where the most important temple of the Goddess lay, and whose omens were considered of great significance.

'I have listened to your suggestions with interest. I agree that we should not be in the position of having to worry about this Englishman and his doings, particularly when monsoon is around the corner. I am old, but I know you would prefer a quiet life too, and we all hope to send our aulaes and bhartotes on their journeys after Diwali. Therefore, we need to solve this problem. Before leaving Dhaka, I consulted our family astrologer, who read the signs and prayed to the Goddess on our behalf. Brothers, I can reassure you that if we decide on the end of this Englishman, we can leave it to the Goddess to effect it herself. We will not need to seek help from the Dhaturias and their unclean poisons. We will not even have to sacrifice a bhartote by sending him to draw blood with a blade.'

'I do not understand, Biswas seth,' said Sahib Khan.

'The omens were clear. The Goddess will take the life of this Englishman during the rains. It is only a matter of time. He will die as surely as you see me, and his death will not be viewed with suspicion by his people. His work will die with him. That is certain. Therefore, we must decide that his death is to happen. That is the only decision we need to take,' said Biswas.

'If the Goddess will act on our behalf and rid us of this problem, and the omens point to this, nothing will give me greater joy, Biswas seth,' said the man from Kota.

There was a murmur of agreement from everyone. The Englishman had to die.

'Biswas seth, you have lifted a great burden from my shoulders. I shall be able to sleep content tonight. And sahib will be happy too, knowing he will have to neither talk to the Dhaturias nor find a suitable bladesman,' said Banshidhar.

The man who was many men smiled and expressed his gratitude to Biswas and the Goddess. But he also looked at all the subedars in turn and wondered why they did not take the matter as seriously as he wanted them to take it. Was it because they saw the British as just conquerors interested in farther fields, without the focus and will to uproot the Phansigars? Did they not understand how thorough this Englishman had been in trying to understand them, and in convincing arrested aulaes to save their miserable skins by betraying others? Only a few layers of separation protected them from the redcoats and the end of this life which their ancestors had built for them. The Goddess, it is true, protected her devotees, and many miracles had been ascribed to her. He knew of all of them. But the Englishman was too earthly an enemy, too real, and therefore, needed to be dealt with by blade and muscle.

He decided to wait for the monsoon before knowing whether he should feel relieved or not. If the Englishman survived the monsoons, the subedar would act on his own. Sometimes divine intervention needed a human hand for assistance. A subedar of Phansigars knew this better than anyone else.

The town which was once known as Jabalgarh waited for the first signs of the monsoons. Brigadier General O'Halloran's engineers raced to widen the carriage road to Sagar before the first bloated clouds gathered in the distant horizon from the south. Sleeman, Reynolds, Moore and the skeleton staff of the new provincial police travelled far and kept long hours, interrogating prisoners and gathering evidence. Sleeman had to accommodate this along with administrative work of the district, and there were days when he did not see Amelie except in passing. His sleep suffered and his back ached because he could not avoid travel by horse.

His reports to Calcutta, and news of the trials in Allahabad and elsewhere began to cause a stir in Government House. With great reluctance, the mighty bureaucratic machinery began to take note. In the tone of the replies from Macnaghten's office, there was a hint of commendation, and abundant caution. There were questions, and petulance, and an unsaid need for reassurance, and the shadow of unarticulated doubts, all of which constitute the grease that lies among the gears of all bureaucracies in all time.

'We shall be required to review your progress,' said Macnaghten, in a rare personal note to Sleeman. The note sounded regretful, as if Macnaghten had been contending mightily against the inexorable workings of his own department, and the review hinted at was a nuisance they could have done without. But such a review, an inquiry, would happen at some point in time, Sleeman was told. It was a necessity, and not a reflection on his work. Sleeman decided to think of it when he would be summoned for it.

After several letters between each other, Brian Hodgson had sent wonderful news. He was in the process of beginning arrangements to travel to Jabalpur in the company of Horace Wilson and James Prinsep, a miracle which brought a satisfied smile to Sleeman's face. Sometime after the monsoon, if all went well, said Hodgson, they could visit.

Meanwhile, the captured Phansigars continued to confess their crimes and reveal others. Amanullah, on understanding his circumstances, was cooperative, but he did not know who the subedar of the Agra Phansigars was, or the location of any of the other subedars. Only his brother knew, and there was no sign of him.

Sleeman kept probing and asking him questions from different directions, but of the subedars, and of the man who was many men, there was no clue. Sometimes it seemed that the stalking of this man had been in progress for years, and perhaps it had been.

'You told me, Amanullah, that every year after the Guna mela you come to Sagar. Is that not so?' asked the captain one evening at the jail.

'Yes, sahib. I have come to Sagar every year for five years.'

'Was it part of an expedition?' It was unusual for a senior Phansigar to lead an expedition along the same long route for several years in succession.

'No, sahib, I brought my horses to Sagar, to trade.'

Reynolds, who was keeping a record of the interrogation, burst out laughing.

'And did you manage to sell any? There are no zamindars or princelings in Sagar who would buy your mares. Only Brigadier General O'Halloran's sowar battalions, and they have the finest horses.'

Amanullah was solemn.

'Leftan sahib, I brought my horses to Sagar every year, and every year I sold them. I do not lie about the horses bred by my family. They are among the best in Agra.'

'Who did you sell them to?' asked Sleeman.

'To the seth known as Hari Singh, sahib. He puts them up for purchase bids by the sowar battalion. They would never let one like me participate, but they know the seth.'

Reynolds uttered an oath. Of course, they knew the seth. Hari Singh was one of the richest and most respectable men in Sagar and Narmada.

'Reynolds, we will have to inform the general about this. Hari Singh would not be the first merchant to be involved in legitimate business with Phansigars. Can you imagine the number of British officers who will be shocked to hear this, and the number who have borrowed money from him at one point of time or the other?'

Reynolds hesitated. Sleeman glanced at him.

'Did you borrow money from him as well?'

'It was only a small amount to tide over an immediate need, sir. I paid him back as soon as I could.'

Sleeman nodded. 'As long as there is no outstanding debt, Reynolds. Try not to take such loans in future.'

Amanullah was staring at the wall of the prison barracks, his expression indeterminate.

'Can you imagine what the seth will feel, Reynolds, if he realises he was doing business with someone like Amanullah? Not to mention the effect on his reputation.'

Far from these revelations, the district continued to suffer. The two litigious zamindars, anticipating a period of enforced quiet during the rains, unleashed their mridhas on each other's tenants. Crops began to catch fire. Carts of produce and oxen drivers began arriving at the Jabalpur mandi with visible signs of damage by hefty men. Allegations arrived by messenger every other day at Sleeman's office.

Moore was taken off an investigation and sent to repair the bunds upstream of Jabalpur, at a village the cantonment's sappers seemed to have missed. It was back-breaking work, for the river had cut into the bedrock and the embankment was a serrated row of boulders. Moore and his unit led the villagers over three days of work under the sun. The young man laboured so much that the villagers were inspired by him, and organised a festival for him at the end of the work. Moore returned to his quarters at the cantonment embarrassed with the praise and attention, and happy for the first time in years.

And then the rains arrived. The first storm of the season caught Sleeman on horseback one afternoon in the countryside, and he was drenched by the time he reached shelter. This was followed by a succession of overcast days and heavy thunder showers.

The Narmada flooded in the way of Deccan rivers, at those places where the bed was shallow and banks more meandering than usual. It flooded villages and fields after a heavy shower or two, but the waters did not stay for long.

The Sleemans' grain stores were ruined within the first week, because the roof had leaked. Sleeman was away and Amelie had to send a messenger to the camp quartermaster requesting supplies. The quartermaster had seen more monsoons in the Deccan than most, and had shifted the camp's stores to an elevated and secure room in the magazine.

Two families of household servants lived in the lower town east of the camp and by the river. Their houses were among the first to be inundated. Amelie helped them take what they could and shift to the residence.

The boy from Seoni had become even more still than

usual with the coming of the rains. Amelie had been letting him free from his bonds for a few hours at a time, and he had begun to respond to her. At least he did not bare his teeth at her if she was not accompanied by the household dogs. She moved him into a room which opened into the rear courtyard, and he seemed to be willing to stay inside when it rained, provided they left the door open and he could stare out at the garden. The children of the families she had invited to stay had been warned not to trouble the boy.

And then the snakes emerged, driven from their holes by the waters. Amelie had to be accompanied by people armed with sticks when she went to take a bath. Crocodiles crawled up irrigation ditches and appeared inside homes or kitchens, and in cattle sheds. Cows were too large for any but the biggest muggers, but for goats it was a season of peril.

The district administration's work increased. Construction of the new jail had not progressed at the pace needed, and the arrested Phansigars continued to be lodged at Jabalpur jail, which at least was on higher ground than the rest of the town.

Sleeman awoke one morning with every joint in his body aching. He was running a mild fever and his stomach ached. He sent word to the munshi to postpone his hearings for later in the day. By afternoon the fever was raging and Sleeman retired to bed.

The rest of the sequence of events was a fevered succession of half-remembered images. Amelie must have sent for Spilsbury even though it was a formality. She knew what had happened and what to do. By the time the surgeon had arrived in the pouring rain, she would have found their supply of powdered Jesuit's bark, which she had kept with her jewellery because it was just as valuable. Only a few ounces remained of the powder a friend had sent from

Calcutta two years earlier. The powder was expensive, for the Dutch who grew cinchona in their plantations in the East Indies prized the tree and sold its bark at inflated rates which exceeded that of cinnamon.

He could hear voices of people around his bed. Amelie must have mixed the powder in wine and fed him. At some point Spilsbury would have come and felt his forehead, covered by a damp cloth. The surgeon did not approve of patients being treated before his arrival, but would not have found fault in what Amelie had done. Beyond advising rest and a repeat of the powder if needed, he had no advice to offer, and said the fever should be allowed to run its course. It should teach Sleeman not to tax his body so.

That was the sequence of events. That must have happened, for by the evening Sleeman was under a mound of blankets, shivering, his body covered in sweat. He could not open his eyes and did not know if he wanted to. The fever induced strange dreams and voices in his head. Therefore, he was not certain if he had dreamed of the Jesuit's bark or if it had been administered to him. He did not know if he had heard Spilsbury examine him, or had only dreamt of it.

Amelie would have refused to leave his side. She would have reassured the household that it was not contagious, but only a cross that he had been bearing since the first time he suffered from malaria. It had almost killed him in the swamps of the terai during the war with the hill people. It had taken the lives of his fellow officers and hundreds of his men, and sent him half-dead to a hospital in Bengal.

The doctors there knew it was fever rising from the swamps, but could not do much to cure it. There wasn't enough Jesuit's bark for enlisted men and officers like Sleeman, who were not the sons or grandsons of significant people. Only the boys of Company notables or aristocrats were sent to hospitals in Calcutta for the best of treatment and fed the powdered bark at great expense. Sleeman endured weeks of terrible fever and pain, but survived. The treatment, such as it was, had not removed the disease from his system. Where did it go? They could not tell him, but said he was fortunate to be alive.

He was released from the hospital emaciated, with thinning hair and a headache that stayed for another few weeks. He was weak and scatter-brained, with aching joints and back which had become worse over the years. The monsoon became a time of trial for him, because he suffered a relapse every few years.

Now he slept, and dreamt, and was no longer sure which was which, for everything seemed real and yet tinged in febrile colours. Amelie must be sitting by his bed. He was certain of that at least.

He saw his father. He saw the Stratton of his childhood and the Bideford of his adolescence. Or perhaps what he thought he remembered of them, for he had spent more than half of his life in India, and had seen so much that he was no longer certain if his memory was reliable. But it must have been, because he saw his father, Captain Philip. All he had ever wanted was to make his father proud. That was all he had ever wanted. He was a captain now, was he not?

He saw his eldest brother, Lewis, on the day he sailed on the naval sloop, HMS Weazle. Sleeman had gone to see Lewis off during the war with Napoleon. Lewis, just a teenager, had drowned with a hundred and four other men and boys only a short distance and two hours later, at the mouth of Barnstaple Bay. Their father had lived for just three more years. Without Lewis he had crumpled inside and given up.

Sleeman dreamt of his mother and his brothers and sister. He saw again the years when the family struggled with the expenses, with running the household. Over the years, he had sometimes felt as if he had been taking care of everyone else all his life. In his fever dreams he saw himself once more taking the officer's commission in the Bengal Army, because he could not afford to pay for a commission in the King's or Queen's regiments. He saw himself sailing to India, not yet twenty, but certain he had to earn and save his family, and by sailing to the land of his dreams, perhaps save himself. All he had earned in these years was a small reputation as a responsible man, and the satisfaction of helping his family get back on their feet.

He had had no plans of marriage or family. Life had demanded too much from him, tried him too often for any residual dreams of having a family.

He saw himself again at the banquet in Jabalpur when he had first met Amelie. He saw himself as he thought others saw him: a useful man, but nearing the end of his prime, one of who much had been taken by family, by the Honourable Company, by duty and two infernal years at Narsinghpur, by fevers untold and work accumulated from those who could shirk better than he. There was much room in India for the mountebank, for the seller of oils of serpents too numerous to define, and not much place anymore for people like him. He was a dying breed. Perhaps, in an empire created by men like Clive of Plassey, his breed had never been numerous.

He saw himself on that evening, and imagined the expression on his face when Amelie had smiled at him. 'The last honest man in the camp,' she had said afterwards. A curious choice of words, for honesty was a virtue much bandied about in those circles, and there were many claimants for it, or at least for moral rectitude of a certain kind, or a reluctance to be purchased. And what, after all, was honesty?

But he had understood at last what she meant. He had never been one of those who thought a hookah, a sherwani and an Indian wife were all that was needed to belong. And he could never be one of those who had a house in the hills because of summer, and a house near the port because the sea waited to take them back home. He saw those who found modesty in covering their ankles, and he saw those who found virtue in covering their heads and understood them both, even if he could be neither, even if all he was happy doing was digging up the remains of long-dead giants in the hills. And he knew this, and was at peace with it. Being conditioned from childhood to take responsibilities, he had asked for nothing much from anybody, least of all from the land he had made his home. If he had disappointments, he had forgotten about them. He was one of those fortunate foster children who saw the inadequacies of their adoptive mother and forgave her, for all mothers are inadequate except in myth and paean, which happen to be convenient fictions written by men.

He dreamt of a monstrous creature which shook the ground as it walked. It wore a crown on its head, and its presence wilted and poisoned the land. From the lessons of his youth he remembered its name, basilisk, from the Greek for 'little king'. Why should he be concerned? Because he was chasing this creature, and he had not yet caught it. What was it that the Nawab Begum had said? About petty tyrants who suffered a bigger tyrant to rule them. Which tyrant did he serve, and who did he chase?

Time stretched on through such visions and memories. Eons passed. Glaciers advanced, scoured the earth and retreated. Fabulous creatures were born and ruled the land, giving way to lesser species. Empires rose and fell, gods and prophets came and went, inventors and scholars assured him they were making their best efforts. At what? He did not know.

Amelie must have kept watch as he wandered through his interminable dreams, and must have listened to his fevered utterances. When he awoke it was afternoon on a clear day. The sunlight filled a side of the room through two open windows. His body was numb, and where it was not, it throbbed with dull aches and complaints. His head was a mass of pain, and the mere act of unlatching his jaw to croak a few words was an enormous effort. Amelie smiled and assured him that his temperature had fallen and he was getting better. He muttered a question which he could not himself hear well.

'It has been two days, William,' said Amelie. He shut his eyes and slept. He went through the motions of being fed gruel in the evening. That, at least, he could remember.

The following day he was stronger, and was made to sit up against some cushions. He could not taste much of the kedgeree they fed him, or the unidentified fish in it. This was the worst fever he had suffered since his recovery from malaria all those years earlier. He was not certain if he could survive another relapse.

'I hope this will help you feel better, William,' said Amelie, after a nurse had wiped his face, which was still damp and fevered. His wife placed a bound sheaf of papers in his hand. It was filled with her neat handwriting. It was a glossary of words in Ramasi.

'You completed it,' he said. His feeble response could not hide the delight in his eyes.

'And towards the end, you will find a list of practices and beliefs of the Phansigars. I was not certain if we should classify them with the words, or in a separate section. A living language, and the beliefs of the people who speak the language should be treated as distinct from each other,' she said, a teacher explaining the axiomatic to a new student.

He turned the pages, marvelling at her thorough definitions, the precision of her explanations, and her honesty in dividing evidence from speculation.

'I am convinced the core of Ramasi, as recorded by the men you have arrested, was born from dialects in Bundelkhand and Awadh. We still do not know how this is different from the language of Phansigars in the south. We have a lot of work ahead, William. Now will you please try to get better soon?'

He smiled and took her hand. It was cool.

'Thank you.'

She nodded.

Sleeman closed his eyes and tried to gather his thoughts. Amelie went back to reading a book.

'My father has written a letter to us. It arrived yesterday. The dak from Bombay was delayed again.'

Sleeman opened his eyes. Comte Blondin de Fontenne now lived on a plantation in Mauritius and entertained himself by devising suitable careers for his son-in-law.

'He worries for you, William. You know he has a lot of regard for your capabilities. He admires you. He escaped from France with almost nothing during the Revolution, and had to make another fortune with nothing but his name.'

'It is a respectable name,' whispered Sleeman.

'It is, and it has helped him. But he just wants what he thinks is best for you. He does not think much about working for the Company, or Government House. They are no better than governments in Europe, he says. He has had his fill of them. He wants us to go and live with him.'

A new vision paraded in front of Sleeman. The old count, Amelie and he sitting on the lawn of a plantation house, perhaps on the sloping shoulder of a hill. He did not know what Mauritius looked like, but imagined a tropical sky and the ocean. Sleeman walking around and supervising a plantation. He tried to remember what the old man was growing at present.

There was no question of leaving. He had never even returned home, for reasons that he could not remember anymore. But to leave for any other place would be exile. He wondered if Amelie's father, who knew the meaning of exile better than anyone else, would understand if he were to explain it in this manner. To leave India and to be transplanted elsewhere would be the end of him, and doubly so on an island of whose economy slavery was such an important part.

'I shall write to him, William, and explain that we cannot go. I would not have it otherwise. He means well, and he is lonely, and says he is certain Britain will end slavery in the empire by declaration in a year or so, and therefore on the island. We shall turn him down, but I too cannot ask him to take such a long voyage to come and meet us. Perhaps we can take a holiday instead.'

Perhaps they could, even though it seemed like an endless journey. Sleeman nodded, dropped his head back on the cushions, and dozed.

A day later, he could walk with some support to the rear lawn. The sky was overcast. He sat on a chair on the threshold, looking at a spotted deer in the distant trees of the forest. The boy from Seoni sat under the spreading branches of a tree some distance away.

Sleeman felt a great sense of sorrow on seeing the child. A sense of futility and disconnect, a feeling of pity for the boy, suspended between wolf and man, and being neither. There was no reason for such a feeling. Perhaps it was the after-effect of the fever, which never failed to leave him despondent about everything. The day was quiet in the way that overcast skies bring. The monsoon breeze was touching the leaves of the trees. It was just his fever and the sense of mortality with which it filled him. Every year, he was diminished in physique and even more in his mind.

'Where is everyone? Where is Reynolds?'

'He arrived from Sagar three days ago and came to enquire about you. Mrs Reynolds says he has locked himself inside his study and has not come out since.'

'My illness does not mean our work should stop.'

'I do not think that was the matter, William. Reynolds can't seem to fall sick like you do, so this could be his way of dealing with fatigue.'

'All right, perhaps he should be left alone. But please send for the munshi. He at least should be at work.'

The munshi arrived in an hour and expressed gratitude to the gods for Sleeman's recovery. The captain, who had started feeling cold and had returned to bed, asked him for news of the district. The monsoon's impact had not worsened, but a village of tenants on the lands of one of the litigious zamindars had lost their supply of grain two nights earlier after the granary's roof collapsed.

'Have you seen the damage?'

'No sahib, but one of the clerks went himself, after we received news.'

'What does he have to say?'

'He says the granary was strong and the roof was built for the rains. It should not have collapsed.'

'What do the villagers say?'

'They do not say anything, sahib.'

Sleeman closed his eyes. His head ached. An arc of pain radiated from his elbow to his forearm and fingers.

'There should be a sheaf of blank paper on my desk, and the stamp.'

The munshi brought it.

'Please write this down. On my orders, by the power vested in me by the government and the agent of Sagar and Narmada, I direct the arrest of both the zamindars, their mridhas and armed retainers and confiscation of all lethal weapons in their possession, as well as any means to cause arson or damage property.'

The munshi wrote this down.

'William, are you certain of this?' asked Amelie.

'I should have done this earlier. It would have saved a lot of trouble for the tenants. I will not tolerate this any longer. Munshi, take this to the kotwal and ask him to send a unit of police to the houses of the zamindars. They are to be taken along with their retainers to jail. If they attempt to resist, tell the policemen to report to the camp and seek a force of sepoys to help them. We will see how they like living in a jail near the likes of Amanullah and his bhartotes.'

The munshi left to carry out the task.

'William, are you certain you are not trying to make amends for being too patient earlier by being hasty now?'

'Amelie, I can't wait for them to destroy all the food supplies of each other's tenants and drive the families to starvation. The zamindars think this is a contest of pride and honour. I should not have let it linger for so long. As soon as I return to court, I shall throw out their suits and order them to compensate the tenants for the damage they have done. If they want to show each other up, they can take lathis, go off to a clearing and have at each other.'

'William, in that event Government House will censure you for encouraging duelling in the district.'

Sleeman tried to smile but his jaws hurt. 'Yes, they might.

We could ask all the zamindars and princelings, not to mention the Company officials in Calcutta, to solve their feuds in this manner, and the people might even pay for the entertainment.'

He closed his eyes and lay back on the pillows. He was not certain if he was beginning to recover his appetite, but giving the orders to the munshi had made him feel better.

'You were muttering in your sleep, William. You had fever dreams.'

He could not remember anything, except vague snatches of people, of faces, of events which he was not certain had happened or of which he had only dreamed.

'Was I calling for Lewis?'

'Yes, you were,' she said, and covered his hand with hers.

'His death broke my father's heart, Amelie. He was never the same till he passed away. I sometimes wonder what we would have been if Lewis and my father had not died and we had not become poor. My mother would have been happy. I could have become a proper man of learning. I could have…I do not know. Please forgive me for speaking of this.'

And since he never spoke of these events, Amelie brushed his hair with her hand and was silent till he fell asleep.

His health improved over the next few days, but Spilsbury told him not to travel for some time and to stay confined at home. He spent clear evenings in the forest, going on short walks, or trying to talk to the boy from Seoni, who had begun to respond to him as well, although with not as much warmth as he showed to Amelie. The munshi brought urgent matters from the office, including a plea from the two zamindars to be let off on payment of hefty indemnities and reparations. Sleeman was inclined to dismiss the requests, but the agent sent a message asking him to be lenient on this occasion. The political department had to live up to its name, so Sleeman grimaced and ordered the two feuding men to be released with warnings. The agent visited him, and agreed with Amelie that Sleeman ought to travel to the hills for a few months to recover. The question was: when.

In Britain, an aged but hardworking and frugal prince had become King William IV. His distant subjects in Jabalpur received the news in due course with grace and celebrated it, awaiting further reports of his coronation.

Amid this and the occasional alarms that the monsoon brought, Sleeman could look forward with genuine enthusiasm to just one event: his friends would visit him as promised, and bring some light into his lately benighted existence. Amelie would notice the look on his face whenever he mentioned the expected visit, and understood his secret joy and anticipation.

They were going away, and passing through, but they came and stayed and lifted some of the moroseness that had settled over Sleeman's world. That they were together was a miracle, that they might never meet again was understood. Thus they arrived at Jabalpur, as promised to Sleeman, after monsoon was over and the rivers had subsided.

Wilson had brought only a few belongings; the rest had been sent by ship to Bombay, from where he would leave for England and a prospective teaching position at the University of Oxford. He was to travel to Ellora from Jabalpur for the cave temples. Hodgson was to spend the winter with him among the natural world of the Deccan before returning to Kathmandu in the spring. And Prinsep was stalking an old elusive quarry, which would take him to Benares, Allahabad and Agra.

Each was a magus in his own right, high priest of specialised branches and pioneer of arcane disciplines. Therefore, each brought a gift for Amelie to rival the precious metal and incense of another age.

Prinsep gave her a carved wooden box, inside which were nestled five silver coins, one of them a drachma of Menander, the great Greco-Indian ruler. The obverse showed the king in profile, and the reverse an image of Athena hurling a thunderbolt. It was the only coin of Menander with Prinsep that was inscribed in Greek on both sides. Amelie would not have it, for it was too priceless to accept, but Prinsep was certain his correspondents in the Punjab would find more.

'Since James laid claim to Menander's treasury, I had to find a gift elsewhere,' said Wilson, producing a thick bound sheaf of papers. It was a copy of the draft of the first volume of his translation of the Vishnu Purana. He told Amelie that it would be some time before he could complete the remaining volumes and send them to his publishers.

Hodgson said he could not hope to match such treasures, and produced a wrapped and framed painting of a forested valley with snow-clad mountains in the distance.

'It is not easy to compress the riches of India's natural world into a single image, but I find the foothills of the Himalayas a place of calm, yet abundant in the variety of trees and animals. I painted this in a valley in the Bengal Duars, where I found a species of antelope called chiru by the locals,' he said. Each tree in the painting was of a unique species and painted in detail.

The agent had been gracious and relieved Sleeman from work for the duration of their stay. Prinsep was known to only a few in the land, but Wilson was an important personage in Calcutta, and even Hodgson was beginning to acquire fame outside the rarefied membership of the Asiatic Society. Jabalpur was not going to take such guests for granted.

Sleeman was struck by the worry that his guests, welcome though they were, would find Jabalpur provincial. Prinsep still had fond memories of Benares with its attendant halo of antiquity, although he would not commit to a date for the settling of the city. Even Calcutta's two centuries seemed to confer on it a degree of sophistication to which Jabalpur's twelve years of existence could never make it aspire.

The agent invited them for banquets, and Brigadier General O'Halloran entertained them in the cantonment in the presence of his most senior officers. What passed for society in Jabalpur opened its gates for the three gentlemen. Prinsep and Wilson seemed to be delighted with the cuisine, although Hodgson, who had suffered another bout of illness in Calcutta, was circumspect. The conversations, Sleeman was mortified to notice, were desultory, for O'Halloran's officers, even in the presence of their wives and the civilians from Calcutta, were limited to talking of military matters and local politics. Here Wilson and Hodgson showed their political acumen by participating in knowledgeable discussions with the hosts, with a smattering of insight on South Asia, but Prinsep was out of his element. His idea of social conversation was to assume that the person he was talking to understood at least half of what he was saying, which was not possible among his audience here. Therefore, his listeners would be puzzled by his remarks until the other two, Amelie or Spilsbury rescued him.

But at last the invitations were all attended, and the hangers-on had satisfied their curiosity, and the guests were left to their own devices. At the top was their wish to see the excavation sites on Bada Simla. The fossils from the find, which Sleeman had kept protected from the damp in his study, were brought out and examined with great attention, while Hodgson made quick but detailed sketches from different angles. They walked around Bada Simla on many occasions and spent days at the excavated spots. Hodgson had many questions about the geology of the hill and Spilsbury told him about his theories. They also examined the new sites at Lameta Ghat. Prinsep thought there was a good chance of finding some petrified remains in the basalt.

There followed an excursion to Narsinghpur, where Spilsbury had been waiting to show the site where the potter had found the petrified trees.

'They are certainly a species of palm, which is unusual

for this region, being so far inland. The only conclusion is this area was at some point of time on the shore of a great water body,' said Hodgson after examining all the remains, and Prinsep agreed. Of this water body there remained not a trace, to their knowledge.

Hodgson was the busiest of them all, for every find and likely mound or midden, every interesting hill and rock formation had to be documented. Every piece of the petrified wood had to be sketched just so, which he would turn into detailed drawings on returning to the house.

'I have no facility in art, I regret to say. Therefore I cannot hope to make such drawings of the finds. If I could use a heliograph, such as Niépce's camera obscura, I could take images to send to the Society,' said Spilsbury one evening.

'Making these sketches is a lot of work, but work which I enjoy. The images made by Niépce's device lack in detail and finesse, and you must consider the expense and labour of carrying the paraphernalia around on trips like these. But still, an improved camera obscura would be a useful aid,' said Hodgson.

Documentation and storage were recurring themes in their conversations. This would not have surprised any other member of the Asiatic Society. Hodgson and Prinsep had been puzzled over an episode that had transpired only a few months earlier. For some time, Prinsep had been trying to decipher some rock edicts which had been found in the Doab, etched in an unknown script. On hearing of this, and reading a paper by Prinsep on his efforts till then, Hodgson had recalled that he had come across two similar edicts in the terai region and in Bihar, which he had examined at length and had sent a report to the Society. This would have aided Prinsep's study to a considerable extent. To their mutual consternation, no record of this report existed in the

Society's archives. They had been thwarted from a priceless breakthrough, and Hodgson had spent the journey from Calcutta apologising for the missing report to Prinsep, who in turn had been contrite at the state of affairs in the Society.

'Nevertheless, James will decipher the script in the end. He always does,' said Wilson at lunch one day. Prinsep was away with Sleeman.

That Prinsep would solve a problem he was labouring on was a certainty, according to those who knew him, for his relentlessness was incredible. He never seemed to sleep. He would retire to his room after supper and work through the night. Amelie sometimes met him in the backyard at dawn, pacing to his thoughts, or standing at the threshold of his room, staring at the morning sky. He was polite, deferential and avuncular in the way of shortsighted men with mild tempers, but Amelie could not help feeling that she was always interrupting some great flow of ideas, as if he was racing to pack as many discoveries and as much knowledge as he could within an inadequate amount of time, and she had intruded where she should have shielded him from the world. And she would feel guilty about the intrusion for the rest of the day, and wonder whether that was how his wife felt all the time.

It was indeed a wonder that he could manage to work on so many disparate projects at the same time. He was on the verge of completing his role in assisting Wilson's translation of the Vishnu Purana, for which Prinsep had some views on the nature of Sanskrit grammar of the period in which the purana was estimated to have been composed. The work on the script of the rock edicts occupied most of his time, but he had also brought a small fortune in coins whose inscriptions he would translate in his leisure hours. Then there was the work for the Asiatic Society, for which he had to read and edit contributions from elected members and correspondents from across the country. Wilson, Hodgson and he had almost formalised the journal they had in mind, the first issue of which would be published within a year if everything went well. Amid all this, he read and edited Amelie's draft of the Ramasi glossary within a few days and presented it to her with his compliments upon joining the group for breakfast one morning.

'I have found some traces of influence from other dialects of Hindustani. It is a most remarkable document, testimony to the process by which a colloquial dialect, or perhaps proto-language, emerges within a group divided by geography but who have a common purpose,' he said.

'A common but murderous purpose,' said Wilson, who had gone over the investigation into the Phansigars and had been fascinated by the findings and the details of the trials. 'This glossary should go a long way towards understanding how they have emerged and spread, not to mention making it easier to detect and apprehend them. I cannot say if a language and belief system of such complexity exists among the criminal classes of London.'

'Perhaps it is because these are ordinary people who happen to engage in a specific kind of criminal activity, which has acquired layers of ritual and myth, in the way that any folk tradition does. They are not what one may call professional criminals, as you would find in a city like Calcutta or Bombay,' said Hodgson.

'The matter of rituals and myth is the most fascinating part of their lore. I wonder why they chose to strangle their victims instead of using a blade or some other implement, like other violent criminals. It is too specific a choice, and seems to go far back into their history,' said Wilson.

'If I may venture a view, for which I have no evidence

beyond common sense. If the stranglers have existed since the earliest days of the Mughal Empire, or perhaps predated it, they would have to travel along public roads where the only armed men who were permitted to pass were soldiers or city militia. A group of peasants with murder on their mind could only have access to their kerchiefs or anguchas, innocent garments to which nobody could object if they were stopped and searched,' said Prinsep, and they agreed that the simplest explanation, in this case, was the most appropriate and likely.

'Captain, with so many kinds of criminal activities of such organisations happening in the hinterland, I wonder how much technology could have made your work easier. If Dr Spilsbury could send samples of tissue or other parts of the victim of a poisoning to a specialist who could determine the kind of poison administered, it would make detection and apprehension of culprits more systematic. Not to mention a dedicated department for the examination of the bodies of victims and scenes of crime could be established. I have been informed that more than thirty universities in Great Britain are on the verge of introducing forensic studies as a specialised discipline for students of medicine and allied branches. We must have similar facilities here if we are to make advances in the field of criminal investigation. Technology should be an invaluable ally in this kind of work,' said Hodgson.

'Speaking of technology, I must tell you about this remarkable young man I met just before we left Calcutta. Brian does not have a high opinion of him,' said Wilson.

'If you refer to the young man I think you do, I should preface the story by saying I have good reasons to be indifferent to the likes of him,' said Brian.

'We seem to have mystified our hosts, so let me begin

from the beginning. The young man in question is a captain by the name of Cotton, now posted in Thiruchirapalli, who introduced himself to me at a social gathering in Calcutta and said he had been expecting to meet me. I was informed later that he has considerable experience as an engineer, and has built dams and other waterworks in Wales and southern India. Of his abilities I have no doubt. After expressing admiration for my work on the economy of Bengal, he said he was looking for an interested group of people to promote the idea of rail transport. He says he has identified places in southern India where such a network can be laid for the transportation of ore,' said Wilson.

'Considerable advances have been made in the construction of pillars and viaducts. We may see such rail networks over short distances,' said Spilsbury.

'Yes, but Captain Cotton appears to be one of those ambitious young men who like to force the hand of history. He said it would be possible to construct railway lines for the transport of raw material and people, and he intended to pursue it with vigour. I had to plead other engagements and leave, but I was intrigued by his sense of certainty about this. He says we may even see rail networks across India in our own lifetime,' said Wilson.

'What do you say, William? Do you see the possibility of a railway line passing through Jabalpur, carrying passengers and goods, perhaps from Bombay to Calcutta?' said Spilsbury.

Sleeman said the Western Ghats might present a problem in terms of construction.

'Captain Cotton does appear to be a man of vision, even though I am wary of his friendship with some Anglican pastors, and his religiosity. As for the railways, if it were to be built at the scale which India deserves, it would change the very nature of travel in the country,' said Hodgson. 'Consider your investigations, captain. If we began travelling by train instead of on horseback or by foot, what would happen to the Phansigars? The basis of their existence and rituals, it appears, is the slow pace of travel over the vastness of India, and the social segregation that travellers experience owing to their jati. The train, gentlemen, by throwing the multitudes of India together, would make the Phansigar extinct,' said Hodgson.

It sparked a fevered discussion about the nature of train travel.

'An immediate problem for an Indian traveller would be whether he is willing to suspend caste considerations, and concerns for ritual purity, if he were forced into proximity with strangers in this manner. What would he eat? What would he drink? I can imagine an orthodox Brahmin would be utterly petrified by the prospect of caste defilement if he were to step into a train compartment,' said Spilsbury.

'But Mr Hodgson, while Phansigars may disappear with the coming of trains, another class of deceivers will not,' said Sleeman. 'I am certain that Dhaturias will flourish, and for the very reasons you have mentioned. They will be delighted to find so many strangers crowded into such a small place, over long distances. If they can convince the victims to share their food, they will gather loot in such quantities as they never have in generations.'

Wilson said this demonstrated a form of social Lamarckism, with a species evolving to survive changed circumstances successfully. And from Lamarck they returned to a subject of abiding fascination for them: the boy from Seoni.

'This Second Lieutenant Moore who rescued the boy is the same young man who we met the other day, is he not?' said Hodgson.

'Yes, it was him. We may owe the child's life to Moore's

reluctance about opening fire on the pack of wolves,' said Sleeman.

'The young man seems to have suffered deep trauma of several kinds,' said Hodgson.

'He survived two battles in Burma, over several days in which thousands of our troops were killed. He suffered severe injuries and illness. But it is the damage to his spirit that worries me. I know that rescuing the child has made him feel he has been of some use to an innocent person, and perhaps that shall make some difference,' said Sleeman.

'Can you imagine how many such promising young men we have lost on misadventures lately? I will not be surprised if Government House finds some new kingdom or princeling to wage war against, now that Burma is not a threat,' said Wilson.

The feral child's case was discussed at considerable length by the guests with the Sleemans and Spilsbury. Hodgson was most interested, although he made no progress in communicating with the boy. He had heard of several cases of feral children in the terai, and at least one involving wolves, whose social structure could, he supposed, have helped the child adapt to life in the jungle.

'Perhaps only a few other species have a social nature similar to ours. Monkeys, for instance, or certain apes found in the depths of Africa. A human child left in the wild would not survive for long if he were to associate with a habitually solitary animal, or even a herd of deer, who might socialise but do not have a complex structure,' said Hodgson. He made numerous sketches of the boy, sometimes sleeping under the jamun tree or on one of its branches, or lapping up water from a wide-brimmed pot, or eating raw meat and sometimes fruit.

'Amelie, I would be grateful if I could follow the

progress of your communication with him. Apart from the humanitarian aspect of it—and I wish him good fortune on returning to the human fold, even if I would advise him against it—it is a significant opportunity for us to understand a few aspects of our own condition,' said Hodgson, and she promised to write to him and to Prinsep about it. To Prinsep as well she gave the assurance that she would write the conclusion of her studies of the folk music of Baghelkhand, and perhaps the Society would take it up for discussion. If the journal ever saw the light of day, her studies could yet be published in it.

'I wonder what he thinks of us. He must have a view, even if he can't articulate it to himself in any language we can recognise. I will not be surprised if he has not formed a favourable opinion so far,' said Wilson one evening, when Sleeman and he were walking past the feral child into the jungle.

He had been thoughtful and silent for a few days, more than he was in the habit of being. Sleeman had been wondering if it was because of the long journey he was about to undertake, and the many partings that lay before it. Sleeman wanted to know how Wilson felt about the prospect of leaving everything behind and returning to England. He mentioned the letter from Amelie's father, and his inability to imagine life elsewhere.

'You should not be surprised at the depth of your feelings, or your fear of leaving all this. James and I have had the good fortune to be involved with language, scripture and mythology. I can carry with me the words and ideas which have defined my life. But Brian needs the natural world of India, as you need its people. Exile, I am afraid, will be hard for you,' said Wilson, as they stopped to watch a small herd of spotted deer graze at a clearing.

'It must be difficult for you, nevertheless, to leave everything behind,' said Sleeman.

Wilson nodded and hesitated before replying, as if he was not certain about the true nature of his feelings even at this hour.

'Things are not what they used to be, captain. People, in fact, are not what they were. Or perhaps the malaise runs deeper. Perhaps it is a universal failing.'

Sleeman waited for him to continue.

'There comes a point in the life of an empire when the people who construct it, or perhaps administer it, cease to be self-conscious about either themselves or the imperial engine, if I may use the term. Finding themselves within such an engine, with so much power, they begin to believe that the historical processes, the numerous accidents, strokes of good fortune, campaigns won by the skin of the teeth or sound judgment, alliances and the inabilities of opponents, which led to the formation of the empire, do not matter. That their empire—note the "possessive"—was inevitable. Therefore there is talk of destiny, of some innate superiority, a sense of entitlement. Every empire passes through this stage of self-regard. I believe Gibbon writes at length of the generations when the Romans began to think thus. I have reason to believe that we have entered that period. There has always been a point beyond which the British and the Indians have not been able to accommodate one another. A dear friend has, I am told, met an Indian woman. She seems to be a remarkable and accomplished person, but has committed the discourtesy of not being born as a princess. Therefore, their domestic arrangement has been the subject of cruel tongues in Calcutta. Now my friend has told me that he cannot imagine the fate of their children, should they have any. They will not be allowed to belong in India, to a casteless father, and they will not be welcome in England, where the only brown people to receive respect are royalty. Where will they go? That, captain, must be the worst exile of all, to be cast out before one is born.'

So the gossips had been correct. There was a woman. But the friends of Brian Hodgson had been steadfast in their loyalty to him.

'Perhaps this has always been so. But I am filled with dismay about many other matters. We have come far from the time of Sir William Jones. Our fall has been precipitate. Every day it becomes more difficult for me to talk to the people in Government House, or find anyone beyond our small circle who is interested in the vastness and richness of India or in dealing with its contradictions. There seem to be just two kinds of British I have met lately—those who will hear no blame about India, and those who will hear no praise. Every day I find youngsters with dreams of discovering the mysterious and exotic Orient, or forcing it into the modern world, two kinds of condescension which I cannot tolerate any longer. There are none among them willing to make the efforts and sacrifices Brian and James have made to understand their disciplines. The scholars are lazy and the rulers, as they call themselves, are blind. I will not be surprised if they believe that the problem of the Phansigars is only about enforcing the law and handing out a few death sentences, and not about the society in which such problems emerge. And the less said about the political department, the better. I fear that they will remove one dynasty too many just because they can. I fear, captain, that the day is not far when we will have reached a point where even the most reasonable and reform-minded Indian will stop talking to us. Can you imagine, then, how the powerful orthodoxy among the Hindus and Muslims must feel? We, in England, arrived at our institutions and ideas on our own and made our own unique set of mistakes over the centuries. Is it fair to expect a land as complex as India to accept our ideas as part gift, part imperial imposition, without a murmur? Is it even possible for these entrenched powerful groups to march hand-in-hand with us into the future, or will they merely accept the simulacrum of modernity and not the substance? What if Captain Cotton's trains and Lord Bentinck's new regulations set off an insurrection aimed not so much at them as against the whole idea of modernity? Perhaps you think these are the words of a man trying to reconcile himself to his sense of loss at leaving India, and therefore being morbid. But I see signs of discontent among the people, and I hear subterranean murmurs, and I am afraid.'

Sleeman thought of the cautionary words from the Nawab Begum of Bhopal, about the qazis in the kingdom. It seemed Wilson too had glimpsed, or thought he had, a disturbing possibility in the future. The truth was they were living in times which were unprecedented in the history of humankind, and certainly in the history of India. Not even a scholar like Wilson, who understood historical tidal patterns that lasted for generations, could predict the outcome.

'And therefore, captain, I envy the child you have found. He is not burdened by the failings of the past, dismayed by the present or stricken by fear of the future,' said Wilson, before they returned home to rejoin the others.

They wished they could stay longer, for such a time would not come to pass again, but the interlude at Jabalpur came to an end at last. Wilson promised Sleeman to make a thorough study of the sculptures at Ellora and confirm whether Phansigars were indeed represented on the temple walls. Prinsep took his leave, but not before completing his commentaries on the Sanskrit of the Vishnu Purana. The air and water had agreed with him, and he had made considerable progress on several subjects, about which he promised to inform everyone in due course. He went by road to Sagar and then onwards to Allahabad. A day or two later, Hodgson and Wilson started out for Indore.

The days seemed a little less bright after they left, although Sleeman, Amelie and Spilsbury tried to keep up the conversations they had started in the presence of the guests. But Sleeman was still weak from his illness, and the surgeon agreed with Amelie that they should not delay the journey to Simla.

'I understand you will not listen to any advice I give you, but please consider not taking up work which will tax your physical condition. To rest and let the world run its course is not a crime,' said Spilsbury, and Sleeman promised to be idle if people allowed him to be.

And thus, there came about a day when Sleeman and Amelie set out from Jabalpur for the long journey to the north. Reynolds and his family would follow afterwards. The household servants accompanied them, as did the boy from Seoni. Amelie had concerns about how he would weather the winter in the hills, but could not imagine leaving him behind. She hoped the interlude would be a new beginning for all of them.

But interludes are hard to come by when orders await along the road, and the lower Himalayas were a long journey away. Two days after Sagar they were met by a dak rider sent from the magistrate's court in that town, informing Sleeman about the capture of a gang of experienced stranglers. Faced with enough evidence and eyewitness accounts to hang them several times over, the stranglers and their assistants, and even the inveiglers and gravediggers were clamouring to be made approvers, and to reveal several other scenes of murders which were yet unknown. Would the captain like to be present for questioning them?

He would have liked to be, and therefore the caravan turned back to Sagar. Amelie wished they had not been waylaid in this manner, and suspected that Sleeman welcomed the extension of his stay in the plains, even though he would not betray his relief at this thought.

If he had hoped for substantial information or revelations from the arrested men, he was disappointed. The evidence against them, gathered and sent by magistrates from three neighbouring districts, was thorough, precise and damning, and none of them held out or bothered to deny their guilt. Amelie's presence was not needed at the jail, because there was no new word in Ramasi or belief that the men had to offer. As approvers, all they had were the names of a few men in far-flung places, including a high-ranking Phansigar in Allahabad about whom Sleeman had already informed McLeod.

All that remained were the graves. Some of the bhartotes in the group had been on expedition for years, and the number of murders and burials they had participated in or witnessed was large. They named all the places and an approximation of the year and day to the clerks at Sagar, and messengers were sent to the districts where some of the graves lay.

And some of them lay north of Sagar, along the winding road that fell to the lowland villages on the road to Orchha and then to Jhansi. The villages along this stretch were separated by considerable distances where the countryside was densely forested, and here the Phansigars had been disposing of their victims at several sites for years.

So it turned out that the Sleeman household resumed its journey north, but not in the manner in which it had intended to. Early on a morning soon after the interrogations, the residents of Sagar witnessed a spectacle that the people of central India were beginning to get accustomed to, but which had additional and unexpected characters participating in it. At the head went Sleeman, his ever-shifting posture forced by backache a secret between his horse and himself, followed by Amelie on a palanquin. The boy from Seoni came after, sitting disconsolate in a wooden palanquin-cage covered with clothes so that he would not be frightened by the crowds. The household staff followed, the men on ponies and looking more comfortable for the duration of the journey than Sleeman.

Behind the civilians came the jamadars and sowars, with the prisoners tied by long ropes to the saddles, and infantrymen behind them. And at the rear came a growing crowd of people the Phansigars had broken over the years.

They walked over the fields to the Orchha road on hearing the news. They came with little hope but with the inertia that lies on the other shore of despair. They came with no reason to believe they would discover the fate of their loved ones, or find enough of the remains for their last rites, but they came nevertheless. They walked under the morning sun, mile after mile, without water or food, waiting for the stranglers to point out the graves.

Here, said the arrested men, they had once come upon a large group of sarafs from Jhansi with purses full of gold from a nobleman's wedding. The sarafs had sentries and servants, but the Phansigars knew of them, and sacrificed them on this meadow, during the night. By that stream they killed a zamindar and his staff, on the way north with taxes from the harvest. Over there lay some guests going to a wedding with fine silk as presents.

'They spoke to us only because they thought we were Agarwal like them. We do not remember whose wedding it was, sahib. This was many years ago. And here we buried fifteen messengers of moneylenders from Ujjain travelling to Agra, with small bundles of silver coins. They said they were poor Brahmins on pilgrimage, and so did we, but neither of us were, and we took everything from them,' said the Phansigars.

On and on it went, through the day into the evening, four different sites beyond the trees, the bodies long decomposed to bones which were now exhumed and strewn along the lip of the pits.

There is no such thing as the dignity of corpses. The extinction of life is the final indignity suffered by the human form. The inanimate limbs are forced to place themselves, through gravity or chance, in poses that the animate never attain. A body at a funeral, with the limbs arranged according to ritual or custom, has only the ersatz dignity of a puppet. But even this does not compare with the indignity of exhumed bones after a few years in dry soil.

Thus they lay, piled where the diggers had thrown them, bleached clear of flesh, with no sign of who their owners were, or how life had fled, for the tongue bone is among the first in the upper body to decay.

Amelie would not stay away, and she would not look away, for this too needed to be witnessed and understood. Thus, those who followed in the wake of the prisoners saw what others like them had not, but of which they talked afterwards: the young memsahib who walked among the corpses, and did not flinch.

But only the curious among the watchers saw this. The others, the survivors and the broken ones also walked among the pits and tried to find a trace of the missing, from the few possessions and clothes still identifiable in the graves.

It became dusk, and Sleeman had to pitch camp in a meadow in the middle of an exhumation. The next village was too far away and they had no wish to travel back and forth with the bones dug up already.

Amelie arranged for food for the villagers still searching through the bones. There were some among them, she had found, who were willing to claim a body on the most tenuous of evidence, for the sake of closure after years. But even they had not found anything. She made sure that they were fed, at least, before she retired to her tent for the night and wept. Not for the victims, but for the mothers who had followed her through the day.

By the afternoon of the following day, all the graves by the road had been exhumed, and the prisoners were taken back to Sagar, to be sent to whichever province claimed them. Sleeman at last said he was ready to continue north, and by the evening they had arrived in Orchha.

They had no wish to halt in Jhansi, and a friend of Amelie's from Calcutta was married to an officer who represented the political department in Orchha. Amelie and Sleeman had visited them before, and wished to explore the architecture of the town further before leaving for Simla. They were hosted by her friend, who had been making elaborate preparations in anticipation of the visit, which embarrassed Amelie and reminded her of the formality of life in Calcutta. It was a quiet, undemanding posting amid beautiful environs, and her friend received her with joy.

Sleeman and Amelie walked around Orchha and saw all the beautiful fortresses, temples and small palaces including one which, they were told, was built for an emperor who had stayed in Orchha for a single night. Such were the histories on which fables of the wealth of the East were built.

They were joined by Reynolds and his family, who were welcomed by Amelie's friend with the same warmth that she had been given. The weather was mild, and Sleeman was beginning to recover his strength, although he had to walk with care and rest after covering short distances. He promised Amelie that he would not tax himself on the way to and at Simla. He also promised he would not brood much on the prospect of being questioned by Government House representatives sometime after they returned to the plains. He would cross that bridge when he came to it, and would accept the outcome and see where his future lay.

Their hosts plied them with excellent food and arranged for local musicians to visit and perform at their haveli, where local notables would also be pleasant. Amelie was effusive in her gratitude to the friend for this, and Sleeman too had to admit that, even for his untrained ears, the songs of Orchha were as attractive as he had remembered them to be.

Thus, the days were long and spent in exploration, and the evenings in the company of gentle people and beautiful music. The perils of the world were far away, or seemed to be so, and on one such evening, sated, tired and drowsy, Sleeman excused himself from the other guests and walked through the lantern-lit passages, up the wide stairs to where his room lay, with the doors and windows open to a terrace and the breeze from the surrounding jungle. The lanterns cast flickering shadows, and the curtains cast yet more, but the passages were lit and bright, and a curtain moved and one of the servants of the house stepped forward, bent and balanced on his toes, a hand extended in what appeared to be supplication, but there was a bichhawa at the end of it.

The man who was many men sat in a room in his house. It could have been the most comfortable, or the best lit by the sun, thus his preference for it over all the others in the haveli. But it could just be a room where he preferred to sit alone, a choice uninfluenced by architectural considerations. He had neither built nor chosen this house, and had never thought about whether he liked it or not.

The British officer was dead, or about to be. The bladesman had inflicted severe injuries on him, but had in turn been wounded fatally by others who had rushed to the scene. There was as yet no further news, but he was willing to wait. He was a patient man. That, like the house, he had inherited from a long line of similar men.

With Sleeman gone, or incapacitated, the arrest of Phansigars would not stop, but would cease to remain the concerted campaign it had become. There was nobody else who had connected the dots with such clarity, nobody among the many administrators, magistrates, officers and Company officials who had at one time or the other pursued the stranglers and others like them. So a few incautious deceivers, some stranglers, poisoners and such would continue to be caught and tried, jailed or hanged. But the world, with all its rituals, beliefs and necessary deaths, would continue.

He wondered if his fellow subedars, who valued tradition and superstition so much whether they believed it in their hearts or not, knew or understood the real meaning of the British, of the changes which were going to happen to the land, to the way people lived. Perhaps they did not. They were harmless in their petty illusions and everyday piety, not different from the masses among which they swam and on who they preyed. But the subedars, like the masses, had no capacity for understanding the abstract beyond a point. Only people like him did.

The shadows lengthened across the floor. There was a faint noise in the distance, the whisper of commotion. It was not the far cacophony of a brawl on the street, or a hawker with his wares in the market. It grew until he could distinguish the cries of several men, either in rage or panic, and the sound of hooves. It came closer, and then the tumult was inside the house, separating into individual shouts and gruff orders.

The man who was many men sighed. It was a little late to get up and rush to do or attempt anything. Besides, someone in his position had his dignity to consider.

His men did not appear, to inform him of what had been happening or to answer his questions, if he had any. The shadows lengthened. The house grew quiet. And then the doors were thrown back and a dusty man in officer's uniform came in. This, thought the owner of the house, must be Reynolds, with a dragon in one hand, a sabre in the other and a Baker rifle on the back. The sword did not appear to be bloodied, which was a good sign. There was no reason for the servants of the man to be killed in a fruitless defence.

Reynolds glanced around the room to see if there were men hiding somewhere, but it was almost bare of furniture and too bright still to hide any secrets. If the lieutenant was dismayed at being denied violence, he did not show it. Nor did he glance at the man sitting on the floor, who had not moved at all. The officer walked to the window nearest the door and looked out into the courtyard. The owner of the house declined the temptation to stand up and see the happenings outside. He would come to know in due course.

A second man entered the room, but did not look around, instead focusing on the man who was many men. He was steady on his feet, even though he looked weak and fatigued.

'So, I was wrong to believe that your injuries were grievous,' said the owner of the house, without preamble.

'Only by the merest chance, and even then I was not certain till my host and Reynolds here came up. The man you sent was good with the blade, just unlucky that he could not get me,' said Sleeman, sitting on the floor some distance away. His riding boots made it difficult for him to sit cross-legged for any length of time.

Across him, seated on a dhurri and leaning against the wall, was the man he had stalked for so long, the subject of so much legend and speculation. He was indeed as beautiful and regal as the stories said, if younger than the captain had been led to believe. Or perhaps he looked younger in the way that some men do. Sleeman wondered how broken-down and obsolete he appeared to the man he had captured.

'And the bladesman is no longer alive?'

Sleeman shook his head.

'He did not survive his injuries from the fight. We needed time, therefore the false news of my wounds. But we moved as quickly as possible, under the circumstances. I am sure you would agree,' said the captain.

'He was not my man. I did not send him. I don't think I ever met him in my life,' said the man.

'I am aware of it. But for all that, as long as you are the subedar of Phansigars in Gwalior and Bhopal, he would be your man. And you should have sent more.'

There was the silence of unasked questions in the room. Outside, the courtyard was filled with voices of soldiers giving orders to captured men.

'We did not know who had sent the assassin, only that he was a servant of our host, and had been so for years. That presented a puzzle. He had never met me, we were told, nor would he have any enmity against me, unless it was because I was a British man, in which case, why not attack his employer? But then my host told me that he had come from Sagar, and his ancestral village was not far from that town, and that he had worked at the haveli of a wealthy seth there. Who was this seth? When I heard his name was Hari Singh, I knew I had found the answer.'

'But how could you know? Hari Singh is one of the most reputed merchants of Sagar.'

'Yes, he certainly is. What you may not know is Amanullah, an Agariya who was captured a long time ago, used to sell horses to Hari Singh, who in turn sold them to Brigadier General O'Halloran's cavalry. So when a blameless wealthy merchant, known to be in business with a veteran strangler also happens to be the former employer of a man who tries to kill me, one has to question whether he is blameless after all, does one not?'

The man who was many men closed his eyes. This he could not have anticipated. A strangler could, of course, have a legitimate business, and know diverse people in the course of it. Amanullah's lawful trade had now caused the subedar's downfall, and Hari Singh had been the unknowable weak link in the chain.

'But still we did not know who the mastermind behind the assassin and the intermediary was. Hari Singh we ruled out. You know him better than we do. He does not strike anyone as a criminal mastermind. But, if such a powerful and prominent crooked merchant did not know who the mysterious subedar of Phansigars was, the mythic man who is many men, then who did? So Reynolds rode through the night to Sagar, and between the general and him managed to put the fear of numerous deities into the merchant, who told us where you could be found. People like Hari Singh should not have been trusted. I understand that he is an initiate into your customs, but not a Phansigar himself. He knew too much, but lacked the personal courage to keep those secrets.'

The subedar of stranglers nodded but did not look at Sleeman. The shadows were lengthening and the room was becoming darker.

'But why plot my murder in the house of a British man? What would that have accomplished?'

Apart from stopping the focussed nature of the investigations, and slowing down the capture of stranglers, the murder would also have fed myths and rumours across the countryside. Now Englishmen killed each other, the people would say. The great new rulers of India were just as petty and vile as all the princelings and rajas, and for even less gain.

'I know how much you know of me, for I too have been asking about you as you have enquired after me. You know what happened on the night I was born, in a forest. My family lost everything when your army attacked our village. Do you think I would hesitate before ordering the death of a single British man of no significance outside his minor office in Jabalpur?'

A brief smile flickered across Sleeman's face. He was almost apologetic at having to explain this.

'Yes, about that. You see, I have written to the officer in charge of the archives of the Bengal Army, and over this time I have corresponded with every single surviving officer who led soldiers at the court of the Scindia from the beginning of this century. No unit is known to have attacked a village within the Scindia's dominions, leave alone for the nonpayment of customs dues, a petty infraction for which even Ujjain's watchmen or militia would not bother to expend force of arms. No British officer has ever sent infantry and cavalry to decimate a village over such a trifle. Whatever the circumstances of your birth, the story of that invasion and destruction is not true.'

The man who was many men, and none of them, smiled, conceding that the Englishman was thorough.

'Do you mean to tell me that your armies have never ravaged the countryside, or attacked the innocent?'

'I did not say that. Their sins are vast and well-chronicled, and I shall not attempt to defend them, for they are indefensible. But this story is not true, and not because officers are inclined to be merciful. It is not true because the cost of such an expedition would not justify any possible benefits from it.'

'Then why does this legend exist?'

'I have thought about it, and I would like you to tell me now if I am correct in supposing this. I believe it does not matter to those who hear this story whether it really happened or not. That is not how stories are remembered and understood in India. Did this event really happen? Did that person really exist? Some call you the son of a family destroyed by British and Maratha greed. Others call you an orphan found with great good omens by a learned Brahmin, and brought up as recipient of vast stores of knowledge and wealth. I think it does not matter who you really are. What matters is which stories are believed by the people. And today the people want to hear stories of British greed, of a great subedar of Phansigars born on the night the Bengal Army destroyed his desh by gunpowder and sword. And so the people think, it must not be beyond the British to have done what the story says they did. It is the myth that is real. That has always been so.'

The subedar grimaced as if the admission that Sleeman was right caused him pain. But the captain was right in his understanding of how stories worked in India, and that angered the man.

'Should I commend your insight into the minds of Indians? Is this wisdom the result of your friendship with the learned Englishmen of Calcutta? Is it not enough that you rule and rob us, that you and your children to come will explain us to ourselves? Your friends write learned volumes explaining how India is being robbed of her wealth. Do you not see the cruelty in this? Do not imagine for a moment that I am like one of the Indians of Calcutta who try to emulate you in everything. You do not exalt us by telling us who we are. I know who I am, and from whom I am descended. This is my home, my land, not yours. You are only a visitor, and one day you will all return. The day is not far. You want to rule, but will not let your subjects be. You have to mould them into your image whether they want it or not. And you are surprised when they are not grateful to you for this. We will take back what is ours.'

'Who is this we?' said Sleeman. 'Who do you claim to represent? The higher varnas, perhaps, because who else owns this land? The zamindars, because of who your family is? Or do you speak for the nawabs and princelings, or Muslim nobility? Do you speak as a subedar of Phansigars or a patriot, for I have not seen much love of the people among your kind. If there was, you would not have been responsible for the murder of thousands, and the ruin of many more. The wealth of your family, the tenants who live on your land, were inherited by you, but do you know how they live? Do they matter to you? A question has bothered me for a long time. When your aulae return home after masquerading as members of any caste or faith that they like, do they begin to understand how others live, and do they change their habits as well? I am told you appear as different men in various places. Have you been changed as well when you return here?'

The subedar looked at Sleeman. His voice was distant, puzzled. 'Why should they change? Why should I? We only wear the clothes or eat the food of other jatis when we are on expedition, because it is an obligation for an aulae. It is necessary for the act of deception. How can we become like others when we return to our homes? Must you be so naïve?'

'It is not I who is naïve. You speak of reclaiming the land from the hated outsider, but do not want to mingle with other castes unless it is for your accursed expeditions. You pose as a victim of the British, calling them casteless rulers who want to impose change although they do not belong here, but you will not embrace your own people and call them your equal. The condition of women in your family is such a terrible omen that it contaminates your expedition, but you will pray to your Goddess. Now you are being churlish because you failed to have me killed, and because I did not believe in the lies and fantasies which you have built around your life and your past. At the end, you are the leader of a band of killers, and you have inveigled poor, powerless villagers to commit untold murders because that is easier than helping them find a way out of poverty. The true deception is what your lore has done to these people. All the myth in India cannot gild that crime.'

'So what would you have liked me to do? Become a friend of the British, like the petty princes who are so admired by Government House, and participate in taxing everyone to death? Or enter the opium trade, like the Rajmata of Ujjain, but on your side? Perhaps then you would host a banquet in my honour rather than hang me.'

'How is either choice, inadequate though it may be, worse than causing the murder of men, women and children by the thousands for a few coins and trinkets, or participating in such murders yourself? At least a Maharaja or a Nawab takes responsibility for his failures, though he will not leave the throne. You hide behind your lore, such that the people you champion do not even know your real name. All you offer them is myth in return for their complicity in murder.'

The man was silent. Now his face was in the shadows as the room became darker. Reynolds shifted on his feet and turned away from the window, but did not speak. This was not his hour.

'And what about you, captain? Do you find fulfillment by telling yourself that you are the saviour of the poor helpless Indians in a way that Government House or these incompetent princelings are not? Do you believe that you are what the law aspires to be? Does that complete you, just as you find completion by adopting children rescued from the forest because you can't be a father yourself? Spare me the piety, captain. Tell me the speech you have prepared for me.'

'Do not speak about the child. You have the blood of children on your hands, even if you did not strangle them yourself. We have evidence and eyewitness accounts about you, and your presence and role in several killings. These will stand the scrutiny of any court. But you can become an approver for the government and help us in our investigations, as Amanullah and others like him have. Tell us everything you know about your fellow subedars and where to find them, and of every single Phansigar you know, and you may yet be spared the noose. You may yet spend the rest of your life in exile or in prison.'

'I will not betray the other subedars. That I will not do, even if your men attempt to beat it out of me. You will have to find them yourself. I will tell you about anyone else that I may know of, and tell you what I have witnessed, if you ask the right questions. I may even tell you about the merchants who have profited from us.'

Sleeman acknowledged the impasse for the moment. He would work on it afterwards. But this was a beginning.

'Then tell me what you may have heard about a group of men from the Scindia's court who were travelling from Poona to Ujjain with some precious gifts, and vanished. That was the beginning of all this.'

'When was it?'

Sleeman told him.

'I do not know of this. There have been so many such Maratha processions and groups. There was once a princess from the Peshwa's house. I do not know if you have heard the story of what happened to her.'

'I have heard the story. We captured the leader of the expedition which killed her bodyguards and her. In this case, there was a fine horse among the missing gifts.'

'A horse. I seem to remember being present on one such occasion. There was, if I recall well, a Mughal nobleman. There was a horse, too.'

'Where are the bodies? Where did you kill them? What happened to the gifts?'

'I believe the valuables were distributed among the aulae who were on the expedition. I think I rode the horse for a while and gave it away. I do not remember to who. It seems like such a long time ago. I have never understood how some memories last and others do not.'

He seemed to be quite amused by this.

'Tell me about the lore, then. I am told your memory of it is not treacherous.'

'What of the lore? I am told, in turn, that you have

compiled words in Ramasi, and some of our more colourful superstitions, with which you frighten our poor bhartotes and sothas, causing them to confess all the crimes they have seen or participated in.'

'Where are the seven original clans of Phansigars? The ones who came out of Delhi centuries ago and spread around the countryside.'

The man laughed. Even his laughter was polished.

'They are gone.'

'Where?'

'They went to the Deccan generations ago, and we know about them no more. They may or may not exist now. There are some clans who claim descent from them.'

If Sleeman was disappointed on hearing this, his voice did not betray it. Now his face too was in the shadows and it was impossible to read the expression on it.

'We will take you back to Jabalpur jail. Along the way, you will point out all the places where the bodies are buried. We know of some already.'

Sepoys entered the room. The man stood up and held his hands out for the expected manacles, which Reynolds placed on his wrists. Shackles were placed on his legs, and connected to the manacles by iron rods. The man shuffled forward and the iron clanked. This was how he would be paraded through the countryside. This was part of the new lore that was being forged. He understood that. He knew how myths worked.

He shuffled forward, out of the room, followed by Reynolds and Sleeman. The last light of the day went out, but the house was empty of people and there was nobody to light the lamps.

There had been one of those periodic upheavals in Government House. Its burrows had sent forth a vulture and a homunculus to sit with a judge in the inquiry. It was not called thus by anybody. Secretary Macnaghten had a few questions, and the judge had a few more, and it was just a part of the process to ensure that the provinces were being administered in the correct spirit, they said.

Therefore they convened at the office of the magistrate of Allahabad. McLeod had vacated it for the three luminaries, and had been given to understand that his role in the matter was limited to the trials over which he had presided, and about which they had only a few minor questions.

Sleeman had been waiting in Allahabad for a week before the judge arrived, on his way from Varanasi to Delhi, for he had combined several official duties into this journey. Sleeman had recovered from his illness after his time in Simla, and hoped he would not have to endure another extended period of seclusion there, although he now understood why a person like Reynolds would grow fond of the place. Amelie had been thankful for the effect of the hiatus on his health, but had confided in him that she was not constructed to live among the ladies of the new town. So they had at last descended to lower Punjab and then through Delhi and Agra by ferry to Allahabad to await the final word from Government House. Although it was understood by everyone that finality was not in the nature of how the administrators of Macnaghten functioned. Therefore, an interim final word.

Sleeman presented himself in front of the three men at the appointed hour and was introduced to each in turn. He wondered which of them would declare that he had known Amelie's father in Vienna. Perhaps the homunculus, whose taxonomy was difficult to determine. The vulture, on the other hand, was a gyps of the accountant genus. It was said that he understood more about the financial circumstances of the princes than they had ever done. But it was the judge who was to be the fulcrum of the three. Edward Ryan knew as much about the sciences as about criminal law, and just as much about rural India, or so it was said. It was inevitable that he would soon be the chief justice of Bengal. He was a man of destiny, and yet younger than Sleeman.

He wished Sleeman a pleasant morning, and asked after his health. Sleeman said he had recovered, and was waiting to return to Jabalpur. The judge, the vulture and the homunculus, in that order, murmured their happiness at this news and settled into poses of appropriate dignity.

'We are assembled here on the request of Secretary Macnaghten to review the reports which you have sent with such admirable regularity to his office. I must confess that while we have also received reports of trials by other magistrates, I have not examined them all in detail, choosing to focus on your account. I would like to begin by asking you to explain for our benefit what a Phansigar is. If I am correct in my understanding, while this problem had been detected by other administrators in the past, your inquiries and results have been the most extensive,' said the judge.

'Thank you for the opportunity to clarify this, my lord. A Phansigar is any of a class of criminal who strangles his victim. This category also includes those who help subdue the victim, and others who deceive him, or help bury the bodies,' said Sleeman.

'And we are given to understand that deception is the key to their peculiar method of waylaying victims?'

'Yes, my lord. As I have mentioned in my reports, Phansigars are among three kinds of criminals who inveigle and deceive their victims. There are also Dhaturias, or poisoners, and kidnappers of children, which go by different names across the provinces. We may refer to all three of them as Thugs, from the Hindustani word for "deceiver", although they are different from one another. Indeed, one may look down on the other.'

'You have drawn a distinction between Phansigars and Thugs, captain, in your reports. Is such a distinction necessary? I have been told that the term "Thug", being easier to pronounce, has already taken hold in the popular imagination, in particular among a certain kind of people in Calcutta and London who revel in what they consider the macabre and the exotic,' said the homunculus, peering at the papers in front of him. His dismay at the tastes of the people gave the impression that his apparent bloodlessness made him immune to such attractions.

'The distinction is necessary if we are to formulate laws specific to such crimes, sir. Of these three kinds of deceivers, the Phansigars are the most deadly and have the most sophisticated hierarchy.'

'Yes, and it is about this hierarchy that I wish to ask you. What do we know about these stranglers? From where do they come?' said the judge.

'My lord, according to their traditions, there were seven original clans of dacoits who used to strangle their victims. They used to live in or near Delhi in the reign of one of the Sultans.'

The vulture raised an eyebrow and exclaimed that this must have been not less than three centuries earlier.

'Yes, sir, it appears to be so, although we do not know if they were descended from yet older bands of highwaymen. During the reign of this Sultan, the stranglers were driven out of the city and reached Agra, from whence they dispersed in different directions over time.'

'And what has become of these seven clans?' asked the vulture.

'We may never know, sir. They, or their original iterations, have passed out of history. I have made extensive inquiries, but only some clans which claim descent from them remain.'

'And am I correct in understanding that these seven original clans were Muslim in faith?' asked the judge.

'Yes, my lord. They were.'

'Therefore, will we be correct in concluding that the problem of Phansigars is, shall we say, a problem of the Muslims?'

Sleeman suppressed a sigh. His throat was already in the process of drying. He was beginning to realise that the explanations might be longer than he had assumed. There was no reason for this, because the three men were said to be wise beyond measure. Perhaps they wanted him to state the obvious, for the sake of the record and their bureaucratic conscience.

'My lord, while a large number of stranglers who we have captured are Muslims, all of them are not.'

'But I also observe, captain, that these gangs practice macabre rituals invoking Hindu goddesses, or is it a single Goddess? Can we then call this a problem of the Hindus?' asked the vulture, who seemed to be unhappy at this thought.

'Sir, we have captured stranglers from all castes, and those outside the caste hierarchy, in addition to Muslims of various biradaris and descent. The problem cannot be held to be specific to a particular faith or community.'

'And yet these rituals, the idea of sacrifice, invocations to the Goddess, which you have mentioned at several places in your reports. Does this not indicate at these men being part of a murderous Hindu cult?' asked the homunculus.

'Sir, no aspect of life in our rural parts is free of religious practice, symbols, myths and ritual. The presence of these alone does not make the stranglers a religious cult. The rituals they follow are meant to appease the Goddess, in the hope of finding what they believe are appropriate sacrifices.'

'You mention caste, captain. I have read your previous reports and I understand you have a specific interest in the castes of India. Can we say that Phansigars may be identified with a specific caste or set of castes?' asked the judge.

'My lord, I have not made a statistical survey of it, but from my understanding of the number of people we have caught and tried, the proportion of arrested men by caste and faith conforms to the proportion of these faiths in the larger societies of the provinces.'

'That is an interesting observation, captain. And yet you do not have sufficient statistical information about the provinces to confirm this with precision?' asked the vulture.

'No, sir, we do not, but we have estimated these numbers.'

'Captain, in your reports I have found repeated references to these gangs and their relation to the caste structure, notably their ability to mimic caste markers of their victims. Must you find caste everywhere?' asked the vulture.

'Sir, no society or group of people here is free of caste, and therefore these observations needed to be made. The manner in which these groups have understood, and in some cases subverted, caste structures is, I believe, instructive. Owing to the segregation imposed by caste structures, a traveller can be robbed and murdered without a neighbouring village or settlement ever coming to know of the crime. The Phansigars use this knowledge, and also pretend to be from the caste of the victims in order to lure them to their doom.'

'I should like to know more about the problems you faced in gathering information about the people of the provinces, Captain,' said the judge.

'My lord, I have mentioned the problem of incorrect information about communities in my report. No administrator or prince, to my knowledge, has accurate knowledge about the people they govern. We should begin the process of census enumeration of all people, regardless of whether they live in areas directly administered by us or by the princes. In the absence of that, any policy for their economic or social benefit, or for advancing the rule of law, will not work to the extent we desire.'

'As you must be aware, captain, that is a subject close to our hearts as well. Given the size and complexity of India, census enumeration might not happen soon, but we can hope that Government House will begin attempts in this direction in a more limited manner in Bengal. I believe Dr Wilson, with who you are acquainted, made some suggestions about this to Lord Bentinck before his departure for England,' said the judge.

The vulture, who was tenacious, cleared his throat. 'To return to my question, captain. Is it your conclusion that the stranglers are drawn from all classes and faiths?'

'Yes, sir. At some point after leaving Agra, the original seven clans met Hindu dacoits. The fear of being searched for weapons by watchmen or soldiers made them take recourse to strangling people with various innocent items of clothing on them. A strangled victim leaves no telltale signs, like blood, on his killer; moreover, his clothes and other effects are also not damaged or marked in the process of the murder, and can be taken as loot. Around this core a myth and set of lore evolved, as well as cryptic terms known only among the stranglers. The two most remarkable aspects of this are, first, the extensive nature of this lore and language, and second, the manner in which the stranglers live among more law-abiding people.'

'I have read your notes on this cryptic language with great interest, captain. Please convey my regards to Lady Amelie, who I am told assisted you in this enterprise,' said the judge.

'And mine as well. I hope to meet her before you depart from Allahabad. I knew the count in Vienna many decades ago,' said the homunculus. This earned him a sharp look from the judge, which he ignored.

'You mentioned how the stranglers live among law-abiding people, captain,' said the judge.

'The stranglers that we have captured are not professional criminals, my lord. They are farmers, herdsmen or involved in other rural trades. They happen to go on expeditions in groups within which caste and faith is temporarily suspended. They are known to their neighbours, and are even protected by their zamindars or local officials, some of whom take bribes for this protection. The stranglers are not isolated from local societies but are integrated with them. This is true for poisoners as well.'

'Speaking of expeditions, I find it remarkable, captain, that they do not appear to target British travellers,' said the vulture.

'That is true, sir. We have as yet found no instance of the Phansigars, or even the Dhaturias, robbing or murdering a British traveller. We have heard of a single instance, and are trying to verify it.'

'That is most interesting. Is it possible that the Phansigars do not consider a British traveller a suitable sacrifice?' said the homunculus.

'This is unlikely, sir. Apart from the sonoka or the

first sacrifice during an expedition, the Phansigars do not discriminate regarding the caste, gender, age or other attributes of their victims. There is no reason to believe they would not strangle a British traveller were he to fall in among them.'

'Then perhaps they do not want to call the attention of the authorities by murdering a British man. Surely they are intimidated by the might of the government,' said the vulture.

'Sir, I do not think they are intimidated by the government. Unlike an erring prince or zamindar, they are difficult to trace and apprehend, and can therefore defy the authorities, if they choose, with some degree of impunity. From our investigations, I have concluded that they do not choose British travellers as their victims because we are not in the habit of carrying valuables on our journeys. The trouble of deceiving and murdering a British man is usually not worth the wealth that may be gained from him.'

There was a brief silence at this statement.

'Captain, are you suggesting that a British traveller is unworthy or not rich enough to be robbed? You present a rather unedifying picture of how we are seen by the people,' said the homunculus. Sleeman did not know how to reply to this, and kept quiet.

The judge cleared his throat. 'A word or two about your methods in the course of this investigation, captain. We have been told that you arrested a large number of villagers on suspicion of being involved in such activities. Should all people not be considered innocent until proven guilty?' he asked.

'Yes, sir, they should. We had to keep some people in jail for questioning till we had evidence about their guilt or innocence. We were not presuming their guilt in any manner. I believe that while this principle is important, it is also necessary to question all suspects in a criminal case to establish their guilt or innocence, and they should agree to put up with the temporary discomfort in the interests of the law.'

'Be that as it may, captain, your suspects will only agree to this if they are fully aware of the law, which in most cases people in rural India are not. Some might call this approach oppressive, although I shall not censure you for it.'

Sleeman expressed his thanks to the judge.

'You have also written to magistrates and agents about captured stranglers in their respective provinces, or have provided evidence.'

'Yes, my lord. We have based our cases against Phansigars on three grounds. The discovery of mortal remains, the eyewitness testimonies of stranglers and next of kin of the victims, and confessions of stranglers. They agreed to become approvers for the government in exchange for a mitigated sentence, which has helped us uncover more such crimes. We have chosen only those cases where the remains of the victim have been located, the murder has been identified by approximate date, and the murderer by name. This means any figure we can provide you for the extent of these crimes will be a fraction of the real number.'

'Please explain that, captain,' said the vulture.

'Sir, a Phansigar such as a bhartote, who actually does the strangling, might go out on dozens of expeditions in the course of his lifetime, rising from novice to expert. On an average expedition lasting months, he might take part in ten or twelve different sets of killings, each of which might have ten or twelve victims. In the course of his life, he will have directly participated in or witnessed the murder of thousands of victims. To bring any such person to trial, we have chosen only those cases where the bodies of the victims have been matched with eyewitness testimony, supplemented by the accused person's confession. The chances of us acquiring all three are small.'

'Captain, you are saying that although the number of victims mentioned in the trials is large, the true number is much larger than all the reports have stated?' asked the vulture.

'Yes, sir. The true number may never be known.'

Over the three august gentlemen there settled a momentary silence as they contemplated the magnitude of the matter.

'In your opinion, captain, how did this malaise become so widespread? If it is neither a Muslim nor a Hindu problem, how did matters come to this pass?' asked the judge.

'My lord, as you have heard, stranglers have existed on Indian roads for at least three hundred years and more. As the Mughal Empire disintegrated and lawlessness spread, common villagers had to fend for themselves. Crops were failing, bandits had been unleashed over the land. In the province where I have been posted, it has not been a decade and half since this anarchy receded. Becoming a strangler was for some the only means of survival.'

'I see. Is it possible that the same political circumstances which led to our involvement in the Deccan Wars also created the Phansigars?' asked the judge.

'It was a difficult period, my lord,' said Sleeman, and hesitated.

'Please, continue.'

'There is, however, another matter related to this. Of the victims we have identified either by name or trade, an unnaturally large number were messengers carrying consignments of money for sarafs or lenders involved in the opium trade. We have reason to believe that the proliferation of the opium monopoly created a huge amount of money in transit, which became the target of Phansigars. This led to their growth in numbers.'

'Good lord, Sleeman, are you implying that we have created the stranglers? Your antipathy to the opium trade is well known, as is your support for abolition of slavery, but you go too far. You are impugning the memory of Lord Wellesley,' exclaimed the vulture. The judge responded with another look. The vulture, not being as stern as the homunculus, subsided under the gaze.

'It is not my intent to make a baseless allegation, sir, nor is it my place to comment on decisions of governance and policy made in the past. Lord Wellesley must have had excellent reasons for establishing the opium monopoly, even if they escape my understanding at present. However, its inadvertent result was to cause a manifold increase in the depredations of Phansigars.'

'Your remarks will be noted in our report, captain,' said the judge, meaning, let us talk about other matters.

'Incidentally, I would like to ask you about the occurrence of a sati in your district, which you are reported to have permitted,' he added.

Sleeman explained the circumstances to them. Whether they understood or not, he could not tell.

'It is my understanding that you were censured for this by the agent of Sagar and Narmada,' said the homunculus, scribbling on a piece of paper. Sleeman confirmed this.

'We ask because you must understand how it will appear to people in Government House if you make accusations about the opium trade. A junior administrator who has been censured for permitting the violation of an important regulation, who is present when a woman commits sati, then questions the wisdom of the Company government in causing the proliferation of the opium trade. They may not welcome your views. However, there are mitigating circumstances regarding the sati incident which we shall place on record,' said the judge.

There was a brief conference among the three before they resumed.

'I believe prior to your departure for recuperation in Simla, you had arrested a prominent Phansigar leader of Gwalior and Bhopal provinces?' asked the homunculus.

'Yes, sir. He has since agreed to become an approver, and we have received valuable information from him about the stranglers' hierarchy,' said Sleeman.

'Captain, in Calcutta one hears stories which strain one's incredulity. I have even been told that you have struck up friendships with some of these captured stranglers, and have on occasion masqueraded as a villager and slipped into these gangs to unearth their secrets,' said the vulture.

Sleeman considered this. It was fantastic, and testament to the fevered speculations of people who had been hearing of the campaign against the Phansigars but had very little idea about the hinterland or about how crime was fought.

'Sir, it would be virtually impossible for me to pass off as a villager, despite appearances and language. Not to mention the physical toil of walking through the countryside with the stranglers during their expedition would be quite beyond my capabilities, such as they are. As far as forming any bond with the arrested men is concerned, whereas I have had and shall continue to have extensive discussions with them regarding their lore and practices, they are my prisoners, and our relationship has never been either collegial or fraternal,' he said.

'I see. Is there any suggestion or request you would like to place before us, which we may pass on to the secretary?' asked the homunculus.

'Yes, sir. My investigations have made me realise that we need a penal code if the criminal justice system is to be established in a permanent manner in India. Such a code must reflect the needs of the people here rather than a transposed British law. Like the Phansigars, the nature and roots of crime in India are unique. The Anglo-Hindu and Anglo-Muslim laws which have survived since the time of Sir William Jones need to be amended.'

'Yes, captain, I have read your suggestions for such a code, and must say you have acquired a commendable understanding of the kind of laws we need to introduce here. Be assured that we shall consult you when we begin the process of drafting a penal code for India,' said the judge.

'My lord, it is also important that legislation be introduced addressing what Thuggee is. Under this definition, Phansigars, Dhaturias and kidnappers of children must be included, for all of them continue their depredations on the basis of deception and inveiglement,' said Sleeman.

The three wise men said this suggestion, too, would be considered, and that he should submit a detailed study of this.

'We have also realised the need for harnessing science in criminal investigations. Dr Spilsbury, the civil surgeon of Jabalpur, has rendered invaluable assistance in examining the bodies and determining their identities or cause of death. In the case of poisoners, for instance, if we possessed the means of identifying and isolating toxins from the bodies of the victims, or from items seized from suspects, we could stamp out this scourge faster than we have been able to,' said Sleeman.

'In that regard, captain, I am happy to inform you that Government House has already taken a step forward. A medical examiner's office is to be established in Madras to study chemicals, poisons and narcotic substances within a short time,' said the vulture.

An office nine hundred miles from Jabalpur was not going to be of much assistance to Sleeman, but he expressed gratitude to Government House for this step.

'My lord, I would also request you to mention the need for strengthening police departments, and teaching new recruits to enforce the law. We have been informed that police departments in the provinces have not yet understood that they are neither the watchmen and militia of princely states, nor are they soldiers. Since they are civilians, and under local civil authority, a culture of responsible behaviour towards the people needs to be established. This has not happened,' said Sleeman.

The vulture made appropriate noises about how culture needed to be imbibed, not reinforced. Sleeman knew he could not expect more from them.

'The secretary has noted your additional remarks in the reports about the deportment of some provincial officials, captain. We can mention this in the strictest confidence: Government House will be replacing the agent of Bhopal in due course. We have received other complaints about him, including his involvement in trade with the Rajmata of Gwalior who, as you know, is not our friend. It also appears that his performance has been unsuitable for such a vital position. We have found a likely candidate to replace him; somebody not different from your circle of friends in Calcutta,' said the judge, shuffling his papers.

'We have also noted your warnings about the possibility of insurrection by clerics in Bhopal, and of discontent among the people about the Bengal Army. Government House is aware of the situation,' said the homunculus.

It could be worse, thought Sleeman. At least they admit reading of my fears.

'The secretary wants you to know that he appreciates the work you have done and will, I am sure, continue to do, captain. Please inform your junior officers that we commend their work as well, including that of Lieutenant Reynolds, who has been instrumental, we are told, in the apprehension of several senior stranglers,' said the judge.

Sleeman thanked him, and added that the efforts of magistrates like McLeod, and the support of Brigadier General O'Halloran, had also been vital.

'Captain, there is also the matter of Second Lieutenant Moore, who was seconded to you by the general,' said the vulture.

'Yes, sir, his assistance has been invaluable for our work.'

'Secretary Macnaghten is of the view that a war hero like Moore, and such a young man at that, should be better utilised on a different stage. He will be transferred to the court of the Maharaja of the Punjab, to assist the Resident. It is an important position, and he can take the opportunity to learn Punjabi and Pashto while in Lahore,' said the judge.

'Pashto, my lord?'

'Secretary Macnaghten intends to be more directly involved with affairs in Afghanistan. He believes Moore would be a suitable addition to his embassy to the Emir in Kabul, whenever it comes about. It will be an opportunity for Moore to see the world.'

'I believe he has seen enough of it in Burma, my lord,' said Sleeman, but not too loud.

'It will be an adventure, captain. The secretary will make a diplomat out of him yet,' said the judge.

Sleeman was excused as the great men began to confer among themselves. He walked out of the office and down the passages, where he met McLeod and accepted an invitation to dinner.

They were sitting in a shaded corner of the grounds when the judge appeared and conversed with them about minor matters. McLeod slipped away in a few minutes.

'It is quite a story, captain. The secretary believes it could not have been handled better by anybody. That is my view as well.'

Sleeman thanked him.

'I wonder if you could do me a favour. A young man posted at the court of the Nizam has written to the secretary. His mother is one of the Mitfords of Northumberland, you see. An excellent family.'

Sleeman had not heard of them, but understood.

'He has read of your exploits, if I may call it that, and has been interested in the Thugs, or whatever you may choose to call them. He says he finds their rituals, the Goddess worship, the atmosphere of the cult and its dark deeds fascinating, and wants to write a book on it.'

'If I may, my lord, the ritual aspects of the matter are relatively minor. There is nothing mystical about the Phansigars, or macabre, except the pile of corpses they leave behind. It is not a tale of who committed such crimes, but why, and what created these circumstances. I would not suggest a sensational account, for it would take away from the true tragedy of the matter.'

'You have enough material to write several books on this matter yourself, captain. Have you given a thought to it?'

'Yes, my lord. A friend has written an introduction to the Military Orphan Press in Calcutta, and I shall send them my writings in due course.'

'That is excellent. A word of advice, captain. Be circumspect in blaming the opium monopoly for the stranglers. Government House does not take kindly to being shown large mirrors. And do not worry about the young man. It is just a novel.'

It was a time of fictions great and small, after all. Of crimes masked by tradition and myth, by cruelty and apathy, by the self-regard of dangerous men in the hinterland and in

Calcutta. If Government House was unwilling to understand the complexities of India, could he expect a young man in Hyderabad to? Perhaps another small fiction would be fitting. Perhaps that was what they deserved.

Sleeman thanked the judge for his advice.

'Also, how is the child that young Moore is said to have rescued from the jungle? Does he make progress? I should very much like to see him.'

The boy from Seoni had survived the Simla winter but had still not taken to cooked food. He sometimes stayed indoors. As for speech, Amelie still hoped for a few words from him instead of grunts. Sleeman said he would be delighted to host the judge and show the boy to him.

'What a marvellous opportunity this is for you, captain, to participate in the civilisation of a human. To learn about what distinguishes us from beasts.'

'I have often wondered about that, my lord.'

The eminent man excused himself after some time and walked away. Sleeman sat under the tree for a little while longer. He was waiting to return to Jabalpur and find time to dig at Bada Simla. The creature in the rocks was waiting to be uncovered one bone fragment at a time. He would never know the whole truth about it. Perhaps there was no such thing as the complete truth. Perhaps each additional part that was uncovered was a small truth by itself.

Sleeman got up and left for his residence, where Amelie was waiting.

Epilogue

The interrogation of the man who was many men, and none of them, would lead to the capture of most of the prominent Phansigars of Gwalior and Bhopal, and some subedars of other provinces. From him too Sleeman would compile the lore of the stranglers, and further words and idioms in Ramasi.

In time, Sleeman would buy some land, but not in Simla. He would purchase it within riding distance of Jabalpur, at a site chosen by Amelie, and give it to the families of people displaced by natural calamities, and those orphaned by bandits. The people would name the place after him.

In time, Sleeman would be appointed to the court of the Nawab of Awadh, where despite his misgivings, he would find himself talking to kings and princes as a matter of course, and from where he would advise the gentlemen of Calcutta not to replace the nawab.

In time, also, the government would enact legislation to define the practice of Thuggee, and to suppress it. Phansigars and Dhaturias would be included in this definition. Despite Sleeman's reports and suggestions, kidnappers would not be. The views of the Nawab Begum of Bhopal about this would not be known.

In time, also, Sir Edward Ryan would meet in conference with Sir Thomas Macaulay, who too was the son of somebody important, and draft what would come to be known as the Indian Penal Code. Their alliance would also introduce English as medium of instruction in India, in what would be the last, and most grievous, defeat for Wilson, Hodgson, Prinsep and their circle.

Sleeman's suggestions about the need for the law to reflect Indian realities would be part of the discussions, although his role in the matter would not be acknowledged, for the discussions would be held at too rarefied a level of government.

But, as it so happened, it would take three decades for the code to come into practice after it was drafted. Macaulay would not live to see this.

Even great men are sometimes denied satisfaction by the workings of bureaucracy.

Some Words and Phrases in Ramasi

Aulae: Any of the different categories of Phansigars. Also called Bora among the river Phansigars of Bengal.

Adhuria: An intended victim who through luck or dexterity has escaped from a group targeted by the Phansigars. From the Hindustani 'adhura' or unfinished.

Agariya: A Phansigar descended from a clan which lived in Agra.

Beetu: Anyone who is not a Phansigar or Dhaturia. A potential victim.

Boog jana: When a beetu becomes suspicious of Phansigars.

Bajuni: Musket or dragon.

Bhartote, bukote: A Phansigar senior enough to be trusted with the task of strangling a victim.

Bel: A designated burial ground.

Bahleem: One of the original seven Muslim clans of the Phansigars.

Bojha: A Phansigar tasked with burying the bodies.

Bilha: A great enemy of the Phansigars. Also, a leper.

Bilia: Literally, a brass cup. Figuratively, a designated place to strangle the victims.

Bindu: Any member of the Hindu castes.

Baruni: An old woman Phansigar who is respected by those who know her.

Baru: A Phansigar descended from a line of reputed stranglers, and himself of renown.

Chiha: A Phansigar who shows sympathy for the victims.

Chaka dena: To make victims look upwards in order to make it easier to strangle them.

Chamosia: A Phansigar who seizes the victim's hands and holds them down during the strangling.

Chamia: A Phansigar who assists the chamosia by holding down the victim, either by the legs or other parts of the body.

Chandu: An expert bhartote.

Chisa: A wealthy traveller, or any good omen.

Dhaga karna: To find out the plans of travellers and intended victims.

Dhokar: A man who pursues and captures Phansigars. Literally, a dog.

Dhurai: The division of the loot. One-tenth would be given to the leader of the expedition, and extra payment to bhartotes, grave choosers and diggers, after which the remaining would be divided among everyone according to rank.

Gobba: Round grave, considered more stable than an oblong one, which is known as karva.

Geeda: Contaminated, such as a Phansigar whose wife and daughter are menstruating; also term for a Dalit victim.

Ganga Ram; Jhawar Khan: A code to signal danger nearby.

Gan karna: To pretend sickness in order to draw attention of traveller.

Ganua: Any of the tricks used by Phansigars to inveigle their victims.

Hilla: Any of three ranks which command respect in an expedition. These include the man who chooses the places of killing and burial; the man who carries the sacred pickaxe for digging the graves, and the man who carries consecrated jaggery.

Handiwal: Eater from earthen pots, pejorative term used by Phansigars of Agra for those from Telangana. A subedar who helped Sleeman work on the glossary told him to explain in his records that this was an insulting term, because the implication that Phansigars of Telangana ate from earthen pots was not true and not good for their image.

Jiwalu: A revenant.

Khachua, kantju: A cutpurse.

Kachcha: An unburied or imperfectly buried corpse; a Phansigar who has turned traitor.

Khidura, thulla: Policeman.

Kallu: A common thief.

Katua: A Phansigar whose duty is to cut the body into small pieces for burial.

Katori manjna: Literally, to wash a bowl; code for choosing a place for the killing.

Mauli: A messenger who carries money from the loot of Phansigars on expedition back to their families.

Morka: An extra portion of the loot set aside to senior Phansigars, such as a jamadar or subedar. This may be in the form of the most precious item in the loot.

Pehlu, ruhmal: Kerchief used to strangle victims.

Pola: Signs left behind at crossroads by a group to tell a following group which direction they have taken.

Pungu/Bungu: A Phansigar on a boat or ferry.

Patli ho jana: To disperse at the sign of danger.

Rehna: Temporary burial of a corpse, caused by haste.

Ruh: The number of people killed in an expedition, also used as a suffix to describe the expedition. If one person is killed, the expedition is an eelu, if two are killed, it is a bhitri.

Rangwa: A redcoat.

Rarein: The howling of a pack of jackals. A good omen if heard on the left at night. If heard on the right on the day an expedition begins, a bad omen.

Sonoka: The first murder of an expedition. The victim could not be a woman or belong to some prohibited varnas and trades, including Brahmins, potters, oil pressers, musicians and singers. Those taking their parents' ashes for immersion were also not to be murdered.

Sotha: The most eloquent and persuasive Phansigar in a group, whose task is to inveigle the victims.

Tonkal: A group of travellers too large for a gang of Phansigars to strangle.

A **Jhirni** is a set of words or phrases from the leader of an expedition to signal the start of a killing.

Aye ho to girhi chalo: If you have come, sit down.

Dhar dal: Pounce on him.

Hukka bhar lao: Fill and bring a hookah.

Superstitions

Eetak: A menstruating female member of a Phansigar family. The male relative cannot go on an expedition during this period. If it happens in the family of the leader of the expedition, it is halted for the time. Also refers to other superstitions like a death or wedding in the family, or birth or death of livestock owned by them.

Kaagara: The cawing of a crow. If it caws from a tree in any direction, it is a good omen. If from the back of a pig, buffalo or atop a corpse, an ill omen.

Kanta: The braying of a donkey. If heard on the left while halting at a place, the group must not stop. A good omen if heard on the right, and terrible if the donkey is moving towards them while braying.

Korra: The low hoot of a large owl, an ill omen.

Lampocha: A snake, whose crossing before or behind the group was an ill omen which could be repaired only by killing it.

Mrigmaul: A herd of deer, considered a good omen.

Pathori: The loud, continued hoot of a small owl. If the owl is sitting, a good omen. If it is flying, an evil one.

Tas: Bluejay. If seen on the right, or walking from left to right, a good omen. In any other position, it is neither good nor bad.

Walgi, Burauk: The crossing of a single wolf or a pack in front of a gang. A terrible omen.

About the Author

Siddhartha Sarma is a journalist and historian. A former investigative reporter who covered insurgency, crime, law and foreign affairs, his debut novel, *The Grasshopper's Run*, received the Sahitya Akademi Award, 2011, for children's literature. His most recent non-fiction work is *Carpenters and Kings: Western Christianity and the Idea of India*. *Twilight in a Knotted World* is his third novel.